Heirdom

Heirdom

Valerie Claussen

Chapter One

As a child, everyone I knew came from a two-parent household. This made fitting in a bit challenging for me. That changed when I met my best friend, Denny and his family who included me in most vacations and parties. His father took on a surrogate role for my own, whose contact was limited to the cards he sent for my birthdays and occasional holidays. Each card had some cute little animal incorporated into the front, with cash inside and was signed, 'With all my love, Dad'. I was consistently disappointed that there was never a letter, picture or other message enclosed, and no return address.

I often wondered about my father and had a million questions, but my mother passed away when I was barely out of diapers. This left my Grandma as my sole guardian. My mother never told her anything about him—not even his name—which was omitted from my birth certificate. I only knew that she had moved back from New Orleans shortly after my birth. Although I wanted to press my Grandma for more information about my mother, I didn't like to bring her up because I knew how much she missed her, and it always made her cry.

When I turned twenty-nine years old, my birthday came and went without a card. I worried the worse had happened and I would never meet him. My fears were confirmed a few days later, when a letter showed up from my father's mother telling me he had passed away unexpectedly. She explained that she did not know I existed but was excited to meet me. I felt numb at first and was not sure what to do. I wondered why he never told her about me or why he did not want to be a real part of my life. I broke down, realizing I would never get to meet him. I cried until my eyes were sore and I was too tired to stay awake.

The next morning, I jumped out of bed having decided I wanted to go meet her. Being the only living family member I had, I hoped she might have some answers for me. I called in to let my work know what had happened. They were great about giving me a few days of paid bereavement.

When I arrived at my grandmother's home, she came rushing out to greet me. Her hair had much less gray than I expected and wore the same kind of trendy glasses as my friend Sam. She reached out to give me a hug. I hugged her back, noticing that she smelled like vanilla and cinnamon.

"Come in, come in," she said, grinning from ear to ear.

I grabbed my bags from my driver and followed her inside. Her living room was full of Victorian style furniture and she had a plate of beignets sitting in the center of her coffee table. The walls were covered with photographs. I studied them for a while before sitting down on her couch.

"That's my son, your father," she said as she smiled at me. "Wasn't he handsome?"

I nodded and continued to stare at them looking for resemblances between us.

"You look a lot alike," she said.

"How did you find out about me?" I asked curiously.

"I was going through Antony's things to see what to donate, save or toss out. Then I came across a birthday card addressed to you. I hope you don't mind that I opened it," she said, handing it to me from a side table.

"Not at all." I put it in my backpack without reading it.

"There's so much I have to tell you." She poured us some tea.

"Well, I have a lot of questions."

"Of course, but first, I need to give you something," she said with her arm stretched, holding a small, old-looking brown book with a worn-out buckle on it. "This belonged to your father, Antony and his father before him and so on."

3

"What is this, some kind of journal?" I asked while carefully opening the book.

"Not exactly." She watched on the edge of her seat.

I turned the first page, beginning to read my father's writing and got a paper cut. Before I could pull my finger away, a single drop of blood fell onto the page. The words slowly faded away to nothing.

"What the hell?!" I jumped up. "Excuse my language."

My grandmother gave out a big sigh of relief, smiled and said, "It belongs to you now."

"Is this some sort of trick? How did you do that? Invisible ink?" I asked, trying to figure out what happened.

"It's blood magic. You just unlocked the book and with it, your ancestral powers."

My stomach knotted up and my mouth became dry.

"It's okay," she said. "I'm sorry. I should have warned you."

"What just happened?" I took a deep breath and slowly blew it back out, trying to compose myself.

"You come from an exceptionally long line of magic. This book helps you connect with your ancestors and their magic," she replied. "This will help make you quite powerful."

I eased my way down onto her couch, sinking into the seat. The only family member I had left in my world was absolute bonkers. I did my best to mask my feelings and prayed it wasn't hereditary. Although she was my grandmother, I would only be able to keep a relationship with her from a distance.

"You think I'm just a crazy old lady, don't you?" she asked laughing.

"Uh, um," I stuttered.

"It seems like a lot to absorb, but I would like you to try something."

"Okay?"

"Do you have a pen?"

"Yeah." I reached into my purse and grabbed one.

"Write a simple message on the first page asking for something small," she said with eyes fixed on the book.

Although I was humoring my grandmother, I already missed Denny and wrote asking for a call.

My phone rang. I gasped when I saw who it was.

"Hello," I answered with my voice shaking and my heart pounding.

"Are you okay?" he asked. "I just wanted to make sure you got to your grandmother's okay. You didn't call me."

"I'm sorry. I forgot. I made it here about an hour ago."

"You sound off. What's going on?"

"Do you mind if I take this outside?" I asked my grandmother.

She smiled. "No, of course not."

I went outside and let Denny know what was going on. He helped calm me down by explaining that the call was merely a coincidence.

"I'm sorry, Alice. I know how much you were looking forward to meeting her," he said with empathy.

Tears welled up in my eyes, but I did my best to hold them back. Denny knew me better than anyone and had been my best friend since the fifth grade. I wanted to teleport myself home and get one of his famous hugs.

"I'll tell you what," he said trying to cheer me up. "When you get back, we'll drive down to Disneyland for the weekend. K?"

"You're the best." I sniffled. "What would I do without you?"

"Just try to enjoy the time you have with her the best you can. She's still your grandmother."

"Thanks for checking in on me."

"Love you girl," he said.

"Love you more. Bye."

When I came back inside, my grandmother told me she had made a lunch reservation at Mable's Ragin' Cajun. This perked me right up, as it was a popular place to dine. I had always wanted to try one of their signature dishes but never got to during my previous visits to New Orleans.

As we entered the restaurant, the tantalizing aroma from the Creole spices stewing made me salivate. After we were seated, an incredibly good-looking man who appeared to be in his late thirties, walked into the restaurant wearing an expensive three-piece suit. He had olive colored skin, neatly trimmed black hair, dark brown eyes and a well-groomed mustache and beard. I couldn't look away.

"Oh good. Dimitri's right on time," grandmother said, looking right at him.

The movie star-looking man walked towards us and put his hand out to shake mine. My heartbeat picked up.

"You must be Alice," he said with beaming eyes. "I'm Moana's, excuse me, your grandmother's assistant."

He gave me a firm yet friendly handshake before sitting down across from me.

"I hope you don't mind me hijacking your lunch. She insisted I come," he said, sounding quite charming.

"I don't mind at all. It's nice to meet you," I replied. I knew a lot of attractive men but had never seen such a beautiful person so close. Without even thinking about it, I picked up the menu and fanned my face.

Dimitri raised his hand, and a waitress came.

7

"Are you ready to order?" she asked, holding her notepad.

"Not just yet," he said. "Could I trouble you with dropping the temperature in here by a degree or two?"

"Of course," she replied. "I'll give you a few more minutes."

"Thank you," I said. I opened the menu and placed it on the table.

"I'm afraid Alice and I got off on the wrong foot today. I was so excited to tell her about her lineage, but I think I've scared her," my grandmother told him.

"Well, it's not every day one learns they're a witch," he whispered to us smiling.

To avoid speaking, I took several sips of water.

"I must ask. Did you not even have the slightest inkling? Have the feeling of déjà vu? A dream that came true?" he asked with a grin.

I raised my eyebrows. "Everyone has that from time to time. Surely not everyone comes from a magical bloodline."

"Indeed," he replied. "But you'd be surprised by how many that do."

I wasn't sure if he was playing along to please my grandmother or if he was nuts too. Either way, I enjoyed my delicious lunch, entertained their silly notions and appreciated some serious eye candy.

8

"I don't see a ring. Are you not married?" she asked. "Do you have a boyfriend?"

"No." I laughed. "I don't have either. I've never had much luck with my relationships. They just don't seem to work out."

"Well…then it's good we found out about you before it was too late. You'll be much happier being with someone of magical blood."

I did my best to not laugh as she seemed to be completely serious.

"Do you think we'll have time to do some shopping today? I'd love to head over to the French Quarter," I said eagerly.

"Dimitri and I have some of your father's paperwork to get finished up this afternoon, but you should go on without us," she replied.

I wasn't accustomed to going out by myself. Denny and I went everywhere together, but I knew I was either going alone or waiting around her house all day until she came back. I decided to step out of my comfort zone. I called for a ride and got dropped off on Bourbon street. There were so many quirky stores, and the people were always so friendly. It was one of my favorite places to shop.

When the afternoon sun peaked, the humidity started to get to me. I bought myself a lemonade with crushed ice. I couldn't find any benches to sit on outside, so I found a shady spot and plopped myself down on the curb to enjoy some people watching.

As I finished my drink, I noticed a commotion in the middle of the street. A large group of young adults drank and knocked into each other as they walked down the center of the road. One of the guys picked up one of the ladies from behind and swung her to where her feet spun around them in a circle towards the crowd. At that point, I decided to get up and toss out my cup.

A clean-shaven man with dark brown hair in his early thirties stepped into my view. He wore an interesting, steampunk/vampirish-looking outfit and walked with his face buried in a book. The crowd moved towards him while the woman's legs swung around. I tried to yell to him to get his attention, but the group kept getting louder and he couldn't hear me. I tossed my cup in the trash can and rushed towards him shouting, trying to get the attention of either him or the guy swinging her.

"Hey! Look out!" I yelled.

A terrible feeling came over me as if I knew something bad was about to happen. I ran as fast as I could over to them. The woman's boots were inches away from smashing into his head. I instinctively shoved the man out of the way. I turned for a second to make sure he was okay when something hard hit me in the eye and knocked me down.

I regained consciousness. The vampirish man sat beside me on the curb. He held one bag of ice over my eye and another against the back of my head. A huge crowd circled us with their phones out, recording everything. A few feet away, a police officer interviewed the guy who had been swinging the woman.

"I'm so sorry," he kept yelling over to me.

I looked at the vampirish man and thanked him for the ice.

"It's the least I can do," he said kindly.

Another officer walked up to us and knelt on the sidewalk. He shined a light in my eyes and examined my head.

"How do you feel?" he asked. "Are you okay?"

"I think so," I answered.

"Do you live around here?" the officer asked.

"No, I'm visiting my grandmother. She lives near the Garden district. Her name's Moana Cabot."

The officer was silent for a moment, looked at the vampirish man and then asked me, "Is she home now? You'll need someone to make sure you stay awake the next few hours."

"I'm not sure when she's going to be home. She's working with her assistant for the rest of the afternoon taking care of my father's estate."

11

"Is there anyone else who can keep an eye on you until she's home?" he asked.

"I flew in by myself from California. I've only been here a few times. I don't really know anyone," I replied while yawning.

"I'll make sure she stays awake," the vampirish man told the officer.

"Thanks Luke," he replied.

"No problem Steve. I kind of owe her for pushing me out of the way."

"Okay. Great," the officer said before walking back towards the guy who swung the girl.

I yawned again.

"Let me help you up," Luke said as he grabbed my hand. "I own the store across the street."

I looked over and saw a Voodoo shop. "Ah, man," I said, thinking out loud. "Not more witch stuff."

He laughed and pointed to the vampire shop next to it. "That one."

"Oh, good" I replied. "Thank God."

We walked into the store and there were a lot of customers inside. People chatted, laughed, tried on capes and carried bags of fake blood and prosthetic fangs. Although my head was killing me, I enjoyed the shoppers' excitement.

"Let's go to my office," he said, leading me to the back of the store. "Have a seat. I'll grab you some water and some aspirin."

"Thank you." I sat down on one of the chairs.

Soon after I took the medicine, my head and eye started feeling much better.

Luke pulled up a chair and sat a few feet away.

"Pretty cool shop you have here. I don't remember seeing this when I was here last time. Is it new?" I asked.

"Very," he replied. "I had the grand opening last month."

"I should probably check my phone to make sure my grandmother hasn't tried to reach me."

I unzipped my backpack and pulled out my phone. "Nope."

Luke appeared to be deep in thought.

"I can ask her to come get me. I would hate to keep you away from anything."

"Oh, no. You're not keeping me from anything. I can sit with you," he replied. "I was just thinking about how funny it was that you got so upset when you thought I owned a Voodoo shop. Not a fan of magic, huh?"

"It's a long story," I sighed. "Normally I enjoy looking at shops like that. I've spent many hours and more money than I should have in those. I love all the supernatural stuff, always have."

"So, what's changed?" he asked. "We've got time."

In that moment, I noticed Luke had the look of someone who was always up to something. It was if a smirk always lurked behind any expression. This made me question telling him anything, but before I knew it, I had told him all about my grandmother and her witchy nonsense. I expected him to laugh, but he didn't. Perhaps he had become accustomed to meeting eccentric people in the Big Easy.

"I have to be honest," he said smiling. "I already knew."

"You already knew? How?"

"When I saw your face, I kept asking myself, where I have seen that face before? You seemed so familiar. Then, you said your grandmother's name and I saw the book in your backpack. I knew you had to be Alice."

"How could you possibly know who I am? I only just met her today," I asked confusedly.

"People love to talk. As soon as my mother learned that your father had an heir, she asked me to stay with a buddy of mine overseas for a while. She'd let me know when it was safe to return."

"Safe? Why?"

"She knows you have your father's talisman and with it, you could become one of the most powerful witches in New Orleans," he said seriously. "Our families have been enemies for many years. She fears you'll do something to harm us."

"For the sake of argument, let's say I believe you. Why on earth are you helping me?"

He grinned. "Now that's a good question."

"None of this is real. Is it? You're just messing with me."

"Seems a prank, doesn't it?" he asked with a mischievous smile.

I took the book out of my backpack and sat it on my lap.

"What are you doing?" he asked intriguingly.

"If this really works, I'm going to ask for something bigger."

"You've already used this?" he asked nervously. "On whom?"

"My best friend. I asked that he call me, and he did. Well, but that was likely just a coincidence because I was supposed to call him and forgot. He was just worried."

"Alice, you can't just use this for petty things. You'll make your ancestors angry, and you don't want that," he said firmly. "This is real. You shouldn't play around with it. I've learned that the hard way."

"You have a book too?" I asked excitedly. "Where is it? May I see it?"

"Buried, to not temp me. It's identical to yours."

"Sure." I snickered. "It's conveniently hidden away. Sounds plausible."

I reached into the front pocket of my backpack and grabbed a pen. I began writing the most random thing I could think of, *'I want some stranger to hand me $3.12.'* I closed the book and rested my hands on top.

"Why would you do that when I just told you not to?" He sounded annoyed with me.

"Because this isn't real," I said, feeling quite sure of myself. "I don't believe in magic."

"You will." He crossed his arms. "It is real."

My head felt better, but my eye started to sting. I picked up a bag of ice and put it back over my eye, as the lid began to swell.

"Sorry, you can't come back here," Luke said, jumping to his feet.

A man with bleached dreadlocks stood behind me. "I found these on the shop floor. The cashier told me I should bring them to you," he said, reaching his fist out in front of me.

"It's not my shop." I pointed at Luke. "It's his."

"*His* name's not Alice," he replied while dropping a handful of cash with my name written all over them.

"Ah!" I screamed. My heart pounded. I don't think I had ever been so scared in my life.

"Most people are happy when someone returns their money," the guy said while walking out of the office laughing. "You're welcome."

"If someone who clearly knows more than you, tells you something, you must listen." Luke scolded me. "Now, quickly pick up the money. We have to return it."

"Return it?" I asked with my voice shaking. "To whom?"

"Follow me," he said as he grabbed his keys from the desk. "Trust me. I'm doing you a big favor."

I picked up the money and put it into my jeans pocket. We got into his car and drove north to a park with a huge tree with massive branches off to the side. Fruit, shells and coins covered the base of it.

"This is what you're going to do," he told me, as if my life depended on following his instructions. "Take the money out of your pocket and add whatever coins you have to it."

As annoyed as I was, I did exactly as he said.

"Now, you're going to knock three times on the tree to let the spirits know you're here."

"Knock? No. Why knock?" I asked, feeling apprehensive. "I don't want to knock."

"Just do it," he insisted. "Knock."

My hands trembled but I did it.

"Now apologize, thank them for the help and toss the money at the base of the tree."

This time I didn't question him. I just did it. I wanted to get away from there as quickly as possible.

"Rule number one: never ask for anything unless you or someone close to you truly needs it," he said, scolding me like a child. "Nothing comes without giving something in return."

"Okay," I whispered. "I'm sorry."

We got back into his car but didn't say a word during the drive back to his shop. I wanted to be home in my bed and forget everything that had just happened. I was raised Catholic and kept thinking how upset my Grandma would be if she knew what I had done.

Once we walked to his store's office, we began talking again. He explained that our books were made from an ancestor tree when a large branch had broken off during an electric storm. There were two given to our great, great grandmothers who were once best friends. The books had always been passed down to their eldest children after their deaths.

It confused me. "I don't understand. What happened to make them become enemies?"

"Power, obsession, and greed, I suppose."

"Well, I don't want power or magic. Maybe they'll stop fighting. Anything that could have happened was many years ago, right?" I asked. "How many people do you have in your family? On my side, it's just me and my grandmother. How can that be a threat?"

"I only have my mother left," he answered.

"I'm sorry."

"It happened long ago."

"I'm only here for a quick visit. Once I'm gone, things should go back to normal."

He laughed. "That's not how this works. You can leave but it won't change anything. Your blood is in the book now and your ancestors have been summoned. I called on mine too before I fully understood what it meant."

I tried to inject reason. "But yours is buried, and I'll never use mine again."

"You called on them," he said, getting frustrated. "Don't you understand? They gave you what you asked for and now they'll expect you to do the same."

"What are you talking about?"

19

"My mother told me that our ancestors craved power and status. If both of our blood lines end, so shall the magic. The books will become worthless."

"Are you kidding me? First you say that our families are enemies and now you're telling me that I'm supposed to make little witchy babies with you?"

"Heavens, no," he replied, acting as if I had said something truly offensive. "Our families want to be stronger than the other, not joined and never equal."

"Then what's the problem? You marry some other witch and have all the magical babies you want. I'll just go back to being happily single in California. Your family wins and you'll never have to see or hear from me again."

"I have absolutely no interest in ever having any children with anyone, witch or otherwise. I plan on living my entire existence doing what makes me happy. I don't want to worry about anyone else," he said coldly. "But you called on them and may have to marry who she told you."

"My ancestors didn't say anything to me about having to marry someone. In fact, they said nothing at all. I just wrote in that dumb book."

"I'm talking about your grandmother, Moana. She wants you to marry a man named Dimitri D'aveau. He's of a magical bloodline."

"Dimitri? Really? I met him today."

"I heard my mother and your grandmother arguing after your father died. Each won't let the other family become more powerful. They'll do whatever they must, including choosing who each of us marries and we won't have a choice in it. They'll call on the other witches if they need to keep us in line. No one we care about would be safe."

"You actually heard them say that they're going to force me to marry Dimitri and you some woman?"

"Isabelle. Her name's Isabelle and yes. My mother said that she's already asked the ancestors to help make it happen. It won't be difficult to get the coven's support to keep you from being more powerful than I am."

An enormous weight suddenly pressed down on my chest, as if it were being crushed.

"What are we going to do?" I asked. "Do they even know about this? Dimitri and Isabelle, I mean."

"Believe me, they know. My mother said that their families are looking to use us to grow their power and status."

I dropped onto the floor and started to hyperventilate. Luke sat down next to me.

"It's not fair," I said, shaking. "I just wanted to meet my grandmother. I don't want any of this."

A beautiful young woman with wavy black hair wearing a well-fitting purple dress stepped into the office. "I thought we had a date tonight," she said putting her hand on Luke's shoulder.

"No, we didn't Isabelle," Luke replied, flicking her hand off as if it were a bug. "What are you doing here?"

"I came by to see my fiancé," she said while batting her eyelashes at him.

"Well, if I see him, I'll let you know." Luke rolled his eyes. "Go home."

"You can't run from this forever," she said. "You might as well stop fighting it."

"Good night, Isabelle," he replied without looking at her.

As soon as I was sure she was out of ear shot, I commented. "Wow, at least she's gorgeous."

"As is Dimitri," he replied.

"True," I said. "Why don't their families want them together? Can you imagine how beautiful their kids would be?"

"Most definitely. But alone, you and I are more powerful than they are combined."

"I'm not powerful."

"You are. You just need to be taught. It's in your DNA, you have the book of power and blood magic is the strongest."

"I'd just rather bury my book and forget magic." I drooped my shoulders.

Luke stood up, reached out with both hands and helped me back on my feet.

"I buried my book, but I still use magic," he said proudly. "If I ever need my book, I can get it."

"It just seems dangerous."

"Dangerous is not knowing how to use your magic when Dimitri and his family come for you. You don't want to resort to using the book against them. I could teach you some unbelievable mind tricks and spells."

My phone rang as he finished his sentence.

"It's my grandmother. I have to answer it."

"Hi Alice, we're just finishing up. Are you heading here soon?" she asked.

"Uh, I can be. I'll call for a ride and text you when I'm on my way."

"Great. See you soon," she said, ending the call.

"What if Dimitri's still with her? I don't know what to do. What am I supposed to say?" I paced back and forth.

Luke racked his brain.

"I'm scared."

"Okay, listen. You need to focus and remember these three words and the order I'm saying them: bridge, blue, Ekul. Now say them back to me."

"Bridge, bowl, uncle."

He chuckled. "No. Not even close. Listen again. Bridge, Blue, Ekul. Ekul is my name backwards. Look at my face and try to memorize every detail. Smell my cologne and try to remember that scent. Focus. Study me, try to recall as much as you can, and listen to my voice. Bridge, blue, Ekul. That's a code I'm giving you."

"Bridge, blue, Ekul. Fine musk with an accent that almost sounds a bit British," I said while studying his face. "You know? You have an interesting, but attractive and well-structured face. Your cheek bones are amazing and your blue eyes kind of sparkle. I've never seen eyes like yours."

He laughed. "Thanks?"

I closed my eyes and remembered his every detail.

"If you get scared or too stressed when you get to your grandmother's or anytime really, close your eyes and focus. Say those words and connect with me. I can take some of those bad feelings away for you."

"What if I'm not alone? I don't want to look like a freak or draw any attention."

"Then focus on me the best you can and say those words over and over in your mind, until you can sense me."

"What if I forget those words?"

"Then do the same thing but keep saying or thinking my name and ask me for help."

"Will that work?" I asked, not having much faith.

"It can, if you can really focus." He smiled. "And because I've created a channel for you to reach me."

"Can I do that for you too?"

"If you can reach me telepathically, the channel will work both ways."

"Could I have your phone number?"

"Ooh, how forward of you." He winked.

"No, no." I smiled. "You offered to teach me magic. It's so we can keep in touch after I go home."

"That's what the channeling is for. You get good at it and reach me, then I will tell you my number."

"I see how it is. Wow, you're going to really make me work for it. Huh?"

"I'm not like most guys." He grinned. "Just focus. Besides, by asking how to reach me, you gave me permission to channel you whenever I want to."

"You don't need me to give you any key words or anything? Like overpass, chartreuse, Ecila?" I asked, starting to giggle.

"Nope, I've already put everything about you to memory," he said cheerfully.

Chapter Two

The rest of my visit was happily uneventful. My grandmother never mentioned magic again and Dimitri didn't come up in conversation. I flew back home with the book and a few keepsakes from my father's childhood, then Denny and I left for our trip. I told him everything that happened during our long drive to Disneyland. He said that if he weren't so good at being able to tell when I'm lying, he would have thought I made it all up.

We went on each of our favorite attractions the first day, but the Haunted Mansion was closed for refurbishment until the second. The line was long up until about an hour before closing. As soon as it was under a twenty-minute wait time, we ran over to join the queue. A couple minutes into the ride, it stopped. I hated when that happened, not because I was annoyed by the waiting but because I always got the heebie-jeebies sitting in the dark staring at ghosts. For many years, I had the eerie feeling of being watched, but after my trip to New Orleans, it felt magnified.

"*Are you okay?*"

"I'm okay," I answered, looking at Denny.

He laughed.

"*Want me to take it away?*"

"Take what away?" I asked.

Denny laughed again. "Who are you talking to?"

My heart sank. "You didn't say that?"

He turned his whole body to face me with eyes wide open. "No one said anything. The carriages next to us are empty."

My muscles tensed and my heart raced like an anxiety attack.

"*Alice, focus and let me help*," I heard in my head.

"Luke?" I shut my eyes.

His face became clear in my mind, and I smelled his cologne as if he sat next to me. An enormous wave of calmness washed over me. My heartbeat returned to normal.

"It's just a ride," I whispered.

"*Tell me in your mind. Focus*," I heard Luke's voice say.

I focused and showed him where I was and who I was with. He laughed in my head. When I realized how silly it all was, I laughed out loud.

The ride started again.

"Now I'm freaking out," Denny said with his eyes wide open.

As we approached the end of the ride, where the mirrors are and ghosts can be seen in the carriages, Denny covered his eyes. "Nope, don't want to see *anyone* hitchhiking home with us."

We both laughed.

Life seemed to go back to normal after the trip. I worked weekdays and hung out with my friends on the weekends. My grandmother called me Sundays after church to check in, but she never brought up anything about magic and neither did I. I enjoyed our chats, especially her filling me in on town gossip.

Around once a week, before going to sleep for the night, Luke channeled me. Although I got better at communicating with him, I looked forward to having him come for a visit in a couple months. Some things he tried to teach me seemed like they would be easier to understand in person. Still, I had learned how to read people better which helped me become a kinder friend and made my work life a bit more bearable.

Denny's 30th birthday came. I threw him a surprise party at my apartment. Because there were going to be so many people over, I made sure to let my neighbors know beforehand and invited them as well. Denny's brother came over to barbecue hot dogs and hamburgers on my patio. We had enough food and drinks to feed twice as many people. I made sure to read Denny the whole time to make sure he always smiled and had everything he wanted. The party was a huge success.

As it began to get dark, a bunch of our friends told us that they wanted to go swimming. Denny grabbed a stack of towels from my linen closet and told me to suit up. Although I didn't feel much like getting wet after straightening my hair and doing my make-up, I got changed and headed to the pool with the rest of the group. A couple swam with their young children. As soon as they saw us, they gathered them, and headed home.

As per Denny's request, we all played Marco Polo which was as much fun as I remembered it being when we were kids. Other than a few of the couples who were way too into each other, everyone participated. When Denny's brother Darren was *it* and moved in my direction, I carefully pulled myself up out of the pool. I tiptoed around the edge, planning to jump back in as far away from him as possible.

"Fish out of water!" he yelled.

He caught me, so it became my turn to be *It*. I did a cannonball back into the water. I swam towards the shallow end away from everyone, went under the water, closed my eyes and counted to thirty. When I rose back to the surface, only a few splashing sounds came from the deep end and then everything went quiet. I couldn't hear anything and felt no movement in the water. I crept around, reaching out in all directions but didn't feel anyone. It was if everyone had left. I wanted to peek to see if they were playing a trick on me, but I didn't.

"Marco," I said.

No one answered.

"I said Marco!" I yelled, scooting towards the edge of the pool.

Still no answer. Being a bit annoyed but trying to not show it too much, I opened my eyes. A couple feet in front of me were a pair a fine men's black dress shoes and black suit pants. I slowly looked up to see who it was and why they weren't wearing a swimsuit, while standing so close to the pool.

"Dimitri?" I asked, feeling surprised.

I turned around. Everyone sat on the edge of the pool with their feet dangling in the water, smiling. '*What a bunch of cheaters,*" I thought to myself.

"Oh, my lord! You weren't kidding, he is hot," Denny yelled out.

I scolded him with my eyes, wishing I hadn't said anything to him.

Dimitri smiled.

I tried to stay calm and focus on what to say. I was genuinely freaked out but also didn't want to make a scene and spoil Denny's party. I went under the water long enough to compose myself.

Luke had already gotten in my head, *'Dimitri doesn't know I told you anything about his intentions. So, act casual. I'll try to figure a way to help if things go awry.'*

My nerves calmed enough for me to come back up.

"What are you doing here?" I asked while wiping the water from my face. "How did you even know where I live?"

"Moana wanted me to look at some property out here and she thought we could spend some time together while I'm in town," he said, sounding especially charming. "She gave me your address. I hope that's okay."

"Yeah, that's fine, but tonight's not the best. We're celebrating my best friend's big 3-0," I said, feeling relieved that I had a way out for the night.

"How about I pick you up for a late lunch tomorrow, around one?" He smiled. "If you're free."

"Uh, okay," I answered, unable to think of an excuse.

"Until then." He smiled and headed toward the gate.

"That was hella rude, Alice," Samantha said loudly.

Dimitri turned around, smiled and said, "I'm the one who was crashing this soiree. It's totally fine. I'll go watch movies in my hotel room."

32

Samantha chimed in. "The more, the merrier. Isn't that what you always say, Denny?"

Denny looked over at me not knowing how to respond.

"He's all dressed up with nowhere to go," Samantha said, smiling. "Please let him stay."

"I don't mind if he stays, but he's not dressed for this," Denny said, waiting for my reaction.

"Would that be alright with you, Alice?" Dimitri asked me. "I could definitely use the company."

Samantha's judging eyes were fixed on me.

"Won't the chlorine ruin your Armani suit?" I asked.

"It's not Armani," he corrected me. "But you're right. Chlorine would destroy this. I'll be right back."

Denny dropped back in the pool as soon as Dimitri walked through the gate and swam over to me.

"Are you okay with this?" he whispered. "I didn't know what to say."

"It just seems a little weird that he's here. Doesn't it?" I asked.

"Only because of what Luke told you," he said. "He actually seems nice and oh my God, he is hot."

I laughed. "You already said that."

"Well, it's still true." He smiled.

The next thing I knew, Dimitri carried a duffle bag into the restroom by the pool. After a few minutes, he came out wearing swim shorts, looking like he stepped right out of a magazine. I had to consciously make myself not stare at him to avoid any inappropriate thoughts from entering my mind.

Denny whispered to me, "If he wasn't after you for your magic, you'd definitely need to hit that."

"What a waste," I whispered back. "My God, he is beautiful."

Dimitri walked over to the deep end of the pool and did a perfect flip into the water.

Samantha looked at me and asked, "Does he have a brother, cousin or even an uncle?"

"I don't know." I laughed. "I barely know him."

Everyone seemed to like him right away. He was smart, funny and ridiculously good-looking but didn't seem full of himself. He went along with whatever random game our friends came up with and even did some silly magic tricks that any non-magical person could do. He was not at all what I expected.

After dark, most of our friends had gone home. I was left with Denny, Dimitri, Darren and Samantha. We all sat in the hot tub talking about random stuff like our favorite theme park rides, stupidest things we had ever done, our favorite bars and bucket lists. Dimitri seemed completely normal, so much so, that I had almost forgotten everything Luke told me about him.

"So, how do you and Alice know each other?" Darren asked.

"Through Moana, her grandmother," he answered. "Her father's mother."

"He's her assistant," I interjected.

"Oh," Samantha said. "So, you help her with her business and run errands and stuff?"

"I do anything she asks of me," he replied cheerfully.

"Anything?" I asked curiously.

He went on to explain that he had a falling out with his parents as a teenager over their spiritual beliefs. He told them he wasn't sure what he believed and wanted to learn other ways. When he came home from high school on his eighteenth birthday, his clothes were put in duffel bags on their front lawn and the locks had been changed. None of his friends' families would allow him to stay with them, so he slept on park benches on top of his bags.

He said that he had been doing it for a week when my grandmother happened to drive by and saw him. Having pity on the young man, she took him in and helped him finish school. He told us that she appreciated the company, as her son

35

was grown, and her husband had passed away many years before.

"Are you and your parents still not speaking?" Denny asked him while glancing over at me.

"No, we've made amends. Moana helped me understand that it's important to them to keep with their own traditions and I should respect that."

"That's really cool of your grandmother, Alice," Samantha said. "My parents wouldn't even let me take in a stray kitten."

"Because you're allergic, Sam. Your face puffs up like a balloon." Denny rolled his eyes. "That's not the same."

"You would do *anything* for her?" I asked.

"Yes, I would," he answered without hesitation.

"So, you said something about looking at property?" Darren asked. "Are you hoping to move out here?"

"It's a nice enough city, but no. It's not for me. She wanted me to find a small house here for her to buy," Dimitri replied.

"She wants to move here?" I asked. "Why on earth would she want to do that? She has such a nice home in New Orleans. There's so much history and culture and don't get me started on the food."

"To be near you, obviously." Darren smiled at me.

"She's not moving out here. She'd never leave her home," he said. "The house would be for Alice."

"Me?" I was surprised by her gesture.

"She wants you to have a nice home with a yard large enough to have a garden," he replied. "Herbs are very important to keep on hand."

"I couldn't possibly let her do that."

"Yes, you can, because it would make her happy. It may not look like it, but she's very well off. Your father and grandfather made sure of that. She just wants to help make your life easier. No more rent and you'd own your own home. Kind of hard to pass up."

"That's kind of her, but I'm fine where I am. Besides, I could never manage a garden. I've killed every plant I've ever had."

Denny laughed. "That's true. She even killed a snake plant my mom gave her. It was supposed to be nearly impossible to kill. Alice did it, in less than a week."

"Well, maybe no garden then," Dimitri chuckled. "But I promised her I'd look anyway."

The next day, Dimitri and I went for lunch at a local diner. Halfway through our meals, our conversation completely shifted gears from talking about our favorite television shows to overly personal topics.

"What are your thoughts on arranged marriages?" he asked as calmly as if he were talking about the weather.

I choked on my water, then managed to force a response. "I'm strongly against them. I think people should choose whoever they want and only marry for love." I took a sip of water and continued. "It's really an old-fashioned notion."

He was quiet for a moment and then took a bite of his stuffed chicken. I ate a couple fries and stared out the window. I tried to think of another topic I could bring up to derail the discussion.

"Did your grandmother tell you that she wants *us* together?" he asked, sounding a bit vulnerable.

"No, she didn't say anything to me."

"Would you consider it?"

"Honestly, no. I wouldn't. No offense."

He looked curious. "You wouldn't even think about it at all?"

"The fact that you said you'd do anything she asked, would leave me always questioning your motives. I would never know if you ever loved me or if you felt like you were just repaying a debt."

"Okay. But do you find me at all attractive?" he asked. "I think I'm fairly decent looking."

"That's not the point."

"I'll take that as a yes, which gives me something to work with," he replied with a smile.

"Dimitri, you seem nice enough and yes, you are incredibly attractive. But I really don't want to waste your time or mine on something that we both know would never work out," I said seriously.

"Are you seeing someone now? Is that why you won't even consider it?"

"Does it matter?" I asked, starting to feel annoyed.

"I'll take that as a no." He smiled.

"Ugh," I sighed.

"You know there are far worse men your grandmother could have chosen for you." He took a sip of water. "You have no idea what your other choices are like."

"My choices?" I laughed. "How is an arranged marriage a choice?"

He leaned in and whispered, "I know she told you what you are and that she gave you your father's book of power."

I didn't know how to respond.

"Do you even have the slightest clue what you can do with it, combined with your God-given abilities? You could have the perfect life you've always dreamed about. I would be your doting husband. We could move anywhere you'd like, find the perfect little house next to a babbling brook and raise our children."

"I've learned the hard way. When something sounds too good to be true, it usually is. Besides, I have no interest in magic or using that book again. So, it doesn't matter."

"It's just something I hope you'll think about." Dimitri half-heartedly smiled. "Did you know there are only two of those books in existence that were gifted with the power to command your ancestors?"

"And where is the other?" I asked, already knowing the answer.

"A deranged wizard that seeks to control everything in New Orleans wields the other."

"Am I supposed to be afraid?" I raised my eyebrows. "Because I'm not."

Dimitri's face grew red. "Your grandmother lives there. How can you not care?"

"Why on earth would anyone want to do anything to her?" I asked. "She's a sweet, church-going granny."

"Not everyone is who they seem, Alice. You must learn who you can trust."

"If she's in any kind of danger, why would she give me the book of power? Couldn't she just use it herself?"

"Because the blood line came from your father's side, not hers. She can't wield it," he whispered.

"Let's back up a minute." I crossed my arms and sat back in my chair. "You said there are only two books of power. Where do *you* think they came from?"

"From an ancestral tree branch."

"That's the part that makes no sense. If the covens knew about the books and where they came from, why weren't other branches taken to create more books?"

"Many tried to cut off branches and even take the whole tree down, but it wouldn't let them. Anyone who tried felt extreme anguish and could feel the little magic they had being pulled out of them."

I kept thinking about everything Luke had told me and realized there was so much more to my history that I did not know or understand.

"If the tree can't be broken, then how did a branch break off?" I wondered.

"The story goes that two neighboring families were struggling to survive. They had little hope and barely enough food to feed themselves. They did everything to help each other and their community. One night, during a terrible storm, the eldest daughters of each family decided to ask the ancestors for help. They heard that they listened to those who suffered the most. The girls tried to make an offering at a tomb of a well-known voodoo witch who was known to help people."

"I've heard of her. I can't remember her last name, but it sounds like yours," I said, thinking back to a tour Denny and I had gone on a few years before to an above-ground cemetery. "Sorry Dimitri. Please continue."

"Desperate for aid, they walked for blocks through a storm with the wind and rain whipping at their faces until they reached an old tree everyone called the ancestor tree," he went on. "Your great, great grandmother and her best friend Mary knocked on the tree three times begging for help for their families. They each took out the last bag of food from their coat pockets and tossed them to the foot of the tree making an offering."

As I listened to him tell the story, my mind went to the tree Luke had taken me to drop the money. I wondered if it was the same one.

"When they turned to walk away, lightning struck the branch over their heads. The girls darted out of the way, as it broke free from the tree. The storm stopped and they carried it back, believing it would bring good fortune. As they approached, their families stepped outside to see what they were carrying. When they told them where it had come from, they decided that the girls should share the gift. Their fathers worked together to break it down and make it into a journal for each of them."

Dimitri finished his meal while I gathered my thoughts.

"What happened to make them turn on each other?" I wondered.

"The girls stayed friends their whole lives. When they passed away, the journals were left to their eldest sons. The men discovered that anything they wrote was communicated directly to their ancestors, so they used it to ask for lavish, unnecessary things. The more one of them had, the other wanted to have more, to be better. That was the beginning of the end of their ties, but what destroyed their friendship was when they both fell for the same girl, Sonya. She was the most beautiful woman either of them had ever known. Each did everything to win her affection, but she never led either of them on, as she was already engaged to a man named Tom who was stationed overseas. When she wouldn't give in, they each decided to use their books of power to win her for themself. She felt like her heart was being torn in three directions. The men didn't notice her suffering and kept using the books to make her feel false love for each of them."

"Oh my gosh," I said sadly. "That's awful. I don't understand why their ancestors would allow such a wish."

"There's more," he said. "Should I tell you or would you like me to stop?"

"I need to know what happened," I responded. "Please continue, Dimitri."

"Rumors began to spread around The French Quarter about Sonya, calling her the Spanish harlot. Although she had never slept with anyone, people began to believe the lies. Upon hearing the gossip, her fiancé's mother threw her out on the street. Having no money and nowhere to go, she reached out to both men begging each to let her stay with them— offering to work as a servant. Because her good name was now tarnished, the men no longer wanted her, but neither thought to remove the love curse. She was tormented day and night. A week later, Sonya's body was found on the dock. The coroner reported that the cause of death was blunt force trauma to the head. Once the post-mortem exam was made public, her good name was finally restored but it was too late."

"That poor girl," I said feeling embarrassed by my ancestor. "Who killed her?"

"Although the two men accused the other of killing Sonya, neither admitted to doing so. No one was ever charged with her murder. Those who knew about the books of power, assumed that one or both were used to cover up what they had done."

"Maybe I shouldn't have asked." I felt sick to my stomach.

"Well, you needed to know," he answered. "After her death, each vowed to do everything possible to learn as much magic as they could to become the most powerful and to keep the other from taking anyone or anything from them ever again."

"But that was so long ago. Why on earth is this still dragging on?"

"Because hate is never born, it's passed down."

"If that's true, then it can end with me and whoever has the other book. Right?" I asked, feeling optimistic.

He leaned towards me and said, "There's a huge flaw with that logic. You've been kept away from this your whole life, but he hasn't. He's been groomed into a monstrous, avaricious, lunatic. His magic feeds on people's minds and is far more powerful and destructive than any before him."

"Well then, I'll just have to stay away. I don't want to fight," I said calmly.

"Word spreads fast in the Big Easy. By now, every coven has heard of you. That vampire wannabe will find you. If he's able to get in your head, he can use his power to get you to destroy your book, leaving him to do as he chooses."

"What?" I asked, feeling startled. "I thought the books can't be destroyed, only buried."

"Who told you that?" he asked.

I didn't answer. "Who told you that they can be destroyed? Has anyone even tried?"

He didn't answer.

"I think I'll take my chances." I placed my napkin on my plate.

"As long as you don't understand how to use your natural magic, you're vulnerable. Until quite recently, no one knew that your father had any children, but word travels fast. Lucas Varlett isn't the only one who'd like to see the end of the Cabot bloodline. For most, magic is taught and not in their blood. People with learned magic want to live without fear, doing simple spells and creating healing charms and potions. Most just want to do good and help people, but make no mistake, they will protect their own. Alice, you're now the second greatest threat to their world."

"Well, I have no interest in harming anyone, even a silly vampire wannabe. If I ever were to use magic of any kind, it would be to help people, not harm them." I tried to end the discussion. "You can tell the other witches that."

"Sooner or later, you will *need* to learn magic. I assure you." He realized I wasn't listening. "You can't hide from what you've already unlocked or who you are."

He reached into his pocket and handed me a business card for his magic shop called D'aveau Enchantments. His cell phone number was written on the back. I put it in my purse, stood up and pushed in my chair.

"Thank you for lunch," I said. "I need to go home and clean up. My place has bottles and cans everywhere and I have loads of laundry to run."

Dimitri stood up, paid the bill and placed a nice-sized tip on the table. "It's a lot to think about and my offer still stands. You can call me any time about anything."

We both walked out the door and stopped at our cars.

"How do I know that everything you said in there weren't lies?" I asked. "How do I know that *you're* not the villain?"

"If you work on your magic, you'll be able to," he replied.

I smiled and said, "Touché."

"Seriously, Alice. If you only listen to one thing I say, promise me you won't let that Varlett freak get in your head."

He got into his car, rolled the window down and told me he'd be in touch.

Chapter Three

The next day, I learned my job laid me off and the company wasn't going to let me cash out my paid time off or leftover sick time. I saved it to take a dream trip to the Fiji Islands with Denny, Darren and Samantha, but without a new job lined up, I needed to keep my savings. My boss told me to use it or lose it, which ultimately meant that my last workday was the past Friday, although I didn't know it at the time.

After hearing about my news, Denny's parents offered to let me stay at their Lake Tahoe cabin in exchange for cleaning it up for their Summer season. I was extremely appreciative and immediately took them up on their generous offer. The cabin had free Wi-Fi so I could continue to job hunt while I was away.

On Wednesday morning, I got up early, filled up my gas tank and loaded my car with my suitcase and two buckets full of cleaning supplies. I closed the trunk. Denny stood behind me.

"You came to see me off." I smiled and gave him a big hug.

"What am I going to do without you for two whole weeks?" he asked, drooping his shoulders. "This will be the longest we've been apart since eighth grade."

"If you didn't have work and your cousin's wedding this weekend, I'd ask you to come with me."

"I know," he said, still looking mopey.

"I'm sorry." I gave him an extra hug.

"Oh shoot, I almost forgot," he said, walking away and reaching into the backseat of his car. "My mom wanted me to give you this and she said to not take no for an answer."

I took the large tote bag from his hands and looked inside. There was an envelope with three hundred dollars cash and a nice variety of healthy road snacks.

"Oh my gosh, your mom is too sweet. She's already letting me use your family's cabin. I was going to do the cleaning for free," I said, smiling at him. "Please thank her for me and tell her I'm going to make the place shine."

"Well, I don't think she'd like me to tell her that."

"Why?" I was puzzled.

"Oh my god, you actually don't remember, do you?" he said while putting his hands on his waist with a slight grin. "How can you not remember?"

"What are you talking about?"

"When we were like twelve years old, she asked us to clean up the cabin and polish the tables while they went shopping. But we only saw the bottles of furniture polish on the counter, so we used them on everything: the floors, the toilet seats, the windows—"

"Oh my gosh! How did I forget that?" I laughed. "I must have blocked that memory. You can't blame me for that. The worst part was watching Darren slide all the way across the floor. It looked like he was going to glide right through the sliding glass door. The look on your mom's face—"

"If it weren't so scary at the time, it would have been hilarious. Well, it's hilarious now. Anyway—don't make *everything* shine. Especially, no polishing the floors," he said laughing as he walked away. "Have a great trip and text me later. Love you."

"Love you more," I said cheerfully and waved as he drove away.

As much as I loved spending time with Denny, I looked forward to getting away from everyone and everything for a while. There was already too much going on in my head before losing a job that I had held since I was nineteen. I had so much to think about and it seemed like there was always someone around. I desperately needed time by myself. Although, when I was alone, it was like there was someone looking over my shoulder. I wondered for years if I was being haunted. If that were true, at least they didn't seem to be there to frighten me.

During the long drive to the cabin, I thought about how Dimitri and Luke each warned me about the other. I had never been a great judge of character and couldn't really tell who or what to believe. Being alone with nothing but my thoughts, I began to feel angry that all that stupid drama had come into my life. As I started to feel it build, I thought of Luke and did not want him to get in my head. I turned on the car radio and set it to an 80's station. I focused on every song and sang along as much as I could to block out any other thought from entering my mind.

When I arrived at the cabin, I punched in the code to unlock the front door, stomped off the dust from my shoes and carried my things inside. There was a neon pink Post-It stuck to the fridge with a local phone number and a note that read, *'If you need or want anything, please call us. Beth and Brian.'* I put my drinks in the fridge and found that it was fully stocked with my favorite foods and several bottles of red wine from Denny's family vineyard. I was always amazed by his family's thoughtfulness and incredibly thankful to have them in my life.

Before I began doing any cleaning, I decided to fill up my water bottle and take a long walk. It was wonderful being able to soak in the warm sun, enjoy beautiful blue skies and the lake's famous, crisp clean water. There was such peace there. I understood why it had always been a favorite place of my Grandma. I had spent many summer weeks with both her and Denny's family. Many marvelous memories danced through my mind; it was if she were walking along my side.

After an appreciative afternoon of strolling and munching on trail mix, I returned to the cabin and ate a Caesar salad. To make the next three hours of cleaning fly by, I played some of my favorite film soundtracks, stopping often to dance. Around 7:00 pm, I took a nice steamy shower, ate some dinner and then headed to bed. Before I could finish reading the first chapter of my book, I fell asleep.

I used to dream a lot about my Grandma right after she died, but I hadn't in a while. Perhaps she returned to my dreams that night because I had her on my mind most of the afternoon. There wasn't a lot I could remember upon awakening, other than her telling me to stay strong and that she loved me. It would have been nice to stay asleep a bit longer.

After being there for a couple days, I could no longer block my troubles out. I decided to have courage and face my fears. I grabbed my water bottle, climbed into the raised indoor hot tub and turned on the jets. I scooted all the way back onto one of the raised seating areas and rested my head. I watched the bubbles pop around me. The water from the jets thumped against my lower back.

Although my heart raced, I knew I needed to try to channel Luke to address my concerns about him and Dimitri. I closed my eyes, took a slow deep breath and pictured his face. It took a few minutes to remember his code words but as I said them, his face became clearer in my mind. I focused on how I remembered his voice sounding. I said his name a few times, but he did not answer. Nothing seemed to work.

I am not sure if the half bottle of wine I drank had anything to do with it, but I was livid that he was able to get into my head whenever he wanted, but I couldn't get into his. I focused all my energy on everything I knew about Luke down to his incessant drive to improve the magic I wished I didn't have. The water went cold.

"*Luke!*" I slammed my fists against the surface of the water.

"*Finally.*" He laughed, as if he'd been waiting a long time for me to reach him.

"*Wow.*" I was startled. "*You finally answered.*"

"*Are you wearing a swimsuit?*" he snickered.

"*You can actually see me?*" I reached behind me for my towel.

"*Relax. There are bubbles everywhere. I can only see what's above the water,*" he teased. "*Unless you're going to stand up and look down.*"

I stopped reaching for the towel and laughed. *"No, I am not"*.

After filling him in on my job loss, I recapped Dimitri's side of the story. Luke didn't hesitate to admit there were many truths to it. He usually began with good intentions, but ultimately does whatever serves his best interest. When my father died, he thought the battle for power would finally end. However, upon learning there was another living Cabot kept hidden away, he dreaded more years of turmoil within the witching community.

We spent several hours trying to figure out how to resolve the terrible situation we were born into. Unable to find another solution, we reluctantly agreed that the only way we could put a stop to all the feuding was to unite the families by marrying each other. He planned to fly up to Lake Tahoe on Wednesday morning and we would do the ceremony at a nondenominational chapel near the cabin. This would force them to let go of a long, over run, ridiculous grudge and keep the ancestors from harming anyone. As we would never procreate, the power of the books would then end with our deaths.

As a young girl, I watched reruns of an old-time show called Little House on the Prairie. I always wanted a big family and daydreamed about finding a man like the father on the show, Charles Ingalls. He was kind, strong, loved his family and cared for his neighbors. We would get married and live in a perfect little home with our sweet children. As I drifted off to sleep that night, I felt an unfathomable sadness and wept for the loss of the simple life and love I wanted but knew I would never have. I prayed that Luke would at least treat me with some level of compassion.

There had only been one time during our entire friendship that I kept anything from Denny. When we first met, I had a huge crush on him before realizing he wasn't attracted to girls. I do not think that keeping a secret like that was too big of a deal. However, telling him about the wedding after the fact would upset him a lot. As much as I had hoped he would someday be the one to walk me down the aisle, I did not want him to try to talk me out of something that would help keep everyone safe.

Sometimes, the universe has other plans. Around 9:00 pm on Sunday, someone knocked at the door. Since I was alone and not expecting anyone, I thought twice before answering it. The knocking continued.

"Hey Alice, can you please let me in?" Denny asked loudly. "You know I can never remember the stupid code."

I laughed, walked towards the door and let him in. He gave me a big hug.

"How do you always forget the code? Your mom changed it to your birthday to help you remember it." I teased him.

"Damn it," he said, laughing at himself.

"What are you doing here?" I asked, grinning from ear to ear.

"I took a few days off work so we can hang out." He opened the fridge and grabbed a beer.

My heart started to race when I realized I would have to tell him what was going on with Luke.

"Something's wrong. You're not okay," he said, walking back towards me.

I tried to get the words out but instead, burst out in tears. He sat his beer down on the coffee table and then gave me a long warm hug.

"What's going on?" He handed me a Kleenex.

After a few minutes, I calmed down enough to tell him about the plan. In doing so, I realized I was completely overwhelmed. I had gone on to Dimitri about not believing in an arranged marriage and only marrying for love, but I was a hypocrite. I did not know Luke well enough to love him and was not sure I ever could love someone so self-serving.

"What if none of this is even real and it's just a trick?" he asked. "You told me he seemed sneaky when you met him. What if your instincts were right for a change?"

"What would be the point in tricking some random person he didn't even know? It's not like I'm an heiress and he's after my money," I replied. "Besides, how do you explain the money showing up with my name on it or how I could hear Luke talking to me on the ride? This whole thing—as unbelievable as it may seem—is real."

"Maybe there was a camera in his store and that guy was watching it to see what you wrote." He put his hands on my shoulders, looking me directly in the eyes.

"And the ride and me being able to channel Luke for hours? How do you explain that? It feels like he's always in my head, whether he's speaking to me or not, just sitting in the shadows of my mind, silently watching me."

"Okay, that's actually creepy," he replied. "Maybe you're having some sort of mental breakdown. It wouldn't hurt to see a doctor."

"And say what, Denny? How would I possibly explain everything without getting locked up in a psych ward?" I took a step back. "I wish I just imagined it all and some pill could fix everything, but you know me. I've never believed in magic and wouldn't agree to marrying someone I don't love unless I had no other choice. I need you to believe me."

"I believe that you believe, but I'm genuinely concerned."

"I have to do this. I don't want to spend the rest of my life being afraid and neither should Luke. I need you to support my decision," I said firmly. "You're the most important person in the world to me, Denny. I need you in my corner, no matter how crazy my life becomes."

"You know I will always be here for you. I just hoped we'd both fall in love, buy houses next to each other, our kids would be best friends and we'd all live happily ever after."

"Me too," I said, starting to cry again. "But as long as we stay friends, we can get through anything."

The next two days were spent trying to not think about what the future held. We were in our own world, swimming, eating and drinking far too much. I wanted time to freeze so we could have stayed at that cabin forever.

Early Wednesday morning, Denny came into my room carrying my book of power and a pen. He sat down next to me on the bed and let out a heavy sigh.

"What are you doing with that?" I asked, sitting up.

"I've agreed to give you away today, but I need for you to do something for me too," he said seriously. He handed me the book.

"Okay," I replied nervously. "What do you want me to do?"

"I was thinking about everything you told me about this book and how your ancestors gave it as a gift to help. The only reason things went wrong is because it wasn't used as it was intended. Right?"

"True."

"So, use it to ask for help," he said, smiling.

"I'm not going to ask for something bad to happen to Luke, Dimitri or anyone," I said firmly.

"Oh my God. Why would you think that?" he replied sounding offended.

"I'm sorry, of course you wouldn't. What do you want me to ask?"

He smiled and said, "Ask for help with your marriage."

"I don't know. I'd rather not use it again. It frightens me."

"If the book's fake, then it doesn't matter what you write. But, if it's real, you won't piss off your ancestors and could get some help." He handed me his pen. "Please, it might help me worry a little less."

I thought about it for a couple minutes and then took the pen from his hand. I said a prayer in my head and then wrote *'Please help Luke and I to have a strong marriage.'*

Afterwards, I got dressed in a plain light blue spring dress and Denny put on black jeans and a red collared shirt. We drove to the chapel and went inside. It was nothing fancy, but it would serve its purpose.

"He's here." My hands began to tremble.

"Where?" Denny turned around.

Luke walked through the door dressed in black pants, a light blue dress shirt and slim black tie.

"Oh my god, he's actually really cute, and you match. Did you two plan that?" Denny grinned.

"No," I whispered. "You think he's cute?"

"Don't you?"

I blushed.

Denny gently elbowed me, smiling. "Now I can see how you might have been talked into this. You had some extra motivation."

He walked towards us. "I'm Lucas. You must be Denny."

Denny shook his hand.

"It's nice to finally meet you," Luke said cheerfully.

"Same," Denny replied before taking a seat.

The ceremony was short and there were no objections. Although I was impressed by the beautiful, purple and gold rings that he brought for us to exchange, the kiss was nothing more than a peck. It reminded me of the type of kiss that you would see on an old sitcom where you knew the actors in real life did not like each other. While I was relieved that he didn't try to stick his tongue down my throat, I was surprisingly disappointed by his lack of effort. I looked back at Denny and he half-heartedly smiled.

As soon as the Justice of the Peace walked away, I thought to myself, *"Marriage in name only, I guess."*

Denny came over and gave me a hug. He had tears in his eyes.

"Are you heading home?" I asked.

"Yeah, I have to go in to work tomorrow," he responded. "Big project I need to finish up tonight."

"Thank you for being here. It means the world to me," I said, tearing up. "I love you."

"I love you more." He walked out the door while putting on his matching, red-framed sunglasses.

I let out a heavy sigh without realizing it.

"We're doing the right thing," Luke said.

"I know." I walked to the back of the chapel trying not to cry.

Luke followed behind and picked up my luggage.

"Thanks," I said, attempting to smile.

"He can come visit us any time you'd like," he said. "Your other friends too."

"Thank you. That would be nice."

We got into his rental car and drove to a nice bed and breakfast not too far down the road.

"I got us a room for the night," he said. "Our flight's tomorrow morning. We'll arrange to have your car and personal stuff delivered. I've already taken care of the rest of your apartment lease."

"Oh. Thanks."

Everything became a blur. I wanted to disappear so that Luke and no one else could ever find me or fast forward to when I would be an old woman with most of my life already behind me.

"Once we consummate this marriage, you'll never have to touch me again," he said out of nowhere. "By this time tomorrow, this will all be a memory."

I wondered if he had read my thoughts. I didn't know quite how to respond. "Oh." My shoulders drooped.

We didn't say much during our late lunch and then headed to our room for the night. We walked inside, set our stuff down and then I went into the bathroom to freshen up. Although he was an attractive man, I wanted to skip the next part and go somewhere to cry. If the lackluster chapel kiss was any indication, Luke had little interest in being intimate. My insecurities overwhelmed me.

As soon as I came back into the room, Luke offered me a glass of wine and soulfully asked, "Can I take it away?"

"Take what?" I replied with tear filled eyes.

"Your sadness, your fear, your doubts," he said kindly. "I can feel how much you're dreading all this."

I looked at him and said, "Only if I can take away yours."

He nodded.

I drank the entire glass of wine in one continuous gulp, then took a step forward until I was two feet in front of Luke. We closed our eyes and focused on each other. Before I knew it, he was already in my head, taking it all away and replacing it with an incredible sense of euphoria.

He took a step towards me, lowered his head until his forehead touched mine and taught me what to do. I imagined an energy field between us, focused on his apprehension and commanded it to leave him. Within seconds, it did as it was told. Without hesitation, he put his hands around my waist, pulled me firmly against his body and we passionately kissed. There were no longer any inhibitions between us, only an immense appetite for the other's touch.

Chapter Four

Upon arriving in New Orleans, we called Luke's mother and my grandmother and asked them to meet us at a park that was halfway between their homes. We wanted to get the uncomfortable conversation out of the way before going home. They were both very punctual people who arrived at the same time. We sat at a graffiti-covered picnic table away from the multi-colored playground and far from the other people visiting the park. We watched as our families approached, each giving the other a nasty glare.

"Please sit down," Luke said to the women.

They sat as far away from the other as possible.

"There had better be a good explanation for this," Luke's mother said, scolding him.

"There is," he said. "We have something important to tell you and wanted you both to hear this from us first."

"What's going on here, Alice?" my grandmother asked.

Luke and I looked at each other waiting to see if the other wanted to be the one to break the news. I hoped he would volunteer, as I tended to get nervous during any type of confrontation.

"Okay, I'll tell them," he told me. "Mother, I'd like you to meet my wife, Alice Marie Cabot-Varlett."

"What?" she asked angrily. "No."

"You didn't?" my grandmother asked, sounding disappointed in me. "Oh, dear."

"Please tell me this is an obscene joke," Luke's mother said with disgust. "Or that it's not too late to get this annulled."

"It's no hoax. She is my wife." Luke took my hand. "This is forever."

"Why have you done this?!" his mother shouted. "She's promised to Dimitri and you to Isabelle. How could you do this to our family?! Marrying a Cabot just to get out of an arranged marriage. You're the same selfish, defiant child you've always been. When will you ever learn there are consequences to your actions?!"

"We promised nothing. There were no engagements broken," I said plainly.

His mother stood up and walked over towards me. "You can't begin to understand what you've done and what makes you think you'd ever be good enough for my son? Your own father was so embarrassed by your existence that he told no one, not even his own mother. It was only a matter of dumb luck that she even discovered he had a child."

I stared directly into her eyes and told her firmly, "I never knew my father so I cannot speak for him. As for me, I vowed to God to stay by your son's side, and I will not break my promise. Deciding whether I'm a good enough wife is for Luke to decide. I answer to him and God alone."

There was an uncomfortable silence for a few minutes that was broken by Luke saying, "Alice gave up a life she loved to join me. We want to help bring things back to the way they once were when our great, great grandmothers were first gifted the books."

"I don't know if that's even possible anymore," my grandmother said.

"But we must try," Luke said while looking at both women. "We want New Orleans to be a place of peace again. Can you both at least attempt to get along? We're all family now, whether you like it or not."

The women looked at each other waiting to see how the other would react.

"Please," I said to my grandmother. "We just want to make things right."

Luke's mother looked at me and said coldly, "You're naïve and in for a rude awakening, Alice. There are others who will see this union as a threat. My son may mean well, but when it comes down to doing what's right or wrong, he will always choose power and control above all else, including you."

I didn't respond, as I could imagine Luke's sadness and how much he deeply wished to seek her approval.

My grandmother came over, gave me a hug and said, "I will let Dimitri know."

"Thank you," I replied. "Everything will be all right. You'll see."

"And I've got Isabelle to tell," his mother said. "I'm not looking forward to that conversation."

My grandmother started to walk away, but turned around to say, "Alice, I'd love to meet you Sunday at my house after church for brunch."

"Thanks," I said half-heartedly.

"They can come too," she said without looking at them.

Luke's mother walked over to him and said quietly, "I'd love for you to prove me wrong."

"Me too," he said, smiling at her.

Luke and I headed home after our big reveal.

"Wow, this is it?" I asked cheerfully as we pulled into the driveway. "I really dig the whole vampire vibe it gives off."

"Thanks," he said. "I'll have to show you some pictures of how I've decorated it for Halloween. The tourists love it."

"It's kind of funny if you think about it," I said. "You're an actual warlock but you're totally into vampire stuff."

"That's what my father used to tell me when I was a kid. He thought I did it to trick the locals."

"Are the people with voodoo and magic shops vampires then?" I joked.

"No." He smiled. "And few actually practice magic, the rest are just especially good salespeople."

We carried my stuff inside and he had me follow him upstairs.

"This is your room." He showed me a large room with a queen-sized bed, a flat screen television affixed to the wall, a desk and a small nightstand. "You have a walk-in closet and an attached bathroom with a shower/tub combo."

"This is *my* room?"

"I'm sure once your things get here, you'll feel more comfortable and can redecorate it any way you'd like."

"Where's *your* room?" I asked, looking out the door.

"Come with me, I'll give you the grand tour," he replied cheerfully.

I followed him down the hallway passing a room with a closed door along the way. When we reached the end of the hall, he opened a door and showed me into another room. This one was set up almost identically to the other but had a wall of books from ceiling to floor.

"This is my room. As you can see, I enjoy reading."

"Have you read all of these?"

"Some more than once. I only keep books on my shelves that I've already read or may want to read again."

"I can't even imagine reading half of those. How did you find the time?"

"There's always time for a good story."

Next, we went back downstairs. The living room and dining area were much like I had imagined. It was like a Hollywood style vampire lived there, yet it was somehow tasteful. The creepy yet posh decor made me smile. It much fit his quirky personality.

"Is the middle room upstairs the guest room?" I asked, pointing up. "The one with the closed door?"

"No," he said, almost laughing. "The guestroom is next to the garage. This way."

I followed him to a modest-sized room, painted pale yellow with two twin beds, matching nightstands, a small flat screen tv, wardrobe and attached bathroom.

"Do you have many visitors?"

"Every few years—usually around Mardi Gras—a couple of my buddies from college fly out from London for the weekend," he said smiling. "They really only come here to crash out after partying on Bourbon Street."

"Did you go to school over there? In London?"

"For almost eleven years."

"That explains your accent."

"Funny, I don't hear it when I speak, but everyone else seems to." He smiled. "You have one too, you know?"

"I do?"

"Definitely a Northern California accent," he replied as he walked out of the room.

"Really?"

"Yep."

I noticed a sliding glass door and was anxious to look outside.

"You have a backyard," I said cheerfully.

"*We* have a cozy, yet very nice backyard." He pulled back the drapes and opened the blinds.

A beautifully landscaped yard surrounded a sparkling clear pool with a waterfall.

"Oh my gosh. It's wonderful." I grinned from ear to ear. "I love swimming."

"That's great," he said, smiling. "It will be nice to have someone to enjoy it with."

After a few minutes, we went back inside. He showed me around the spacious, stainless steel kitchen and the laundry area. Never having to go to the laundry mat again sounded great.

"Oh, I almost forgot," he said. "Follow me."

We went back up the stairs, stopping at the middle room. He opened the door and said, "Come in."

I followed him inside and was amazed to see a bedroom much finer than either of ours. It had a king-sized bed with hand-carved, cherry wood bed posts. The bedding was dark maroon made of the softest fabric I had ever felt. The attached bathroom had a tub with built in jets and a giant rainfall type shower head above it. The tile was black, gold and sparkly, like something you would see in a five-star resort.

"This room is stunning," I said with my mouth wide open. "Did someone die in here or something? Is it haunted?"

He laughed. "No. It's not haunted. What a peculiar thing to say. Why would you ask that?"

"Because you never mentioned having a roommate and I can't think of any other reason why this isn't your bedroom. I mean, come on. It can't get much better than this," I said, confused by his choices. "This is perfect."

"I'm glad you think so because this one is *our* room," he said. "I figured we're both accustomed to living alone. The other rooms are so we can each have our own space."

"So, where do we sleep then? There are beds in every room. How will I know where I'm supposed to be?"

"You be wherever you feel comfortable. No pressure. If you need space and want to be left alone, just say good night and go to your room. That way I'll take the hint and sleep in mine."

It took me a couple minutes to process the strange arrangement before replying. "It hasn't even happened yet, but I can imagine how crappy I'm going to feel if I'm waiting for you in our room and then hear you say goodnight, as you head to yours." I flopped down on the bed. "I understand that you're going to do whatever you want, but this could be extremely awkward for me."

Luke took a couple steps toward me and held my hands. "That would never happen. I have a great appetite for you and will always come if I know you're waiting for me."

"How do you know? We won't always agree. You're bound to get angry at me from time to time."

"Naturally, but I will never punish or try to get even with you by withholding my affection." He knelt in front of me. "I will always check to see where you are before I lay down for the night. If you're not in your room, I'll be waiting for you in our bed."

Chapter Five

We took a raincheck on the brunch with my grandmother and spent the next two weeks at home getting used to each other and working on perfecting my channeling. My magic abilities strengthened every day.

One afternoon, during one of our longer sessions, something peculiar happened when a stranger rang the doorbell.

"Can you hear that?" I asked.

Luke laughed. "How could I not? I'll get it."

"Wait," I warned him. "His car isn't broken. It's a trick to get inside."

Luke scratched his temple. "How do you know that?"

"I can hear what he's thinking. He's after something. Don't open it."

"You can actually hear what he's thinking?" His eyebrows squished together. "What's he after?"

"I don't know. He's jumpy and keeps thinking about how important it is that he gets something."

The doorbell rang again.

"Is anyone home?" the man asked loudly. "My car broke down and I need to use your phone."

Luke's lower jaw dropped. "That's incredible. Can you tell him to leave?"

I took a step towards the door, but Luke put his arm out to stop me.

"I thought you wanted me to answer it?"

He shook his head. "Try to get back into his mind and make him think he has the wrong house."

"I don't know if I can do that. I have no idea how I heard him in the first place."

"Try." He snickered. "Better yet, make him ask us if we want to buy some Girl Scout cookies."

I covered my mouth, attempting to muffle my laughter.

"Focus," Luke said while trying to gain his composure.

I concentrated on the man. He had shaggy blond hair and wore a faded, tie-dyed t-shirt and baggy black jeans. He drummed his right hand against his thigh. I took a deep breath while imagining I was drawing energy from all the water on earth, then told him he was only there to sell cookies for his daughter. I exhaled.

"Did you reach him?" Luke asked, bouncing from foot to foot.

The man pounded his fist against the door. We walked towards it and opened it. The man was dressed exactly how I had pictured him. I took a step back.

"Oh great. You're home," the man said with a relaxed smile. "I hate to bother you, but my daughter hasn't had much luck selling cookies this year. Do you think you might be able to order a box or two? It would really help her out."

Luke smiled. "Sure, we'd be happy to. Do you have the form with you?"

The man emptied his jeans pockets. "Maybe I left it in my car," he said as he rushed to check.

Luke and I giggled to ourselves.

After a couple minutes of searching, he said loudly, "I can't seem to find it."

"Perhaps it's with your daughter," Luke said, trying not to laugh. "What did you say her name was?"

"My what?"

"Your daughter," Luke replied. "The one who's selling cookies."

The man became irritated. "I don't know what you're talking about. I don't have any kids."

"That was fun," Luke said, putting his arm around me.

The man sped down our narrow street.

Realizing I was able to do something like that gave me such a rush. If I had been able to do that when I was younger, I could have gotten out of all sorts of predicaments. I never would have had to sit through a bad date or been forced to give a speech in front of a classroom of judging eyes. I wondered how different my life might have been if I had met Luke sooner.

We walked back inside and sat down on the couch. He was deep in thought.

"Well, that was weird but awesome," I said. "Do you do that a lot?"

"No. I can get into people's heads and mess with their emotions, do counter-spells and stuff, but I've never been able to do what you just did without great effort."

"Really? Channeling seems to come so easily to you."

"Hey, do me," he blurted.

"Do you?"

"I want you to try to make me do something random," he said eagerly. "But don't tell me what it is. Write it down or something."

He handed me a note pad and a pencil.

"It's not going to work because you can get into my head and know what I'm writing." I pointed out the flaw in his idea.

"Just use a counter spell on me before you do it," he said, turning his knees towards me. "Block me out."

"How?"

"Use my code I gave you and then command me to stay out of your head. It's basically reversing what I taught you to get in."

"No. You'll still be able to." I took a sip of water.

"Just try it." He took my hands. "Let's practice. I'm going to try to get into your head in ten seconds. Start chanting my code over and over in your head. Ten, nine, eight—"

"Fine," I said reluctantly.

Before I knew it, he was already in my head.

"You aren't focusing enough," he scolded me. "Try harder. You have incredibly strong blood magic in you. Draw on it. This will work for you if you make it."

"I am trying."

"You're not. Use your strongest emotions. Get angry and command me to stay out of your head."

I tried for a few minutes, but my mind kept going back to how handsome he had grown with each passing day. His eyes were like LED lights were behind them, beckoning me like a lighthouse to a sailor lost at sea. As eager as I was for Luke's teaching, I wanted to stop practicing and kiss him, a lot.

'No wonder your father didn't tell anyone about you,' he said, mocking me in my head. 'You're weak and could never hold a candle to his power. You're nothing but a—'

My anger skyrocketed. I immediately vacuumed him right out of my head.

"Well done," he said proudly. "And sorry about that, I did it to force you to push back. You need to be able to block anyone out."

"Well, I hated that." I let go of his hands. "I hope I never actually need to do that to you."

"Me too." He smiled. "Now let's try this again. Don't think of or write down anything until you've gotten me out of your head."

He turned on the video recording on his camera and pointed it towards where we sat on the couch.

"Okay," I said. "Go ahead."

He got into my head instantly, but I fought it. I focused on how angry and hurt I had just been. I hated that my father never once tried to see me even though he clearly knew where I lived. I screamed at him inside my head for doing it. Luke was blocked in less than a minute. I went into his head, demanding he do exactly what I told him and wrote it down.

Before I could finish, he stood up and began singing my favorite retro love song by the Bee Gees, 'How Deep is Your Love.'

He snapped out of it. I handed him the paper and played back the video.

"You actually did it," he said as he watched himself sing.

Luke leapt to his feet. "Let's grab something to eat and get you some more practice."

We got in his car and drove towards the French Quarter. We parked in a multi-story covered garage, took the elevator down and then headed out on foot. We went inside one of the eateries, grabbed a couple of cold drinks and a basket of catfish and French fries to share.

"Over there." Luke pointed across the street at a bench. "That's a good people-watching spot."

I followed him across the street, and we sat.

"What do I do?" I asked.

"Watch as people go by. Read their expressions, study their body language and try to pick up on any that are showing strong emotions. Once you've found someone, try to get into their head and turn it around. If they're angry, calm them down. Scared, take away their fear, and so on."

"Isn't that wrong? I mean, getting into someone's head without them knowing? Without their permission?"

"It's not wrong when you're doing it for a greater purpose," he said with confidence. "You're not taking away anything good from them or causing them harm. You're helping them. How can there possibly be anything wrong with that?"

"Aren't those feelings sometimes necessary though?" I wondered if we might be crossing a line.

"It's our job to know when it's appropriate to help and how much to take away," he continued. "For example, a person that's sad because they did something terrible, should be left alone to feel bad for what they've done. Otherwise, they won't learn from it. Whereas a person who's sad because they lost a loved one or got dumped should have their suffering eased up. You can lift enough to help them feel better while still allowing them to grieve."

"That's beautiful, Luke. I hope I can do this too." I was impressed that it was something he did to help people.

"You can. Just watch and focus," he said, kissing my cheek. "If you can get into my head, you can easily do it to someone without magical blood."

"But you told me yourself, I was only able to get in your head because you let me. None of them will even know what I'm going to do, so how can they let me in?"

"The same way you did to that idiot at the door. Human minds are easy to manipulate. To get into a witch or warlock's takes skill and practice."

We sat together eating and drinking while watching people go about their daily routine. As we finished our fries, a man in his fifties shouted obscenities at the bouncer who pushed him out of a bar.

"He's one we let be?" I asked.

"Definitely not," Luke replied. "This one's actually different. You'll want to get in his head and tell him to call for a ride home. Look at his body language. He's stumbling, swinging his car keys around his fingers and then dropping them. He shouldn't be driving."

I tried to do it, but his intoxicated brain made it too difficult. "I can't. His mind is too sloshy for me to invade."

"It's okay. I'll do this one, but you'll get the hang of it over time."

I studied Luke as he focused on the guy. A minute later, the man walked to the edge of the sidewalk. He put his keys in his pocket, leaned against a pole, slowly slid down to the ground and fell asleep.

"Dang!" I put my hand up to give him a high five. "That was awesome."

"Your turn." He gave my hand a good slap and gestured to our right.

A teenage girl wore a large backpack over drooping shoulders. She dragged her feet as she walked past, adjusting the sunglasses that masked her tears.

"Can you feel that?" I looked at Luke. "She's miserable, it makes me want to cry too."

"I can feel it. Are you going to help her?"

I went into her mind to learn what happened and how much to fix. The girl wished she had never told a boy named Michael that she liked him. They had been friends since kindergarten and had finally worked up the courage to let him know how she felt. However, her feelings weren't reciprocated. I decided to take away all her embarrassment and sadness and replace it with confidence and joy. Letting her retain the pain might have kept her from expressing her feelings when the next boy comes along. Vacuuming all that out of her and watching her demeanor improve gave me such a high.

"Well done." Luke proudly patted me on the back.

We spent the rest of the day helping people, which made the hours fly by. As the sun began to set, we decided to head back to the parking garage to get the car and go home.

We waited near the elevator, discussing other places we could go to practice the rest of the week. The doors opened and Dimitri stepped out. My heart raced.

He immediately reached down and grabbed my left hand, looking at my wedding ring. "I just had to see for myself."

"Don't touch her," Luke said defensively.

As he let go of my hand, I wondered if I should have told him instead of letting my grandmother.

Dimitri began to walk away, but then turned back around and said with an empty stare, "You know, Alice. I want you to always remember that I offered you a good life despite your corrupted blood line. I agreed to marry a woman I had never even met, without question, simply because it's what your grandmother asked of me."

"Dimitri, I appreciate your offer and admire that you were willing to be with someone like me just to appease my grandmother. But I really don't understand why you seem upset. Me being with Luke got you out of a marriage you never even wanted," I said. "You're free."

"That's not the point," he said, crossing his arms. "I warned you about him and told you specifically not to let him get in your head. How could you possibly choose a life with him knowing you've set yourself up for misery."

"Luke and I got married to help bring peace," I said, taking a step towards him. "We're trying to build bridges Dimitri, not burn them."

"No, Alice. You're just a pawn. Your marriage was just part of their elaborate plan to ensure that the Varletts would be the only family of power. He's just using you. Why can't you see that?"

"That's not true," Luke said. "My mother knew nothing about our marriage until after it was done. She hated the Cabots but she's beginning to understand that all we want is peace for everyone, including you and Isa—"

Dimitri snapped. "Wrong! Isabelle and I were the ones who were trying to make peace by marrying into your families. It was an olive branch."

"What are you talking about? My grandmother loves you; she took you in when you had nowhere else to go."

"She's a Cabot by marriage only. I've never had a problem with her," he said.

"I don't understand then. I'm her granddaughter. Where is all this anger coming from?" I began to feel hot.

"I told myself it wasn't fair to blame you for what your ancestors have done. You seemed nothing like the power mongers in your bloodline, Alice nor his. You told me you wanted a simple life. Because of that, I told you everything I knew about Lucas to give you a chance to take a different path. Instead, you chose darkness. Moana asked me to always look out for you, no matter what, but you've made your choice. Now no mercy will be given to either of you."

"Are you trying to threaten—" Luke began as Dimitri started to walk away.

"We barely know each other. I've done absolutely nothing to you, Dimitri. What's really fueling your anger?"

He turned back around. His face and neck had turned bright red. "Your families destroyed my Aunt's life then went on as though nothing ever happened. Do you have any idea what losing her did to our family and to her fiancé? Your families grew in power and status without remorse while ours weakened. Until now, no one has been held accountable. It's my right and duty to make sure your families never harm another living soul."

"Your aunt? Who is she? I do enjoy messing with people, but I wouldn't say I've ever destroyed anyone's life," Luke said, defending himself. "What's her name?"

"Sonya," he said coldly. "Her name was Sonya."

I felt a huge knot in my stomach. "Your aunt was *the* Sonya? Why didn't you tell me?"

He turned and walked away without responding.

"Dimitri!" I called to him. "I'm sorry about what happened to your Aunt. Please tell us how to make things better for your family; we're not using our gifts to hurt anyone. We just want to help."

He kept walking without saying a word or looking back.

"I need to go see my mother," Luke said. "It's best if I go alone. I'll drop you off at home first."

I knew how his mother felt about me, so I didn't protest. As soon as Luke pulled out of the driveway, I wondered what Dimitri meant by not showing mercy. What was he planning on doing? Was he going to destroy the shop, our home, us or everything? It made no sense to me and seemed so out of character.

An hour later, my phone buzzed. Dimitri called me.

"H-h-hello," I answered. "Dimitri?"

"Ask Lucas what he told Isabelle about why he married you," he said.

"Why can't you just tell me?"

"He's your husband. You need to hear it from him," he replied. "This is the last time I'm going to offer my help. If you leave him and go back to California, I'll consider both family's debts to mine paid."

"And if I don't?" I worried. "What then?"

He ended the call. I immediately tried to call him back, but he wouldn't answer. I paced back and forth, pulled at my hair thinking about how Luke might answer the question. The room felt like it spun. I wanted to call Denny and tell him everything, but I didn't.

I ran up the stairs as fast as I could, pulled the book of power out from under my dresser and placed it on the bed. I wiped away my tears, grabbed a pen and started writing. I begged for the ancestors to intercede to God for me, asking to keep us safe from Dimitri and Isabelle. Then, I took a shower before going downstairs to wait for Luke to come home.

"Well, that visit was futile," Luke said as he walked into the house.

"What happened?"

"She thinks his ego is bruised by you turning him down. Says he's harmless and told me to just let him cool off." Luke tossed his keys on the counter. "I swear to God; she thinks he some kind of saint."

I didn't know what to say. I kept replaying the phone call in my mind.

"You're not okay," Luke said, walking towards me. "What happened?"

My voice trembled, "Your mom's wrong about Dimitri. He called me. He was irate."

"What did he want?"

"He wants me to leave you and go back to California. He's says he'll forgive our families if I do."

"Well, that's not going to happen." Luke kicked his shoes off and sat on the couch. "Was that it?"

"No. There's more."

"He said to ask you what you told Isabelle about why you married me."

Luke's face turned pale. I could tell he didn't want to answer, but he knew if I really tried, I could get into his head anyway.

"Shit." He scooted forward to the edge of the leather sectional. "What did he tell you I said?"

"He wouldn't tell me anything. He said I needed to hear it from you."

"I say a lot of stuff just to get a rise out of people." He turned to face me.

"I'm not naïve. I know you don't love me, but I at least thought we were on the same page about our marriage. I need to know what you told her."

"All right," he said reluctantly. "I told her I did it to have control of you and your book. This way the Cabot blood line would end and the Varletts would be memorialized as the last great coven in New Orleans."

"Did you mean any of that?" I teared up.

"Some."

At that moment, I realized how naïve I was. Hopelessness consumed me. Impulsively, I put on my jacket, grabbed my purse and headed for the front door.

"It's probably for the best," he said, without getting up or even looking at me. "I don't know what I was thinking. You and I were never going to work."

"I was only going for a drive to think—to calm down. I wasn't leaving you." I slammed the front door and drove away in tears.

Chapter Six

I didn't call Luke, my grandmother, Denny or any of my other friends and no one called or texted me. I considered driving back to Sacramento like Dimitri wanted me to do, but I couldn't bring myself to leave New Orleans. I checked into a clean, but run-down motel, a few blocks away from the house, trying to figure out my next move. Luke tricked me but even apart, he was still my husband. I was raised to honor that vow until death. I hoped he would reach out to me.

After hiding out and crying for two days, I began working at a touristy gift shop in the French Quarter that sold mostly dolls, potion oils, gris-gris bags and t-shirts. I enjoyed being at a place where I could secretly vacuum pain from anyone who came in seeking cures for their troubles. The more people I helped, the easier it was and the stronger my magic became.

One night while walking to my car, I approached a small group of men playing jazz music on Bourbon Street. Their melodic, bluesy sound danced through me. I threw a few dollars into the hat, sat on the curb and stayed a while to listen. Despite their struggles being tightly interwoven with their happiness, they were grateful souls, proudly embracing it all as their story. It was one of the most beautiful things I had ever experienced.

"Thank you." I teared up. "That was wonderful."

I started to walk away when one of the men handed me a flyer for an upcoming gig.

I smiled. "If there's any way at all I can get off work in time, I'd love to be there."

After I turned down the next street, an ice-cold chill raced down my spine and all the tiny hairs on the back of my neck stood up. It was if I were being warned about something. No one was around, but I could hear their thoughts. They were coming for me. Before I could grab my phone from my backpack or try to vacuum out their dark thoughts, everything went black.

I woke up in a private hospital room with a pounding headache. Stitches ran along the side of my forehead and my right eye was swollen shut. My first thought wasn't what had happened or if the men were caught, but how I was going to pay for the visit. It would more than exhaust the rest of my savings.

"You're awake." A kind-sounding woman walked towards me dressed in light blue scrubs. "How are you feeling, hun?"

All I could do was laugh. My body hurt. I imagined I resembled the bride of Frankenstein.

"I'm sorry. Silly question. I meant to ask how your pain level is right now. One being no pain and ten being the worst pain you've ever had."

"Um, about a seven." I tried to open my right eye. "Mostly my head but my knees quite a bit too."

"Are you allergic to any medications?" she asked while writing down on my wall chart.

"No. Not that I know of."

"Great. I'm going to speak with your doctor and see if we can get you something soon to help with that pain." She handed me a white remote that was attached to my bed. "My name's Christi and I'll be your nurse for the next six hours. If you need anything at all, push the red button."

"Could I maybe just have a Tylenol or Ibuprofen?"

"Yes, but that's barely going to touch that pain."

"Oh." I worried. "How much more will it cost for stronger pain meds?"

She smiled. "Don't worry about that. It's already been taken care of. We'll try to get them to you as soon as possible."

As soon as she left, I noticed the table near the window had a few colorful bouquets of flowers and a large doll. It was nice that anyone would care enough to try to brighten my room.

Ten minutes later, a doctor came in to examine me. When he finished, he explained that I had a concussion and was in a coma for three days. They would need to monitor me for at least the next 24 hours before considering releasing me. Although she said the bill was somehow covered, my concerns about paying for it made my head hurt even more.

A few minutes after the doctor left, Christi came back in carrying a small, white paper cup. "This should help," she said, handing me the cup and some water. "This is the best we can do. Sorry we can't give you anything stronger while you still have a concussion."

"Thank you," I swallowed both pills. "I appreciate anything to help knock this down a bit."

Fifteen minutes later, the pain subsided, and I fell asleep.

"Sorry, we need you to stay awake a while longer." Christi said as she gently nudged my shoulder. "And I need to check your vitals again."

She took my temperature, my pulse and blood pressure and then started to leave the room.

"Could I possibly have a snack, please?" I was so hungry that I didn't care about how I would pay for it down the road.

"We can do one better than that," she said cheerfully. "I'll grab you a snack and dinner will be served in about an hour."

"Oh, good." I smiled.

Two police officers stood in the doorway peering into my room.

"May we have a moment with her?" the male police officer asked.

"Of course," Christi said as she walked out of the room.

"First of all, we want to say that we're terribly sorry about what happened to you," the female police officer said. "There should have been an officer on that street. We've been a bit shorthanded this week with a flu running through our precinct. But we wanted to let you know that the men who did this to you are in custody and your belongings should be returned to you tomorrow."

"Oh?" I was surprised. "That's good."

"We'll still need your statement for the record." The male police officer took out a note pad. "What can you tell us about the night of the incident?"

"There's really nothing I can say. It happened so quickly. I wouldn't be able to give you any type of description or point them out in a line-up. I never saw anyone. I just woke up in here."

"Okay. Thank you for your time," the female officer said, handing me a business card. "If you think of anything at all, please give me a call. We hope you feel better soon."

They left the room and the nurse returned with apple juice and two containers of Jell-O.

"Thank you so much." I raised the back of the bed. "I feel like I haven't eaten in days."

"You haven't, poor thing," she said, patting my hand.

After dinner, I could barely keep my eyes open. I knew I was supposed to stay awake, but the pain medicine made me drowsy. With only one strained eye working, I could no longer fight it.

I woke up. There had been a shift change and I had a new nurse named Paul. I staggered to the restroom, brushed my teeth and cleaned up the best I could for the night. Every movement hurt.

When I stepped out, Paul came in to take my vitals. "Aww. How sweet. He brought you lavender orchids this time," he said, looking out towards the nurse's station.

Instead of going to sit on my bed, I slowly walked towards the doorway with my IV pole in tow. Luke stood at the desk, speaking to the charge nurse. My heart started to pound.

"Luke?" My voice shook. "What are you doing here?"

"Hey," he said, turning around. "I know I'm probably the last person you wanted to see. I did call first. They told me you were asleep. I didn't come here to upset you."

I started to cry.

"I'm sorry," he said. "I should go."

"Please don't. I'm not angry you're here."

"I need to take her vitals and then I can give you two some privacy," Paul said.

Once he was done, he closed the door behind him.

Luke sat down on the chair next to the bed. "You didn't move away."

"No, I didn't," I said with tears in my eyes. "And you've been coming here every day? How did you know what happened to me?"

"The night of the attack, I felt how terrified you were and wanted to help. I tried to see what was happening and where you were, but then everything went dark. I couldn't feel you at all. I feared you were dead."

"You thought I died?"

"Yes. A few minutes later I got a call from Dimitri. He told me that you were beaten unconscious and taken to this hospital."

"Was he angry that I didn't go back to Sacramento?"

"Not at all. He was worried about you. He even bought you that giant stuffed Mickey Mouse." Luke picked up the doll from the table and handed it to me. "He's been asking me about you every day."

"Really?" I laughed.

"About an hour after I left the hospital, I got a call from a buddy of mine at the police station telling me that the two suspects were in custody."

"At least they're not getting away with it." I tried to get comfortable, though my knees hurt.

"They definitely aren't getting away with anything." Luke grinned. "When Dimitri saw what they were doing to you, he beat the living shit out of them. Those guys are huge. I have to say, I have a whole new respect for him."

"Oh my gosh, Dimitri? I can't believe he did that. He seems so proper, and I thought he hated me."

"I guess not." Luke smiled. "It's a good thing he was there. They could have killed you trying to steal your book."

"They were after my book? That's why this happened? I don't even have it. Did they think it was in my backpack or know it won't work if they try to use it?"

"Anyone who knows about the books, knows that we're the only ones who can use them."

"I'm going through all this for nothing." I was infuriated. My empty cup of water and pitcher shook on the table.

"Oh, you're not going through this alone. I made sure of that," he said, sounding a bit sinister.

"What do you mean? What did you do, Luke?"

"I simply mirrored what they did to you," he said, sounding proud of himself.

"What exactly did you do to them?"

"All the pain and fear that you feel, I've made them feel it twofold."

"I wish you hadn't. They're already in jail. We shouldn't play God, Luke."

"I could have done much worse. You have no idea what I wanted to do to them for what they did to you. They're getting far less than they deserve. Think about what they did and what else could have happened if Dimitri hadn't shown up."

I suddenly felt less sorry for them. "How long did you put a hex on them?"

"Until you stop hurting," he said.

"Hmm. Maybe I won't take my pain meds next round," I joked.

Luke laughed.

"Thank you for standing up for me, Luke. I may not agree with your methods, but I appreciate that your heart was in the right place."

A nurse's aide knocked on the door.

"Come in," I said.

She walked in, introduced herself and asked if I needed anything. I let her know I was tired and a bit thirsty. She left and returned a couple minutes later with water, a pitcher of ice and a couple of snacks, in case I got hungry in the night. Then, she left the room.

"When they release you, would you consider coming home with me?" Luke asked nervously. "I'd like to look after you. If you'll allow me."

"Yes," I smiled. "I'd like that very much."

"I'm so sorry for everything, Alice. I don't know what's wrong with me. I didn't mean to hurt you and I never wanted you to leave," he said, starting to choke up. "I know I'll never be that Charles Ingalls type you dream of, but I promise I will keep trying to be a better man."

"That's all I could ever ask for." I smiled.

He leaned forward and we kissed gently on the lips.

I half-laughed. "Ouch."

"Oops." He searched for a spot to kiss that wasn't banged up. "They really messed you up. You must be tired. I should go and let you get some rest."

"If it's not too much to ask, would you mind staying with me, just until I fall asleep?" I asked, feeling afraid of being left alone. "It shouldn't be long. I'm very tired."

"Of course." He smiled.

I scooted over so that he could lay down next to me on top of the blankets. Despite everything Luke had done, it was comforting being there in his arms. I thanked God for bringing him back to me.

The next morning, I woke in a different room on a new floor. To my surprise, Denny sat on a chair staring out the window.

"Denny!" I squealed with delight. "I can't believe you're here."

He got up, walked towards me and sat on the bed beside me.

"You look terrible," he said, looking at my face and my bandaged knees.

"Hey!" I covered my legs with the blanket.

"Do you have any concealer you can put on, well, all of that?" he asked, gesturing my whole face. "Apocalypse zombie girl is not working for you."

We laughed and then he gave me a gentle hug.

"Seriously though. How are you?"

"I've been better," I replied. "How did you know I was here?"

"Luke called me and told me what happened. I flew out as soon as I could."

"How long can you stay?"

"I have to fly back tomorrow afternoon. I have a big-wig client coming to town and need to be there for a meeting."

"Ooh, how exciting." I smiled. "Thank you so much for coming all the way out here. It's so good to see you."

"I've missed you. I'd been meaning to call but didn't want to interrupt what I thought was your honeymoon phase." He raised his eyebrows. "Obviously not. My mistake."

We both laughed.

"Hey, can you keep a really big secret?" I whispered. "I mean, you can't tell *anyone*."

"No," he chuckled. "You know I can't."

"Come on Denny, please. I really want to tell you, but I don't want anyone else to know. I trust you more than anybody."

"Oh my god. Are you pregnant?" he asked excitedly.

"No. Why would that be a secret? And I told you Luke doesn't ever want children."

"Okay, I promise." He leaned closer. "What is it?"

"I can do magic without using that book," I said, waiting for his reaction.

"What do you mean? Like pulling a rabbit out of a hat or turning people into rabbits?"

"Neither. Even if I could, I wouldn't do that. I'm not psychotic."

"Did you think you were a sorceress before you hit your head or after?" he teased. "How many fingers am I holding up? One, two, eleven?"

I could tell that he was going to need some proof. I thought about it for a moment and then asked him if he still missed his stuffed bear that his mom accidentally threw out last year. I could feel him thinking about it.

"Why would you ask me that?" he said sadly. "You know I miss Mr. Bearikins."

I immediately took the sadness away and replaced it with joy. "Sorry. Feel better now?" I asked.

"Um, what just happened?"

"I can change people's moods to make them feel better. I've gotten pretty good at it. I can vacuum their sadness right out of them." I smiled.

"No, that was just a fluke. I'd need to see this again to believe it."

"Do you want me to show you using a different emotion? Think of something that makes you angry and I'll make you happy."

"No, not on me," he said while thinking. "If you can really do this, I need to see you do it to someone who doesn't know you."

"I don't see how I can do it from here and have you notice."

"Uh, you're in a hospital. This place is full of unhappy people," he replied.

"Okay. Let's do this."

I pushed the call button and asked the nurse if my friend could help me go for a walk. She happily agreed. A few minutes later, Denny and I headed down the hallway at a snail's pace. My knees hurt with every step, but I was determined to show him. I held onto the IV pole with one hand and Denny's arm with the other. We searched for someone who needed help, but most patients were asleep or just watching television. No one seemed upset.

"You'd think somebody here would be crying or moaning. For God's sake, it's a hospital," Denny whispered. "Geez."

I elbowed him and laughed quietly. "That's not funny."

We reached the end of the hall and were about to turn around to head back when we heard a child whimpering in pain. We took a couple steps to the left, following the sound. A young girl with sparse blond hair rested alone, facing away from the door.

"Her," Denny said tearfully. "If you can really do this, you should help her."

Without saying a word, I sucked out all her sadness and despair and turned it into peace and hope. She stopped crying immediately. When I tried to leave, an incredible energy came from her begging me to keep helping. She turned and looked right at me. Scary little globs had invaded most of her body. I focused as hard as I could, commanding it all to get away from her. Finally, after a few minutes of struggling, it all left.

"Oh my God." Denny's jaw dropped. "You can really do it."

"I feel sick." I panicked, trying to find a non-patient restroom close by.

When I couldn't find one, Denny helped hurry me back to my room. Barely making it to the toilet, I pushed the door shut behind me and violently vomited.

"Are you okay?" the nurse asked, knocking on the restroom door.

I couldn't answer. I kept throwing up.

"I'm coming in. Okay?" she asked.

She came in and held onto me for the next few minutes until it finally stopped. Because I shook so much, she assisted me with washing my face and kept me stable while I brushed my teeth. Then, she helped me back into my bed and told me she would ask the doctor to come in to check me.

Denny worried. I tried to take it away from him, but I started to see black spots, and everything went dark.

"Alice, Alice," I heard someone say.

A doctor stood next to my bed. Denny sat in the chair watching.

"How are you feeling?" she asked.

"Worn out and sore, but otherwise I feel okay," I answered.

"We're going to need to run some tests, additional brain and abdominal scans. We'll need to keep you overnight. If you need to use the bathroom or want to get up at all, use your call light so a nurse can assist you," she said. "Understand?"

"Yes." I yawned.

"I'm sorry." She looked at Denny. "We're going to have to end visitation for today while we monitor her. You're welcome to check back in the morning after 9:00 am."

"Oh, okay," Denny said. "I understand."

"I'll give you a few more minutes with her," she said and walked out of the room.

Denny's eyes filled with tears. "Please text me if you have any updates. I'll check back in with you tomorrow morning. Please get better, Alice. I couldn't stand it if anything else happens to you. I love you lots."

"I love you more." I smiled.

After Denny left, they took me to another floor to do a CAT scan. Afterwards, I was brought back to my room to have some blood drawn and have my vitals taken again. I wasn't hungry and my pain intensified, so I skipped the meal. They gave me morphine in my IV drip, and I barely finished texting Luke back before falling asleep.

I woke up the next morning feeling much better and stronger. The doctor told me my tests all looked good, and I should be discharged around 2:00 pm. I watched television while waiting for Denny and Luke who were on their way for a short visit before heading to the airport.

There was a knock at the door. A nurse stood in the doorway. "Would you be up for a quick visit?" she asked cheerfully.

"Sure." I figured she had come to talk to me about an aftercare plan.

Much to my surprise, she walked in with a little girl wearing a pink hospital gown holding a piece of yellow, folded construction paper.

"Anna made you a beautiful card," the nurse said smiling.

As the girl got closer, I recognized her from the day before. She smiled and gave me a handmade card with hearts and happy faces drawn all over it with crayons.

"Thank you for helping me," she said, reaching out to hug me.

"Thank you for this pretty card. It's wonderful."

I gave her a gentle hug and she squeezed me back firmly.

"What's your name?" she asked sweetly.

"Alice." I smiled.

Her face lit up. "Like from Wonderland?"

"Exactly."

"I love you, Alice."

"I love you too, Anna," I said, feeling the love behind her words. "I'm so glad you're feeling better."

The nurse took her by the hand. "Let's go get you ready for your visitors."

"Bye, Alice."

"Bye Anna."

As she started to walk out of the room, Denny and Luke showed up.

"Hey," Denny said, smiling at the little girl. "You look so much better today. How are you feeling?"

"I feel great," she said as she jumped.

"That's wonderful." Denny smiled. "I'm so happy to hear that."

"If you ever get sick, have Alice help you. God listens to her prayers," she told the nurse as they walked out of view.

"What was that all about?" Luke asked.

"Alice showed me what she can do," Denny said. "I honestly didn't believe her until I saw it myself. It was amazing."

Luke raised his eyebrows. "What did you do exactly?"

"That precious little girl was crying in her room yesterday morning. She was in so much pain, alone and frightened. I was able to go in and vacuum it all out. Just like you taught me."

Luke was surprised. "You were able to take away her physical pain too?"

I nodded.

"Was that right before you got so sick yesterday?"

"Yes, I felt ill right after. That's never happened before, but it's probably just the injuries and all the meds I'm on. But hey, it worked. She seems to be much better."

The three of us spent the rest of the morning playing cards, until they needed to leave to make sure Denny got to the airport on time. We all agreed that Denny should come back for a longer visit or plan a trip together as soon as possible.

Chapter Seven

It was strange going home with Luke after being apart for so long. A plethora of thoughts rushed through my mind. There were so many layers to him. I wondered if the ones that stirred madness would someday consume those that sought to be good. I also contemplated what having growing powers would do to me. I had always thought of myself as a good person but never had the ability to control another living being. As much as I prayed for his soul, I feared for my own.

Being gone from my job for as long as I had been, the shop owner had no choice but to hire someone else. I fully understood and wasn't in any rush to be back on my feet all day. For the time being, I needed to stay home and recuperate.

"I'm going to run some laundry," Luke said, carrying off my clothes.

"Thank you."

I made my way to the backyard and lowered myself into a lounge chair beside the pool. After being stuck inside a hospital, I welcomed the fresh air and cool breeze on my bandaged face.

Luke carried out two tall glasses of raspberry iced tea. "Thirsty?"

"Yes, please," I said, reaching for a glass. "Thank you."

He sat down in the chair beside me, and a wave of emotion came over me.

"Oh, I'm sorry. Did you want to be alone?" he asked.

"No." I smiled. "I'm just so happy to be home."

"Me too," he said while reaching out to hold my hand.

We stayed outside until around six o'clock and then went inside for the night. As a special treat, we ordered dinner from our favorite Chinese restaurant. By Eight o'clock, the pain medication I had taken with my meal began to kick in.

"I don't think my knees can make it up the stairs just yet." I worried about how I could get cleaned up or get to bed. "Would it be too terrible if I slept on the couch until the swelling goes down?"

"Oh, of course not. I want you to be comfortable."

He left the room and brought back some sheets and blankets. "Are you sure you wouldn't prefer the guest room?"

"I can stay in there if you wish."

He rubbed the back of his neck and sat the bedding down on the couch. I pulled myself up, gathered the bedding and headed to the guest room. A couple minutes later, Luke brought in my polka dot pajamas, clean underwear and toiletries.

"Thank you." I went into the guest bathroom to get cleaned up.

I was concerned when I discovered it had a tub attached to the shower. I turned the water on and got the temperature adjusted. I had difficulty stepping in because my knees could barely bend enough to enter. To minimize my standing, I hurried the best I could. I grabbed a towel, dried myself off and put on the soft white robe that was hanging on a hook. I kept trying to climb back out, but my knees were so painfully swollen, I had to keep stopping.

There was a knock on the door.

"Would you like some help?" Luke asked.

I tried not to cry. "Yes, please."

He came in and carefully lifted me out of the tub.

"Thank you."

"I'll be listening in case you need me." He left the bathroom and closed the door behind him.

After I got dressed and brushed my teeth, I went back into the guestroom to find that all the bedding was gone. I walked out into the living room. Luke made up both sides of the sectional with bedding and our favorite fluffy pillows.

"Are you going to stay out here with me?" I asked hopefully.

"Yes, if that's okay with you," he said with a kind smile. "This way, I'm close by if you need anything."

I gave him the warmest smile and carefully stretched out on the side with my pillows. Luke turned up the air conditioner to how cold I liked to keep it, covered me up with a big fluffy blanket and then laid down on his side with a book. I fell asleep right away.

The next several days, we spent together talking, watching old movies, binge-watching tv shows and playing board games. My knees hurt less with each passing day and the bruising and swelling on my face slowly went back to normal.

By Saturday afternoon, Luke and I were able to take a walk around the block and do some light grocery shopping. We came home, cooked dinner together and watched a little bit of television. Afterwards, I took a shower in the guest bathroom and dressed for bed. Once I was done, Luke went upstairs to take his.

While I waited for him, it occurred to me that I might be able to make it up the stairs. I knew I needed to hang on tight to the railing just in case my knees weren't as strong as I thought they were. I took a few steps. Though they were still a little sore, I figured I could make it the rest of the way. I went back down, took the bedding off the couch and put it in the laundry. With my right hand, I grabbed our pillows and went up the stairs.

Once I reached the top, my hands began to shake. I considered going back down with our pillows and remaking the sectional with new bedding. My heart raced trying to decide what to do. Although things had been going well with Luke, there had been so much that had gone wrong between us; I wasn't sure if either of us were ready to be physically close.

"You made it up the stairs," Luke said cheerfully as he towel-dried his hair.

There was a moment where I could sense him in my head, feeling my apprehension. He turned around, went back into the bathroom, hung up his towel and came out.

"Which way are you headed?" he asked with anticipation.

I took a deep breath, walked into our room and tossed our pillows onto our bed.

"Are you sure?" He waited in the doorway.

I walked towards him and took him by the hands, leading him to the bed. He smiled, then put his hands around my waist gently pulling me close to him. I ran my fingers through his thick damp hair and kissed him firmly and deeply. Passion consumed us as we fed off each other's desires. Having learned to create a much greater channeling connection and knowing exactly what the other wanted moment by moment, created a level of ecstasy I had never known possible.

Still riding high from the night before, I told Luke I wanted to do something special for Dimitri. Although I could never repay him for saving me or make up for what our great, grandfathers had done, I needed to do something. Luke happily agreed.

Although he was successful, we decided to go into town and secretly steer more business to his shop. It didn't take much to get into the tourists' heads. We would say over and over, '*Buy something at D'aveau Enchantments*'. As they would leave, we would suggest that they post everything on social media and leave positive reviews. By 4:00 pm, a line wrapped around the street to get into his shop.

Next, we went to visit my grandmother, bringing her a mixed bouquet of daisies. I hoped she would be able to provide some additional insight on things we could do for him. The idea was to do everything in secret, as I didn't want to take credit for our actions.

"I wish I could offer you some suggestions, but Dimitri is a bit of a lost soul right now," she said sadly. "He's asked me what I'd think about him leaving New Orleans and moving to Massachusetts. He's been looking at properties online."

"He's leaving?" I asked. "Why?"

"He doesn't like the person he's becoming and fears for his soul."

"He saved me, despite who I am and everything that's happened." I started getting worked up. "He could have just pretended not to see anything, looked the other way and never had to worry about me again. That is not the soul of someone who needs saving."

"Dimitri blames himself for what happened to you," she told me. "He's having trouble moving past it. He has nightmares about the attack nearly every night."

"Why?" Luke asked. "He had nothing to do with it and he saved her life."

"He said that if he had just forgiven our families like he had planned, as a good person would have, she wouldn't have left you and been walking alone that night. She would never have been hurt."

"What happened to me wasn't at all his fault. It was those two assholes," I said, clenching my fists. "I need him to know that and how much I appreciate what he did for me."

"Alice, he doesn't just feel ashamed and responsible. He feels abandoned," she said, taking my hands. "His parents disowned him when they heard that he saved you— a Cabot. Isabelle isn't speaking to him either and has threatened him for his betrayal."

"That's horrible. Poor Dimitri," I said. "What can we do?"

She looked at us. "Reach out to him. Let him know that he has more than an old woman who cares for him in this world."

Luke and I thanked her for her insight and went home to figure out what to do next. Neither of us could see him simply embracing our friendship and I worried about what might happen to him. We came to a consensus that we would use our books to request protection from any harm and then for an indestructible bond between Dimitri and us.

Early the next morning, Luke and I went to visit the ancestral tree. We left a bounty of fresh fruit in baskets and around five hundred dollars in small bills around the perimeter of the tree. We knew that anyone visiting the park would be welcome to take what they needed, and it was always important to give back whenever possible.

We headed to a local café that was only a few doors from Dimitri's shop to grab a bite before heading over to see him. I wasn't terribly hungry, so I grabbed a coffee and a mini apple scone. Luke ordered a Po' boy breakfast sandwich and some chai tea. Once finished, we headed out the door and down the street.

"Let's see if it worked," Luke said, smiling.

We continued until we got to his shop, but it wasn't open yet. Through the large glass windows, we saw Dimitri speaking to one of his employees. He noticed us waiting outside, walked towards us and opened the door.

"Hey, look at you," Dimitri said, gazing at me. "You look human again. How are you feeling?"

"Great. Thanks to you." I smiled.

"Did you want to come in?" he asked us.

"Actually, we were hoping that we could steal you away for the morning," I said eagerly.

"Uh, where to?" he asked cautiously.

"To go on a swamp tour," I said cheerfully.

Dimitri started laughing. "Really? That's kind of random."

"I've always wanted to go on one but could never talk Denny into it. He's terrified of reptiles. I want to see the gators but in a safe *controlled* environment," I continued. "We booked a private boat for just the three of us at 9:45 this morning. Please come."

"You're not planning on feeding me to them, are you?" he joked.

"There aren't that many, are there?" I asked, second thinking our plans.

"Oh, I don't know," Dimitri replied. "I've never been."

"You grew up here and you've never been on a swamp tour?" Luke asked, ribbing him. "Then you absolutely must come."

"I don't know," he said, looking back at his store.

"Please," I begged. "It'll be fun."

"Won't I be like a third wheel? I would hate being that guy."

"I promise you will never feel like a third wheel when you're with us," I said smiling. "Please, Dimitri?"

"Come on," Luke said. "We could all use some fun."

"Alright, alright," he said. "But I'm going to need to change first."

"Let's meet back here around 9:15?" Luke asked.

Dimitri agreed.

I don't know if I was more excited to see live alligators or that the three of us were taking the first step towards being friends. Either way, I couldn't stop smiling when I saw Dimitri approach his storefront wearing jeans and a t-shirt.

"Dropped the suit. You almost look like a regular person," Luke teased.

"And you almost don't look like a vampire wannabe," he said, laughing. "Almost."

We got in Luke's car and headed out to meet up with our tour host/air boat driver. We parked the car and took out our medium-sized ice chest loaded with beer, water bottles and snacks.

A man with red hair, a face dotted in freckles and wearing a baseball cap greeted us. "You made it," he said cheerfully.

"Are we late?" I took out my phone to check the time.

"Nah, this is a private tour, so you're right on time," he replied. "My name's Scotty. For the next couple of hours, I'm your guide to all things gator."

Everyone smiled. We followed Scotty to where the airboat was docked, and he helped us climb on. It was a small vessel with a captain's chair and two rows of seats. He instructed us to sit in the front and put the cooler on the row behind us. Luke got into his seat first and then I sat next to him and Dimitri to my right. Life jackets and headphones for the noise were under the seat but weren't required.

"Wow, this is closer to the water than I expected." I realized how low the boat was.

"That way they can just climb on up and join the party," Scotty said grinning.

I nervously laughed. "Good thing I'm in the middle then, huh? It'll be full after eating one of them before it reaches me."

"Hey." Dimitri laughed. "Is that why you invited me along?"

Scotty started up the boat and a couple minutes later, we pulled away from the shore. A nice breeze helped with the humidity, which I hadn't yet become accustomed.

As soon as we were clear from the other boats, we picked up speed, going about thirty-five miles an hour. My hair whipped against my face. I gathered it into a ponytail and put on my sunglasses.

After we had been going for about fifteen minutes, Scotty slowed the boat down to a stop.

"This is my favorite spot," he said, looking down at the green, murky water. "They like to cluster here."

I didn't see any. "Where?" I leaned over Luke and then Dimitri.

"All around us," Dimitri said with nervous excitement. "How can you not see them?"

About ten different gators came into focus.

"Oh, my gosh! There are so many of them," I said, biting my lip.

"And boy do they look hungry." Scotty reached into his tiny cooler.

"I'll go first to show you how it's done," Scotty said, placing a half of a hot dog on a long stick.

"Won't its friends get jealous and try to swarm the boat?" Dimitri asked.

"Nah, they know if they don't get something this round, there'll be another boat through here soon. They're always getting fed."

He walked up next to us, reached the stick out just above the water and one came up and gobbled the hot dog.

"Ah!" I squealed.

They all laughed.

"She's definitely going next," Luke said, elbowing me.

Scotty grabbed another hot dog and put it on the stick. "Who's next?" he asked smiling.

The guys looked at each other and then me. Each offered to let anyone go ahead of them.

"Fine, I'll do it." I took the stick from Scotty with my hands slightly shaking. I scooted closer to the edge to decide on which one to feed next. I reached the stick out towards the smallest one, but another nudged it out of the way and ate it.

Scotty smiled at me. "Awesome. Like a pro."

"You were supposed to let the little one have it," I scolded the big one. "Do you have a second stick so we can distract the big one while the others eat?"

Scotty grabbed a few more sticks and placed marshmallows on each so that all four of us had one.

"Do they eat these?" Dimitri asked.

"They love them."

We stayed in that spot feeding them until another airboat approached.

"Off to the next spot." Scotty got back into his seat and started the boat up again.

Along the way, we spotted turtles slipping in and out of the water, several species of birds and a family of raccoons hanging out on the banks. After about an hour, he took the boat close to the land and turned off the motor. He stepped out of the boat in his boots with a stringy piece of meat in his hands and picked up a small gator. I had never found them to be cute creatures but this one was. He fed it in his hands and then pet it.

"Want to hold him?" Scotty asked us. "He's friendly."

"Won't his mama be upset if we do?" I worried.

"Nah." Scotty pulled the bill of his cap down over his forehead. "He's about twenty months old. Besides, his mama and I are old friends. She won't mind."

I waited to see what the guys would do.

Luke took a step forward. "I'll do it. Haven't held one since I was a kid."

He picked him up and turned it so that its face was inches from his.

"I wouldn't do that. He's small but he could still snap at your nose," Scotty warned him.

Luke calmly rested his head on the reptile. The gator treated him like a dog to its human. My heart pounded.

After holding him for a couple minutes, he reached out to hand him to Dimitri. He waited until he had the gator completely transferred before letting go. Dimitri didn't follow Luke's lead. He held the gator the way that Scotty showed us.

"Do you want to hold him?" Dimitri asked me shortly after.

"Can you hold onto him too? I'm afraid I'll freak out and drop him. I don't want to hurt the little guy."

"Sure," he said, hanging on to the front half.

Its skin wasn't as rough as I expected. Luke took out his phone to take a picture.

"You've got to get in the picture too," I told him.

"I can take it for you guys," Scotty offered cheerfully.

We stood together smiling, crowded around the juvenile gator for the picture and then handed it carefully back to Scotty.

"Can you send me a copy of that?" I asked.

"Sure," Luke replied. "Want me to send it to you too, Dimitri?"

"Oh, I'm not into the whole social media thing."

"Do you mind if I still post it?" I asked. "I mostly want my friends in California to see it. They'd never believe it otherwise."

"Sure. That's fine."

Luke sent me the picture and I couldn't stop smiling. I made it my cover photo.

"Actually, yeah. Would you send me that too?" Dimitri asked.

It was nice to see his face light up when he looked at his phone and saw the picture.

Scotty started the boat, and we were on our way back.

"Checking this off my bucket list." I took out a little notebook and pen out of my backpack.

"What else have you got on there?" Luke asked, as I crossed swamp tour off the list.

"Lots of stuff, but I'll never have time to finish them all."

"You never know," Luke said while looking over my extensive, multi-page list.

"Maybe the three of us can do some together," I smiled. "What's at the top of your list Luke?"

He was quiet for a moment. "Camping," he blurted out.

"Camping?" Dimitri asked. "That's a bucket list item? You've travelled the world but never gone camping?"

"My mother hated the outdoors, so my parents put it off for years. When I made sure it was the only thing that I asked for my twelfth birthday, my dad finally agreed to take me without my mother," Luke said somberly.

"What happened? Why didn't you get to go?" I wondered.

"We had the car all packed up with everything we needed. The campground was about forty minutes away from our house and we were on the road by ten in the morning," Luke continued. "We sang along with the radio. My dad never could sing on key, but I still loved to hear him. Then, he stopped. The car slowly veered to the right. Before I could grab the wheel, we were in a ditch. I thought he had maybe fallen asleep, so I kept saying his name over and over trying to wake him. Then I realized he was gone, just like that."

"Oh my God, Luke. That must have been very traumatic," I said, feeling sad for him.

"I never knew about that," Dimitri said. "I heard his heart stopped, but he had died peacefully at home in his sleep."

"That's because of my mother," Luke said. "She paid off the local newspaper to have them write that it happened at home."

"Why?" I asked. "What difference did that make?"

"She said she did it for me, to keep the other kids from asking too many questions," Luke answered. "I didn't even hear about what was in the paper until much later. She sent me away to school the same day it happened. New school, new friends."

"Oh my gosh. The same day?" I asked. "Did you get any grief counseling?"

"No, she just mailed me my father's book of power and told me to use it if I needed anything. She said it was mine to control and my ancestors would help."

"You weren't even able to mourn your father," Dimitri said sadly. "I can't even imagine what you must have felt."

"How did you cope with the loss?" I asked.

"By blocking it out of my head and using the book to get anything I wanted. I always had the coolest clothes and the most expensive shoes. I was the most popular guy in school, never once had to do any homework and got to go on class trips that were above my grade level."

"How often did you come home to see your mother?" I asked.

"She had me come home for Christmas and for my sixteenth birthday."

"That's it? She had to be grieving too. Wouldn't she want you home with her?" Dimitri asked.

"No, she said I reminded her of him. Said I look just like him and it was too painful to be around me."

I could imagine all the sadness from his memories and started to tear up.

"One Christmas, I became so angry at her for keeping me away. It felt like a volcano would erupt inside me. I felt all this energy around me rushing towards me and then out of nowhere, I could hear every thought in her head. She didn't keep me away because of how I looked. She kept me away because she found me to be annoying. My mother liked being alone and enjoyed the freedom of doing whatever she wanted," Luke said.

"That's when all the mind sorcery started?" Dimitri asked, sounding surprised.

Luke nodded.

"What did you say to her?" I asked.

"Nothing. I didn't want her to know what I could do. I wanted to stay angry but all I felt was depressed. I tried to think of what I could have possibly done. I thought about how things were before my dad died. I remembered that I complained a lot, didn't try in school and hated doing my chores. I could see why she didn't want me around."

"You were a child," Dimitri said. "You should never have been made to feel that way."

"No, but she was right," Luke corrected him. "I focused on how she was feeling about me and wished I could make all of those thoughts go away—at least until I went back to school. The next thing I knew, she gave me a hug and invited me to stay a few more days. We played every board game in the house and watched a couple dozen Christmas movies. It was perfect."

"That's tragically sad but also amazing," Dimitri said. "I always thought you'd used your book to be able to get in people's heads. Never found a spell that worked for that."

"Well, that was the first and last time I used that on my mother," Luke replied. "I went back to school, focused on my studies and made sure I got into a good university by my merit alone. Whenever I came to visit, I did all the shopping, cooking, cleaning and yardwork. I'd go on long walks to give her space and stayed in my room a lot. As soon as I was eighteen, I moved all of my things out of her house to storage until I finished college and found a place to live."

"Wow, you've been through a lot," I said, taking his hand.

There was a moment of silence before we reached the docking area.

"Well, I'm in for camping, if you'll have me," Dimitri said. "But it's got to be somewhere nice, worth the drive, and there needs to be fresh water nearby."

"Sounds good," Luke said cheerfully. "Alice and I will look for a place, but if you find one first, let us know."

When the tour ended, we gave Scotty a generous tip and thanked him for being a fun host. The three of us piled into Luke's car and headed back to town to drop off Dimitri.

After Luke and I went home, we made a couple sandwiches and went for a swim to cool off.

"Thank you for being so kind to Dimitri," I said. "I'm so glad the book worked."

"I actually had a lot of fun," he replied. "I wouldn't mind having him around more often."

"Me too," I smiled.

Chapter Eight

Two weeks after the swamp tour, Dimitri told us he had found a campground with dozens of hiking trails. I missed Denny, Darren and Samantha. I called and asked if they would like to fly out and join us. It would be our treat. Although they said it sounded like fun, they had already made plans with Denny's family to go to a resort in Cabo. Instead of booking a group site, we reserved a tent site with electricity for the three of us. It had a port-a-potty and shower stall within a short walking distance.

However, a few days before the trip, we all agreed that our camping need be less sleep-on-the-ground rustic and more glamping. Fortunately for us, a family had cancelled their reservation last minute and we secured a two-room, A-frame cabin for the week. It came fully equipped with a queen-sized bed downstairs, a full-sized bed in the loft, a small working kitchen, and a bathroom with shower.

The morning of the trip, we packed up our SUV and stopped in town to gas up before heading out on our two-hour drive northwest.

"Would either of you like anything cold to drink?" Dimitri asked before heading into the convenience store.

"I'd love any kind of lemonade," I said. "Thanks."

"I'm good," Luke answered. "I filled up my water bottle before we left."

While Dimitri went inside and Luke filled the tank, I decided to use the restroom to avoid having to stop along the way. I went inside the store, got the key from the cashier and headed to the side of the building. There were two any gender bathrooms. Both doors were closed, so I tried to put the key into the one closest to me.

"Excuse me?!" a woman yelled.

I immediately took the key out and apologized. I put it in the other lock, and it unlocked. I went inside, used it, washed my hands and came out. As I walked away, the other bathroom door opened, and the woman sighed heavily behind me. I turned around to apologize again for startling her.

"You," she said. "That figures."

"Isabelle." I was surprised by the coincidence. "Sorry about the door. The key isn't labeled."

Dimitri walked up carrying my lemonade as Luke called for us to get on the road.

"Thanks, Dimitri," I replied, taking the drink.

"What's this bullshit?" she asked angrily. "Are you guys like a throuple now or something?"

"A what?" I asked.

Luke saw what was going on and came over. "What's the problem?"

"I wasn't good enough for you," Isabelle said heatedly. "But you're fine sharing her with him? That witch has both of you wrapped around her finger."

"It's not like that," I answered. "We've become friends."

"You don't need to defend yourself to her," Luke said, looking down at her. "She's beneath you."

"Isabelle, why don't you come along on the next trip?" I asked, trying to make peace. "It'll be fun."

"Um, no. I don't want any part of this horror show."

"Horror show? What are you talking about?" I asked.

"This, whatever you want to call it, won't work. I may not be able to do that mind shit that Luke does, but I assure you, this *thing* you three have can't end well."

I frowned. "You're not making any sense. We enjoy hanging out together. We've been having a lot of fun."

"Let me spell it out for you," she replied. "Those two idiots are your great-grandfathers and in case you still haven't figured it out, you're Sonya. Now that's karma with a twist."

"You're being ridiculous. That doesn't make any sense at all," I said angrily. "What's wrong with you? There's nothing inappropriate going on with us."

She tuned me out and started humming to herself.

My face burned red as she walked towards her car. I wasn't a violent type of person, but I wanted to take a good swing at her annoying, condescending face.

"Oh, did I touch a nerve?" She turned around, wiping blood from her nose. "Nice. That's very lady like. Did Luke teach you that?"

"I swear, I wasn't trying to do that," I said, raising my hands in the air.

"Oh, it's fine," she snickered. "Watching how this all plays out is well worth some dumb mirroring trick. However, you will eventually have to choose between them. Sounds fun."

"Choose?!" I yelled. "Luke and I are married, you psycho!"

She placed one hand on her hip. "Psycho, no, but I am a bit psychic."

"If you were than you would know that what you're saying is bullshit. You're bitter because the three of us get along now.

Instead of working things out with us, you're trying to make us turn on each other. You can't predict shit."

She walked back toward us and stared directly into my eyes. "I may be no seer of my own life, but I can see yours crystal clear."

I took a dollar bill from my pocket. "Okay Miss crystal ball, what do you see? What does my future hold?"

"Don't answer that," Luke said firmly. "Let's get going."

"He doesn't want me to speak because he knows I can do what I say." Isabelle grinned at Luke. "Tell them what I told you before your camping trip with your dad."

"Let's go," Luke repeated.

"What did you tell him?" Dimitri asked curiously.

"I warned him his father would die before they reached the campground. But he went anyway and didn't say a word to anyone, not even his mother. I wonder if Mr. Varlett would still be alive if he had seen a doctor? I bet you think about that every single day Luke. I know I would if I could have saved mine."

Luke lunged at her. "How dare you speak of my father!"

Dimitri held him back.

"Listen," she said to Dimitri. "I know I've been made out to be the bad guy here, but at least I gave you a warning. I could have said nothing and just let you two destroy her or the other way around. Well, honestly, I really have no problem with that either."

I wanted to ask her exactly what she saw but didn't. I thought about how awful Luke must have felt all those years since his father passed. I went inside the gas station and returned the key, then the three of us got into the SUV.

"What's a mirroring trick?" I asked curiously.

They both tried to answer at the same time.

"Go ahead," Luke said. "I need to focus while I'm getting on the freeway."

"It's basically when someone tries to harm or put a hex on you and you turn it back on them," Dimitri said.

"Huh?"

"Isabelle must have been trying to give *you* a bloody nose," he explained further.

"I didn't mean to do anything. It wasn't on purpose. I was just really pissed off."

"Well, somehow you did." Dimitri took a sip of his iced coffee. "Have you done that before?"

"Done what? Accidently given someone a bloody nose?"

"No. Reversed a spell."

"If I did, it wouldn't have been on purpose. I don't want to ever use magic to harm anyone," I replied.

"Interesting," Dimitri said, looking out the window. "If you didn't mean to do that, I wonder how it was mirrored back to her."

The rest of the drive, we put on the radio and sang along. We tried to give Luke the experience he missed as a kid without mentioning his father again.

At 10:30 am, we arrived at the campground. After checking in, we followed the map to our cabin. The interior was exceptionally clean but smelled stuffy, so we opened the windows and the door while we unpacked for the busy week.

"It's says that the waterfalls are about a six-mile hike from here," Luke said while eagerly reading the map.

"Did you want to go now?" I asked. Although I secretly hoped to go early the next morning when it would be cooler.

"We can go tomorrow, if you'd prefer," he answered.

Dimitri smiled. "Nah, let's go right now."

We all agreed, and each grabbed our own backpack with two water bottles, snacks, sunblock and bug spray. It was already warm out but not too hot.

"Maybe we should bring something to eat," I said. "We're not going to get back here until dinnertime."

"Good thinking," Luke said.

We threw together some sandwiches and Dimitri offered to carry them along with an ice pack. Luke grabbed a large flannel blanket and put it in his backpack.

"Almost forgot my phone." I grabbed it off the counter and then followed them out the door.

It took us three hours to get to the waterfalls. They weren't anything like the pictures online and not much more than a trickle. However, we were surrounded by gorgeous, towering pine trees that filtered the afternoon sunlight, which made it the perfect place to stop and rest.

Luke used his boots to clear loose pebbles from the dusty soil, then took the blanket out of his backpack. I helped him stretch it across the ground. We sat down in the shade with a sigh of relief.

"We still have to walk back," Dimitri laughed while taking out the sandwiches and passing them out. "Whose idea was this again?"

It's funny how great a plain turkey sandwich can taste when you're hungry. I was thankful we brought more than granola bars and trail mix.

"This is nice." Luke smiled at us. "Thanks for doing this with me."

"It's beautiful here," Dimitri said. "I know you'd never have to twist her arm to come. If she had her way, she'd build a cute little house out here next to that stream."

"You know her pretty well."

"Well, I think she has the right idea," Dimitri said dreamily. "I could happily live a life out here."

"I never took you for a nature kind of guy," Luke replied. "You always seem so proper."

"You never can tell." He smiled.

After lunch, we headed back to the cabin. Although it took us under three hours to get back, it felt like ten. My feet throbbed, and my thighs ached, despite stopping to rest along the way. We sat down outside on the porch chairs while taking turns to use the restroom inside.

"I hope there's plenty of hot water tonight," I said, patting the dust off my clothes. "I'm definitely going to need a shower."

"Same," they said at the same time.

Right before sunset, the guys layered some short branches and twigs in the center of the fire pit. They soon realized that neither had brought anything to get it going. I teased them while they failed miserably trying to start it using a stick and a stone. I took a lighter out of my make-up bag and started it myself. Once we had a nice crackling fire, we took out hot dogs and roasted them. Luke burned his first two but then got the hang of it.

As the night grew darker, we could barely see past the crackling campfire. The air was cool but not enough to need a jacket.

"Do you guys want to sing campfire songs?" I asked cheerfully.

They both laughed as if I had said something outrageous.

"Alright then, let's tell ghost stories," I said eagerly.

Luke smiled. "Okay. That sounds fun."

"I don't know," Dimitri hesitated.

"Too scary for you, huh?" Luke teased.

"No, but it might be for you."

Luke laughed. "I don't frighten easily."

"Well then, why don't you tell one?"

"I'm not good at this," he replied. "You tell one."

"I don't think it's a good idea. I should go last. Mine can be a bit intense."

"Great," Luke said cheerfully. "Try to scare us."

"I don't know." Dimitri said ominously. "Are you both sure?"

"Please," I said, hoping to hear a good tale. "I almost never get scared."

After a couple minutes, Dimitri closed his eyes and started humming. Luke and I smiled. We couldn't wait to hear what he would say.

"About sixty years ago before this was a campground, it was the home to an experimental psychiatric hospital for some of the most deranged killers. The staff lost many patients who were being treated for different psychoses through electric shock therapy," Dimitri continued with his eyes shut. "One of the patients was a man with shaggy blond hair and a muscular build. He was wrongfully convicted of murder and had been going through their treatments for almost two years. Then one stormy night, the power went out and he snapped. In the darkness, not being able to differentiate between those who had tortured him and the other patients, he killed everyone. When the power came back on, he saw the massacre he had caused. In denial of what he had done, he ran from body to body begging his victims to wake up. He slipped in a pool of blood, split his head open and died. Years later, the building was demolished, and this campground was built. Campers say he still walks these grounds. In the darkness of the night, as they lay in their sleeping bags, they can hear his voice whispering, *Wake up.*"

Luke and I looked at each other and smiled. I was a bit disappointed. It wasn't that scary.

"Not bad," Luke said to Dimitri who still had his eyes closed. "Nice to hear something different. I've heard that golden arm one a hundred times."

I agreed.

Dimitri sat still with his eyes remaining closed and didn't say anything for a couple minutes.

"Is he asleep?" I whispered.

"He can't be." Luke chuckled. "He was just talking."

"Should we check?" I reached for Dimitri's shoulder.

A human-shaped thing appeared right beside Dimitri shouting, "Wake up!"

Luke and I practically fell out of our seats.

The figure faded away. Dimitri opened his eyes and laughed hysterically. "I warned you."

My heart pounded so hard. I could barely catch my breath. "I've never been so scared in my life. Well done, Dimitri."

"How the hell did you do that?" Luke asked. "I'm impressed."

"You channel the living, I channel the dead," he replied as if it were nothing.

"The dead?" I asked nervously. "Was that the murderer?"

"No." Dimitri smiled. "I made that story up. You just saw Bob's essence. He was a ranger here and isn't ready to cross over. He's harmless."

Luke patted him on the back. "Man, I wish we'd been friends sooner. You would have been a blast at my Halloween parties."

Dimitri smiled.

"How did you do that?" I wondered. "Did you learn that or were you always able to do that?"

"I can't remember a time when I couldn't," he replied while adding a couple of short branches to the fire. "There's almost always a spirit nearby. You just need to know how to listen for them."

I was beyond curious about what he could do. Although I didn't want to have ghosts in my head all the time, I wanted to be able to see how it was done.

"Can I ask you for a weird favor?"

"Maybe," Dimitri replied, sounding a bit uneasy. "Depends on the favor."

Luke looked at me suspiciously.

"Can you let me see how you do it?" I asked. "Like let me in your head?"

Dimitri stiffened up. "If I let you in, you'll be able to see *all* of my thoughts."

"Can't you just focus on getting in touch with a spirit and keep the rest tucked away?"

"I don't know if I can," he said, rubbing his hands together. "It might make things weird between us."

"Never mind, Dimitri. I'm sorry," I said apologetically. "I was curious, but I shouldn't have asked."

"No need to apologize," he replied. "I just don't want to accidentally cross some line because some random thought pops into my head."

Luke unsuccessfully tried to get into his head to find out what he meant, but I knew without invading his privacy. It was like having dreams. You usually can't control who is in them or what happens. They can be completely random.

We sat in the chairs, made smores and drank beer.

"So, what's up with you and all the vampire stuff Lucas?" Dimitri blurted out.

"They fascinate me." He tossed his second burnt marshmallow into the fire. "Don't get me wrong, I love being a warlock. I've spent many years studying magic and it's who I am. We can do great things, but at the end of the day, we're mortal. Vampires are not."

"Aside from being gruesome killers, doesn't the thought of living forever seem monotonous?" he asked.

"Not at all." Luke put a new marshmallow on his skewer to try again. "I'd never run out of things to do because everything evolves. People, places, music…everything changes. There will always be something new to learn or do."

"But wouldn't that be awful to watch the people you love die over and over?" Dimitri asked seriously.

"True, but I wouldn't want to be one unless those closest to me were also. Think about all the things you could do without worrying about getting fatally injured or growing old."

"What are your thoughts on all this, Alice?" Dimitri asked.

"Hypothetically speaking—since vampires don't exist—I think the three of us could have a lot of fun if we were." I smiled. "Well, other than drinking blood. That would be gross, but I guess if we were vampires, we'd probably like it."

"I'm sorry but I can't picture someone who wants a Little House on the Prairie life ever being happy as a vampire. You'd either get bored or feel guilty draining the townsfolk," Dimitri snickered. "Except for maybe a Nellie Oleson type."

"True." I laughed. "However, if I had unlimited lifetimes, I could live out all sorts of fantasies."

"Oh really?" Luke said flirtatiously.

"Well, I see one huge flaw in your logic. What would happen to any children you two have? Would you turn them into vampires too?" Dimitri asked. "That wouldn't be right."

I didn't know what to say, but it made me stop and think. Luke and I were not going to have any children, so it didn't matter whether we were vampires. There would never be a cute little house with kids running around and no small town filled with kind country folks. I was angry that the sadness I had kept buried found a way to creep back in.

"Well, none of that's ever going to happen so it really doesn't matter." I finished another beer. "No vampires, no kids, no small town."

"Have you ever asked in your book of power to be turned into a vampire?" Dimitri teased Luke.

"Can't ask for something that isn't real nor for anything that could kill or cause harm to anyone. Basic laws of the book," Luke replied, as he finally toasted a marshmallow to perfection. "Vampirism falls into both categories."

"So that's a yes— you've tried?" Dimitri chuckled.

"Maybe?" Luke smiled.

"Really?" I asked incredulously.

"Figured it couldn't hurt. I was thirteen and still thought that Earth was flat. Every time I tried to write it down, the book erased it."

"Being stuck looking like a thirteen-year-old forever would suck," I said, thinking back at being that age. "Spend an eternity in middle school or avoiding truancy officers. Ugh."

"I guess I didn't think it through."

We all laughed and drank some more.

145

Dimitri appeared to be in deep thought. "Couldn't you ask for immortality without all the blood sucking?"

Luke immediately paced back and forth aside the campfire with his eyes fixed on the flames. "You don't suppose that's possible, do you?"

I took another drink. "No, I don't think so. You said you can't ask for anything that isn't real. Immortality's not."

He continued to pace back and forth.

"You aren't seriously considering asking for immortality, are you?" Dimitri asked. "I was just kidding."

Luke stood still. "What harm would it do to ask? The worse thing that could happen is they'll make my request disappear from the book, just like every time I've asked for something outrageous."

"Um...no," Dimitri said firmly. "The worst thing that could happen is that you get your wish, and you never grow old or die, but everyone else around you will."

"I'd ask the same for Alice—you too—if you'd like. I do owe you for saving her life, after all," Luke replied. "What do you say? Want to sign up for forever with us, Dimitri?"

"Haven't you ever heard the saying to be careful what you wish for? That book is like a genie, except much worse. You both get unlimited wishes."

Luke seemed obsessed with the idea and kept talking about it for another hour while Dimitri tried to talk him out of it. All I could do was wonder what would happen if he did it and it worked. We'd never have to get sick or watch our bones and flesh grow old and wear away. The more I drank, the more sense it made to do it.

"Would you both join me if I did?" Luke asked seriously.

"You're crazy," Dimitri said. "No, we're not going to do that."

"Until death do us part." Luke said, taking my hand. "What better way to end generations of family feuds than by us staying together for an eternity?"

I imagined what it would be like and there was nothing I wanted more. Aside from the mind-altering sex, I would never get bored with someone as intelligent and fun as Luke nor too old and weak to join in his adventures. My heart raced.

"Join us," Luke said while looking at Dimitri.

"I can't." He shook his head. "It's immoral to even ask."

"How?" I handed him another beer. "We're not asking to be vampires or hurt anyone."

"You can't be serious," Dimitri said as he chugged it down. "Weren't you raised Catholic? What do you think God would think of this?"

"God allowed the book to happen and we're not asking for anything evil," Luke said opening a bottle of rum and taking a drink right from the bottle. "If God doesn't want it to happen, he won't let it. He'll make our ancestors erase it."

"You're asking to suspend your judgement day indefinitely. That can't be acceptable." Dimitri grabbed the bottle from Luke and took a drink.

"It probably won't even work," I said, trying to sell it. "But in case it does, I want you there with us to experience all that we can in this world and beyond. Can you imagine living long enough to see travel to other solar systems? Meet other lifeforms. How amazing would that be? I wanted to be an astronaut since I was around six years old. With all the time in the world, I could be everything I ever wanted to be and so could you. Besides, God can pass judgement anytime. If he gets angry with us, he's not going to say, *Oh, I forgot. You're immortals. I'll just have to wait.*"

"I don't want to go to hell," he said taking another sip.

"Well, I don't believe in hell and we surely wouldn't be sent there for asking to live forever. But, how about this?" I felt brilliant yet highly intoxicated. "If we don't like it, we'll ask to be mortal again. This way, there's an out. What do you think?"

"I don't know," Dimitri said, starting to give in.

"Come on, we'll have so much fun," Luke said, trying again to persuade him. "We could explore the deepest depths of the seas or climb to the top of Mount Everest without a care in the world. Who needs to worry about oxygen, air pressure or freezing to death? We won't. Can you imagine the view from on top?"

"Dimitri, it probably isn't even going to work, but in case it does, I want your permission before asking for you too," I said. "What do you say? Please?"

"I suppose we can try it for a little while. Exploring sounds nice." He smiled. "But, if I ever want it to end at any point and go back to normal, you have to promise me that you'll reverse it."

"I promise," I cheerfully replied.

We all laughed.

"So then, are we doing this as soon as we get back?" I asked.

"We'll have to," Luke said, sitting down. "We didn't bring our books."

"We both don't need to write it, do we? I mean, either it works, or it doesn't," I said.

"Did you bring yours?" Luke asked.

"I did." I smiled. "Want to do it now?"

They both agreed.

I went inside, took my book out of my tote bag, grabbed a pen from my purse, came back out and sat down.

"Last chance," I said, holding the pen above a page.

Neither of them changed their mind nor tried to stop me, so I began writing: *Please give Luke, Dimitri and me the gift of immortality where no pain, aging, illness or harm can come to us.*'

"It's done," I said while staring at the ink.

"How will we know if it worked?" Dimitri asked.

"Well, it didn't get erased," I said. "Does that mean it worked?"

"Try grabbing one of the logs out of the fire," Luke said to Dimitri, laughing.

"Um, no," Dimitri replied. "If it didn't work, I'll get burned."

"How can we test it without risking getting hurt?" I asked.

We talked about ways to see if my ancestors accepted our request, but the drunker we got, the less anything made sense. We soon realized we were all too scared to test it out. We went inside around midnight and passed out.

The following morning, we got up around eight o'clock. Much to our surprise, none of us had a hangover and we were all full of energy. We decided to drive to a town about thirty minutes away that had a lakeside diner. After breakfast, we rented kayaks and paddled out together.

"The water's so clear," I said, surprised by the transparency. It reminded me of Lake Tahoe.

"That's because there's no one else here to muddy it up," Luke said.

"It's nice," Dimitri said. "I never knew this place was here."

Once we reached the middle of the lake, we realized we left our water bottles in the SUV. The guys decided it would be fun to race back to the shore.

"Ready, set, go!" Luke shouted and we all paddled off.

Before long, the guys had a hefty lead on me, but I didn't care. I wasn't particularly interested in competing against two men with strong arms. They egged each other on as they paddled like maniacs trying to be first.

"Alice!" Dimitri yelled back towards me. "Are you taking a nap back there?"

They goaded each other as I tried to catch up. I laughed and paddled faster.

"Hey look!" Luke laughed. "She's gaining on us!"

Something moved beneath me. I stopped to stare into the water but didn't see anything. Although we were in a lake, I began to get an irrational fear that there was a shark in the water. I knew deep down that there couldn't possibly be, but I started to panic and paddled like crazy again.

"Wait!" I called to them, but they were too far ahead to hear me. "Shit."

I kept going, pushing myself as hard as I could, until my oar hit something. "What was that?" I asked myself, looking in the water around my kayak and turning to see if anything was behind me. There was a splash nearby, but I didn't see anything. My heart raced.

The guys had reached the shore and waved back to me. They seemed a mile away. I kept telling myself to keep paddling and before long I would be with them.

A loud thunk against my kayak flipped me out and tipped it upside down. There must have been something in the water. I tried to think fast but stay calm. I took ahold of the kayak and turned it right side up. The oar floated nearby. I grabbed it and tossed it inside.

"Damn it." The waterproof lanyard that held my cell phone had somehow fallen off my neck.

Whatever had knocked me over was out of view. I dove under the water to look for the lanyard. Ten feet below, it laid on top of a large rock. I took a deep breath and swam down and grabbed it. When I turned around to swim back up, a large alligator moved past me towards the surface. I wondered how the hell was there an alligator. There were no warning signs posted and I thought we were far from gator country.

I waited, hoping the gator would swim away but it kept circling the kayak. The only experience I had with gators was on the swamp tour. I didn't know if it would chase me, but it seemed to be leaving me alone. I had no choice but to try to swim back to the shore. I stayed under water, turning back every few seconds to make sure it wasn't following me.

About a hundred feet from the shore, two kayaks went by above me. I swam to the surface. Luke and Dimitri paddled around looking in the water.

"Whew!" I was so thankful to be closer to them.

They both screamed.

"There's a huge gator next to my kayak," I said. "I wouldn't go out there."

"A gator?" Luke asked. "Out here? Are you sure?"

"Yes, I'm sure."

"Thank God you're okay. How did you do that?" Dimitri asked, breathing fast.

"I don't know. It didn't follow me. Luckily, he seems to want the kayak, not me."

"How did you stay underwater so long?" Dimitri asked, puzzled.

"I was only under a few minutes."

"You've been under a lot longer than that," Luke corrected me. "We saw you go under, but you didn't come back up. We've been worried."

"I'm a strong swimmer, but I can only hold my breath for three or four minutes at the most. I couldn't have been under long. I came up because I saw you two paddling over me."

"Yes!" Luke cheered like someone who had won the lottery. "It worked!"

"What worked?" Dimitri asked.

"Oh, I get it. You're trying to make me think that we're immortal." I rolled my eyes and walked out of the water. "I feel the same as yesterday. Well, except sober."

I grabbed a towel and dried off, while the guys brought their kayaks back to the shore.

"I'm going to swim back out and grab her kayak," Luke said happily.

"I don't think that's a good idea. There's a gator guarding it," Dimitri said. "Let's just let the rental people know what happened. They can probably take a boat out and pick it up."

"It can't hurt me. I'm invincible."

"Please don't," I begged him.

"You may not believe it, but you were under water for a very long time and you're not the least bit winded." Luke hugged me. "I need to know if it worked on me too."

"No," I insisted. "I can't let you go out there and do that."

"I'll go with him," Dimitri offered.

"That's even worse. Then I could lose both of you," I said angrily. "We're not immortal!"

An older couple walked past, giving us a strange look.

"Cosplay," Dimitri said, smiling at them. "We get a bit too into it."

"Right on." The guy smiled. "Good times."

As soon as the couple were out of earshot, I told them that even if the book somehow worked for me, there was no telling if my asking for them also worked. I hoped that putting some doubt in their minds would discourage them from facing a large gator.

"Okay, fair enough, but we all want to know if it worked. Right?" Luke asked.

Dimitri and I nodded.

"Let's swim back out together with Alice leading," Luke suggested.

"Do you have a massive life insurance policy out on me?" I asked, half-joking.

"I'm being completely serious," he said. "This seems like a fairly good way to test it. You couldn't have possibly stayed under water that long unless it worked."

"Please don't."

"I'm going whether or not you come. You can't stop me," Luke said, sounding like a child.

I rolled my eyes and immediately, Luke ran back into the water and started swimming out towards the abandoned kayak.

Dimitri walked towards the lake.

"Well, this is just great," I said sarcastically. "I know that I wanted the three of us to be inseparable but dying together wasn't what I had in mind."

"You don't have to come. Stay here. I'll look after him."

"Yes, I do," I replied. "He's my husband and I don't want anything to happen to you either, Dimitri. I'm not going to just sit here and hope you both don't get eaten."

Much to my disapproval, we swam out together to catch up with Luke. It was remarkably easy and none of us needed to come up for air. We reached the kayak. The gator still circled it. My heart raced as Luke reached out past the gator to grab the kayak. He seemed completely fearless, as if he were sure the gator couldn't hurt him. I swam in front of him and nudged the gator out of the way. It looked me right in the eyes and then swam off.

We all went to the surface laughing.

"How do you feel?" Luke asked Dimitri.

"Fine." He smiled. "I'm not tired at all."

"Let's see how long we can stay under," Luke challenged us.

We swam to the bottom of the lake and sat together playing rock, paper, scissors. After a while, Luke checked the time on his waterproof watch, then motioned for us to go to the surface. "Wow. We've been under for almost an hour."

We all laughed, not one of us feeling winded.

"You know, we can't tell anyone about this," Luke said seriously. "This has to stay between us three."

I couldn't imagine keeping a secret from Denny, but part of me liked the idea of no one else knowing.

Chapter Nine

We came back from our trip to find that our home had been ransacked. We didn't notice anything missing but assumed they looked for our books of power. I never asked Luke where he kept his, but he assured me that it was safely hidden. It took us about three hours to clean up everything. After a long day and a brand-new security system installed on our home, we decided to go out to dinner.

While we ate, Anna passed by with her parents. Her cheeks were rosy, and she had enough hair to wear a small pink barrette that matched her dress. As she skipped down the road, I couldn't help but wonder if she would be doing as well if we hadn't been at the hospital at the same time. I knew it wasn't my magic alone helping her that day, but I was pleased she was happy and healthy.

Seeing her again, made me remember how I was as a little girl. I loved hearing stories about Aladdin and the genie. I would daydream about how wonderful life could be if I had a magic lamp and the great wishes I would make. I never could have imagined that I would have my own genies and power of my own to help people. Of all the things I could ask for, the one thing I wanted the most had remained the same. I wished I had someone who genuinely loved me, but that was something I would never ask of my ancestors.

"You've barely touched your food," Luke observed. "Everything okay?"

"Do you think we should have done it?"

"Which thing are you referring to?" He sipped his wine.

"Asking to be immortal."

"Are you having second thoughts?" He sat his glass down.

"Forever is a *really* long time," I replied, staring out at the sunset.

"Hmm, it is."

After a few minutes of silence, the waitress came up and asked if we wanted to order dessert. When we declined, she offered to bring us the check and some to go containers.

Once we got home, I decided to take a bubble soak in the jetted bathtub. My mind kept circling back to spending forever married to someone who didn't love me. My faith and religious upbringing would never allow a divorce, but I could imagine how Luke would grow tired of me and eventually leave. Maybe having Dimitri around would help but he wasn't Denny—in time—he would disappear too. The idea of living forever without ever being loved frightened me.

"Do you want some space?" Luke asked at the bathroom door.

I wanted to say yes, but I couldn't. I never wanted to be the one to turn the other away. When everything would eventually fall apart—as Isabelle predicted—I didn't want any guilt on my conscience.

"Come in," I responded.

Luke got undressed, climbed into the enormous tub and sat across from me, "It's not too hot. I'm surprised."

I smiled the best I could.

"Want to talk about it?"

"I don't know," I said with my lips quivering, trying not to cry.

"Do you want to take it back?"

"I do." I teared up. "I'm sorry."

"What's changed?" Luke said with disappointment behind his words. "Have I done something? Have I *not* done something?"

"No. I just think it was a mistake."

"Just tell me," he said.

I didn't want to hurt him or take away something miraculous that he'd fantasized about his entire life, but I also needed him to know how much I wanted to take it all back. Luke, Dimitri and I got along so well, it didn't seem like our marriage was ever necessary. Being stuck for eternity in a loveless marriage, doomed to ultimately be alone was something I dreaded.

"Will you let me in?" he asked.

"You won't like what you see," I said, trying not to cry. "I don't want to hurt you."

"Please. Let me see what you're thinking. I can already feel your pain."

I closed my eyes and let the energy flow between us. I let my thoughts run freely where he could know everything. Then, I opened my eyes. His eyes were also filled with tears.

"I'm so sorry, Luke" I said, feeling terrible for letting him know how I truly felt.

He sat without saying a word for a couple minutes.

"I know how much being immortal means to you, Luke," I said kindly. "I'll ask to take it away from just me. You and Dimitri can still live on forever."

"Without you? You're not willing to see how things go between us before giving up?"

"I don't want to spend an eternity in an ever-changing world just to feel an excruciating solitude."

"Why do you assume the worst will happen? Why would I agree to doing this if I didn't have faith that it would work?"

"Because you're obsessed with vampirism, and this is the closest thing you'll ever get to being one. You'd have fun with Dimitri and me for a while, but it won't last," I said defensively.

"Ah." He frowned. "You're okay with me living on for a billion lifetimes without you, after having to watch you die?"

"No, I'm not, but forever apart isn't something I want to suffer either."

"But it's okay if I do," he said sadly.

"What? Do you want me to wait around until you grow tired of me and then ask to be made mortal?"

"No, I want you to keep to your vows and stay by my side forever," he said angrily. "You made a promise to me *and* to God. If you weren't planning on honoring that, you shouldn't have married me."

"I would never break my marriage vows, but I don't understand why me becoming mortal again bothers you so much. When we got married, you barely knew me."

"Barely knew you?" he asked, as if I had said something absurd. "I've known you long before we ever got married."

"What are you talking about?" I asked, feeling uneasy. "We met on the street when I got kicked in the head. That wasn't even a year ago."

"That's the first you knew of me, but I've known you for nearly ten years."

"Known me? How?" A chill went down my spine.

Before he could answer, I became angry and insisted he show me what he meant and not hold anything back.

Though neither of us touched the button, the jets stopped, and the water suddenly turned cold. I wanted to get out and dry off, but I couldn't move.

"First, promise you'll keep to your vows," he demanded.

"You know I won't break my word." I began to shiver.

"Promise, first!"

"You're scaring me, Luke."

"You are right to be frightened. Truth can be paralyzing."

My anxiety climbed, but I needed to know. "Okay! I promise. I'll keep to my vows no matter what you show me."

Luke slowly closed his eyes and opened his mind completely. This time, the room of his mind seemed like endless mirrors reflecting almost every memory he held. He pulled some into focus, one at a time, beginning with his earliest memory of falling from the sky during a storm right into the Mississippi River. He wasn't a child; he was a man who looked the same as he did when I met him.

He showed me what appeared like countless decades of his life, unageing, searching for answers to why he was still alive, unchanged and the sorcery he had within him.

Finding no one who could help him understand who or what he was, he learned everything possible about witchcraft, telekinesis and hypnosis. Eventually, his wickedly playful side took hold. He drew on his new and exciting abilities to manipulate the witching communities into believing two books of power existed—there was only one—given to my ancestors. It was passed down one by one through many generations. He found enjoyment in watching the other witches believe that the Varletts had control of a book that never existed. In fact, he had no memory of any of his real family but somehow knew his own name. Wishing for some connection to humanity, he had pity on a childless spinster's loneliness and made her believe he was her long-lost son. He took pride in how easily he could manipulate anyone he met, including Dimitri and Isabelle who were exceptionally gifted in necromancy.

Next, he showed me the terrible loneliness that consumed him and how he happened to notice my father mailing a card out in the middle of the night. His boredom and curiosity got the best of him. He opened the mailbox and read the card before resealing it. He learned that he had been keeping a child in secret and wondered why. He copied the address and spent the years up until my father's death studying me. He followed me around, memorizing everything about me until he was able to secretly channel me. He was there feeling and exploring my every emotion. He knew the pain I went through being without any family and from my many failed relationships.

When my father died, he made sure that my grandmother found the birthday card he had planned to send. He took the book of power out of my father's well-hidden safe and put it with his things. He showed me how he devised a plan to make us meet in the street but didn't intend on me getting hurt.

The last thing he let me feel was that everything he did was so that I would too be immortal, bound to him by marriage and unbreakable by my faith. He would never have to be alone, as no request could be undone once written in the book of power.

The jets turned back on, the water turned very warm again and he opened his eyes. My jaw dropped and my heart pounded. I was angry and had so many things I wanted to say, but I sat in the bubbles staring at his face thinking about my stupid vows.

"Tongue tied?" he asked. "Understandably so."

"You were in my head all this time, seeing *everything?*"

"No, I'm not a pervert." He said defensively.

I paused for moment, then asked fearfully, "What are you?"

He said calmly, "I can only share what I showed you."

It felt as though the bathtub was dropping like a broken elevator and I couldn't get out or even move. All those years of feeling like I was being haunted was Luke. It was impossible for me to understand how or why God would allow any of this to happen.

"You remember no age before looking like you do now? You have no family? Everything was a lie?" I was frightened. "Or was all that you just showed me another one of your mind tricks?"

"No tricks. I told you everything I could," he replied.

"What I wrote in the book of power can't be undone? Does that mean what I did to Dimitri too?" I sank my shoulders just below the water. "I told him I'd reverse it if he ever wanted me to. I promised him."

"I'm sorry, but no. You can't take back what you write in the book. I've watched your ancestors try over the years."

"Why didn't you stop me from writing Dimitri in there too? He was talked into doing it while he was drunk?" I asked tearfully. "He's going to hate me."

"I actually hadn't planned on that happening, but I agreed to it for you."

"For me? Are you kidding me?" I asked angrily.

"If whatever this is that I am someday ends, I don't want you left alone. You'll have each other. Besides, he would have eventually gone along with it, even if he were sober. I saw into Dimitri's soul before he figured out how to block me. He cares deeply for you."

"If you just wanted me to end up with Dimitri, then why did you interfere? My grandmother wanted me to marry him. Why didn't you just get into my head and make me love him instead of you?"

Luke's face lit up.

"Don't smile," I said, scolding him. "Why are you smiling? This isn't funny."

"Despite everything I've done, you actually love me. Don't try to deny it. I can feel it."

"Well, I don't *want* to love you. I'm furious with you," I replied. "You're a terrible—whatever you are."

"You're right to be angry." He smiled. "I am terrible."

"Well, I don't find this amusing."

I stood up, turned on the shower head, sprayed him in the face, rinsed the bubbles off me and stepped out.

After I dried off and put on my robe, I glared at him. "Why did you have to get us so deeply involved in all this? You had been alive a really, long time. Why didn't you just wait until you found someone you could love? Anyone in my bloodline could have easily been tricked into making her an immortal."

"I did wait—you have no idea." He rinsed off and grabbed his robe. "Do you think I went through all this scheming if I didn't love you?"

"My God, that's not how love works!" I pulled the hood over my face, screamed into the fabric, then flopped down on the bathroom floor crying uncontrollably.

"Alice—"

"Please don't." I trembled.

After a few minutes, I pulled some toilet paper from the roll and blew my nose. I stood up, walked out of the bathroom towards the stairs and stopped to sit on the first step. I leaned my head against the wall and continued crying. Luke sat a few feet away not saying a word. His guilt, worry and sadness weighed him down.

"I'm not going to leave you—I can't." I looked over at him, feeling some sense of empathy. "But now, I don't feel like I know who you are Luke. I don't see how we can make a marriage like this work and for such an incredibly long, long time."

"You can sense how I feel for you though?" he asked, scooting closer.

"I'm not sure of anything anymore." I began to feel numb. "Your feelings don't make sense to me. You've been in my head for so long. You know my thoughts, my mistakes, my *many* breakups, my insecurities and every bad habit. When I met you, I felt absolutely broken, Luke. I was always the test drive, the woman men dated before meeting their future wives. That's why I wasn't dating anyone when I met you. It's not that I didn't want to have someone to love. I was tired of being lied to and used. *Every* man I've ever dated told me he loved me but none of them did. We're married, but why on earth should I believe that you're any different?"

"You're right. I went about this the wrong way. I was there feeling your heart break so many times, yet you kept trying to meet the one. When you stopped dating, I saw an opportunity. But then, I learned about your grandmother's plan to have you marry Dimitri. If there ever were such a thing as your perfect man—your soulmate—it's him. He's just like you: kind, selfless, loyal, brave and loves unconditionally. He even wants a big family. I could feel his deep fondness for you as soon as he met you." Luke sounded lost. "And when I felt how attracted you were to him, I knew it wouldn't be long before you fell in love with each other. I know that I probably should have done the right thing and just let you and Dimitri happen, but I just couldn't. I'm sorry."

"All those times I visited New Orleans with Denny, you were already in my mind, watching me?" I asked, feeling drained.

"Yes."

"You could have met me years ago. Every time we came to this city, I was single. Why didn't you just behave like a normal person and come up and say hi? Let me get to know you naturally? My grandmother didn't even know I existed yet."

"I knew you wouldn't have liked who I was at that time. It was easier to not have you know me at all."

"But it was okay that you knew every detail of my life?" I asked and then sat quietly for a moment. "I'm tired, Luke. I don't want to talk about this any more tonight. Can we just stop for now?"

"Okay." he said, standing up.

I stood up, walked into our room and climbed into bed. Luke took off his shirt and got in, staying as far to the edge as he could. After a couple minutes, I scooted towards the center, and he moved closer to me until he cradled me in his arms. Although I sensed that he wanted to take away my sadness, anger and disappointment, he knew I needed to work through it on my own. All he could do to help was hold me until I fell asleep.

When I woke up the next morning, Luke told me he had arranged for me to fly out to Sacramento that afternoon to visit my friends who had returned from their trip. He knew how much I missed them and that a short time apart might be good for us. It sounded like a good idea to me, so I didn't protest.

"When you get back, I'd like for the two of us to take a trip somewhere," he said. "Would you be okay with doing that?"

"Yeah. I feel like you know me. It would be nice to get to know the real you," I said, feeling a bit more hopeful. "Can you just plan it all out while I'm gone?"

"Where would you like to go?" he asked cheerfully.

"Maybe somewhere you've never been, if that's even possible."

I could tell he was trying to think of a place, but he was well travelled.

"Anywhere is fine." I went to pack.

Chapter Ten

When I landed in Sacramento, I walked out of the terminal to find Denny wearing reflective, cerulean blue sunglasses. He held a sign that read 'Wonderland Express.' I immediately laughed and ran to give him a hug.

"You're here!" He smiled and hung on tight.

"Thanks for picking me up."

"Did you want to stop to get something to eat before we head to my place?"

"I'm not hungry but we should pick something up if you are," I replied.

"I had a massive lunch."

I grabbed my luggage from the baggage claim, and we were on our way.

"I hope you don't mind that it's just us tonight," Denny said.

"No one else wanted to see me. I see how it is," I said jokingly.

"They do, but I thought we should have tonight alone to talk," he replied, sounding serious. "Luke didn't really fill me in on much, but he made it pretty clear that you needed your best friend right now."

"I do." I did my best not to cry.

After we got to his house and I put my things in his extra bedroom, we sat down on his giant red bean bag chair to talk. I told him everything that had happened. His eyes filled with tears.

"Okay. I promise I won't ever mention this again, because I know your beliefs and that you've already made up your mind. But...I'm your best friend, so I must say something. What Luke has done warrants an annulment. You do *not* have to stay married to him. He's marathon stalked you, deceived you and pretty much everyone he's met just for the hell of it, but it's all supposed to be okay because he says he loves you," he continued. "I don't know what that is exactly, but that is most certainly not love. I know you believe marriage is a promise to God, but I think he will let you off the hook on this one."

"Do you think I'm going to hell?" I asked sadly. "I never really believed in it, but after what I've done, I'm afraid."

"Listen. Your heart has always been in the right place. You didn't do that to Dimitri to hurt him and you only married Luke

173

to try to bring peace. Even if hell does exist, how could God put you there for that? Seems a bit extreme."

"What if Luke's a fallen angel or something worse than that? He's done a lot of ornery stuff and he doesn't even know where he came from. Could I be damned for loving him?" My hands trembled. "Even if there is no hell, I'd never be able to go to heaven and see my family again."

"What did your Grandma always tell you when things weren't going well?" he asked.

"God still runs the world," I replied.

"Yes, and you need to have faith in that."

"You're an agnostic Denny. How can you possibly ask me to have faith?"

"That's exactly why I can say that. Would you have believed any of this was possible a year ago?"

"I barely believe it now."

"The only thing you need to focus on is being a good person."

"I'm not, Denny. What about Dimitri? I've ruined a good man's life and he will hate me for it," I said, tearing up. "I made him a promise, but I can never undo what I did to him. How can I ever possibly make things right?"

"You can't change anything, but you can do everything imaginable to make his immortality feel like a gift, instead of a curse," he said kindly. "Spend your life doing what you always have, trying to make others comfortable and happy. Go above and beyond for Dimitri and keep helping people like you did for that little girl. There's so much good you can do with your powers. If you're going to stay with Luke, you've got to focus on that."

"Thank you, Denny," I said, feeling more hopeful. "I don't know what I ever did to deserve a friend like you. You always make me feel better."

We hugged for a few minutes and then he said out of the blue, "Okay, now that I've said my peace, you have got to show me this underwater thing you can do."

I laughed. "Okay, do you want me to do it in your bathtub or the sink?"

"Neither. Put on your swimsuit and come out back," he said cheerfully.

I changed and walked out to his backyard. It was dark out by then and he had turned on a bunch of twinkling patio lights. To the right, Denny sat in a hot tub with turquoise lights.

"When did you get this?" I asked excitedly. "This is awesome."

"Last week," he replied happily. "I sold my app to that big wig client and wanted to treat myself."

"That's great! I'm so proud of you!"

"Aww, thanks. Now get in," he said anxiously. "I have got to see this."

I climbed in and scooted towards the center. "How long do you want me to stay under?"

"Until I tap you on your shoulder or when you run out of breath," he said excitedly.

"Okay." I slipped under the water.

Before I knew it, he tapped me on the shoulder, and I came up calmly without gasping for air.

"That was amazing. You were underwater for like ten minutes. What else can you do?" he asked eagerly. "Can you try something else?"

"I don't know. Do you want to try to cut my head off?" I joked. "Or one of my hands?"

"Eww, Alice. No."

I laughed.

"Are you like a mermaid now?" he asked, wide-eyed. "Could you make me breathe underwater?"

"Do you want to be immortal too?"

"No. I meant like they do in the movies. As much as I love you and think your new superpowers are badass, I get bored far too easily to ever want to live forever," he said while watching the bubbles pop. "But if you had absolutely no one else, I would do it for you."

I hugged him. "I'm going to hate it when the day comes that you're up there and not with me."

"I'll tell you what." Denny smiled. "When my time comes—if there's a God—I'll ask if you all can be let off that immortality hook, when you're ready."

I smiled at him, leaned my head on his shoulder and we sat together staring up at the stars.

The next few days were spent with friends dropping in and out before and after work. We barbecued and drank a lot, but I never got more than a slight buzz. It was nice to get caught up with their lives. But time flew by and the next thing I knew, it was the night before I had to go home. Denny and I stayed up late talking.

"I wasn't going to bring this up, but this is the second time that you've kept stuff from me. You can't do that. I'm your best friend. You've got to tell me when you're going through stuff," Denny said seriously. "I worry about you every day and now that I know what Luke did, I'm going to worry even more if I don't hear from you."

"I'm sorry. I'll make sure to keep you in the loop, no matter what's going on."

"Promise me there won't ever be secrets between us," he said, looking directly into my eyes.

"There are some things I can't tell you because I'm married now," I said, laughing.

"I don't mean about that kind of stuff, gross," he shuddered. "I definitely don't want to hear any of that. That's what Sam's for."

"Okay," I smiled.

"No more secrets between us." He put out his pinky finger. "Let's swear on it."

"Okay, but after I tell you something and you promise not to laugh at me or act weird," I said, feeling a bit uncomfortable. "It's really not a big deal or anything but you said no more secrets."

"I won't laugh. What is it?" he asked eagerly.

I took a deep breath and said, "You were my first crush."

"What? For real?" He laughed hysterically. "You're just messing with me. You never had a crush on me. You told me that your first crush was Matthew Bradford in the first grade."

"That's different. A crush at six and a crush in middle school are vastly different. I had the biggest crush on you when we first met and up until seventh grade. I cried like a baby when I overheard Samantha telling her sister that you only liked boys. I was so upset—I even faked being sick so I could stay home until I got over it."

"Oh my God." He stood up and walked around with his hands over his mouth. "Shut up."

"It was a long, long time ago, it's not like I've been pining away for you this whole time. I love that we're best friends. I wouldn't have it any other way," I said, feeling slightly embarrassed. "It's really no big deal. Why are you overreacting?"

"Because all this time I thought you knew me better." He sat back down. "How did it slip past you?"

"What are you talking about?"

"I'm bi, Alice."

"What? No, you're not."

"Who did you think Missy was in high school?"

"A girl you were kissing to make your ex-boyfriend jealous."

"I was *dating* her," he said. "I went out with her for like two months. She went with us to Six Flags. You're my best friend. How did you not know that?"

"I just thought you really wanted to get back at Ben for breaking up with you."

"So, let me get this straight. No pun intended," he said with his eyes wide open. "If one of us had said something back in middle school, we might have been a thing this whole time and avoided all the crazy drama? *We* could have been married with kids right now?"

We both started laughing uncontrollably.

"Well, I'm thankful you've put up with me all these years. You're my favorite person in the whole world." I gave him a big hug.

"I love you, but you've got to learn to pay better attention to social cues. Good lord, Alice." He smiled.

Denny and I never spoke about it again. However—in a small way—it was nice to know that someone so amazing could think we might have worked out. At that moment, I thought that whomever he chooses one day, would be the luckiest person in the universe. Denny was most certainly Earth's greatest treasure.

When I returned home the next day, I found out Luke had donated the beds from our separate rooms and made each more like an office/workout space.

"No more awkwardness," he said, explaining what he'd done. "Okay?"

I smiled and nodded.

"I let Dimitri know that we'll be gone for a couple weeks but he should call us if he needs anything."

"Did you decide where we're going?" I asked.

"It's already booked. We have a flight at 10:00 am tomorrow," he replied.

"Where are we headed?"

"Tennessee."

"Really?" I sort of hoped he was kidding. "Like Nashville?"

"No, Santa Fe and that's all I'm saying for now."

I walked upstairs wondering why on earth he would pick a place like that. Was that the only place he'd never visited in his long life? At first, I was a little bummed out, but then I realized I had plenty of time to see the rest of the world.

"Trust me," I heard him say loudly from downstairs. "And no trying to get in my head to find out. It's a surprise."

Although I had little interest in going to Tennessee, other than seeing the Great Smoky Mountains and being able to say I visited every state, my curiosity was peaked. I ran my laundry, finished getting packed and came back down the stairs to find Luke answering the delivery guy at the door. He took the pizza into the living room and sat it down on the coffee table.

"Have you seen this yet?" I asked, looking at the movie paused on the television. "It's so good."

"Not as many times as you have." He laughed.

"Hey." I smiled.

We stayed up late watching The Lord of the Rings trilogy, before falling asleep on the couch. Neither of us set our phone alarms, which caused us to sleep right through the one upstairs. Somehow, we managed to make it to the airport on time.

Our flight landed around 12:30 pm. The driver picked us up to take us to our vacation rental shortly after 1:00 pm. I was curious to find out what Luke had planned for us. I had a childlike excitement that reminded me of when Denny's family invited me along to visit Disneyland for the first time.

"We should be there in about ten minutes," the driver said.

"Yay," I said cheerfully.

It wasn't long before we were away from the city and we were surrounded by fields and small farms. We drove down a dusty, dirt road.

"Excited?" Luke asked.

"I am." I smiled.

The driver turned right onto a long, private driveway paved with cobblestone. Our destination came into view, and I squealed with delight. There were tiny Hobbit style houses built into the hills, all sitting on a working farm. I had always wanted to go to New Zealand to visit the movie set, but this hidden gem was much closer. It was like we stepped right into the books I so loved.

"You're pleased?" Luke asked, already knowing the answer.

I sprung up on my tippy toes and kissed his cheek, forgetting about our recent troubles. "Yes."

"Is this your first time visiting?" the driver asked as he pulled the car up to the parking area.

I waited for Luke to answer.

"Yes, we've never been," he replied.

As soon as the car was fully stopped, I flung the door open and stepped out. Luke grabbed our luggage from the trunk, and we thanked the driver. I couldn't stop smiling.

"Good afternoon," a man welcomed us from the office dressed in hobbit-style attire. "Come on in."

We followed him inside. He checked our IDs, then gave us a map of the property and our keys.

"Meals are served in the dining hall every day from 8–10 am, 12–3 pm and 5–8 pm. There is no dress code, but we ask that you bring a good appetite and a smile," he said cheerfully.

"Sounds great," I said.

"The office is open every day from 8:00 am until 10:00 pm, but you can always reach someone on our staff at the number on the bottom, if you need anything."

"Thank you," Luke said, looking at the map.

"Yours is circled. It's the green and yellow one at the end of this row," he said cheerfully.

Luke and I rolled our luggage down the path to our little hole in the hillside. The windows and front door were round and had two rocking chairs out front with a small fire pit. The inside was cozy with a kitchenette, wooden dining table, king-sized bed and bathroom with shower. It was quite charming.

"Want to unpack and then go for a walk?" he asked.

"Sounds good."

Once we finished, we filled our water bottles and headed out. Following a trail that ran adjacent to the property, we headed towards a creek. About half-way there, we passed a family of three going the opposite direction.

"Afternoon," the dad said.

"Good afternoon," we replied.

Their son—who appeared to be around ten years old—had been complaining all day. He didn't know they had planned to meet up with his best friend and his family at Universal Orlando in a few days. The mother debated about telling him to make the boy behave better, but the father didn't want the surprise spoiled. I decided to quickly go into the kid's mind and improve his mood.

"I'll race you back," the boy said cheerfully to his parents.

They all ran off laughing.

Luke gently elbowed me and smiled.

About fifteen minutes later, we reached the creek. This was perfect timing, as we were both starting to feel a bit warm. I kicked off my sandals and put my feet in the cool water.

"You were smart to wear shorts," Luke said, rolling up his pant legs and stepping in.

I cupped my hands with water and splashed my face. "It's actually really nice in the shade."

Luke skipped a few stones and then stared into the water. "When I found this place, I was so excited to bring you here, but I also wondered if you were ever going to come home."

"I already told you that I'll never leave you." Why are you bringing this up now? We're having such a nice day," I said sadly.

"What do you see when you look at me?" he asked quite vulnerably.

I took a moment to think before responding.

"I need you to be completely truthful."

"All right, I will." I stared into his sad, sparkly blue eyes. "I see someone unimaginably powerful and likely unstoppable, a man who's capable of doing both great and terrible things to attain anything or anyone he desires."

Luke's eyes filled with tears.

I walked up to him, took his hands. "But I also see a man who is physically exquisite with an incredibly tender heart.

Someone I look forward to having an eternity to fully understand and enjoy."

"Thank you for coming back to me," he said as he kissed my cheek.

Luke and I spent the rest of the first week mostly alone. We took a lot of walks and picked up all our meals and brought them back to our room. It was nice to have no distractions and focus on each other. During this time, we talked a lot about what we were going to do with our extraordinarily long lives. I told him how important I felt it was to continue helping people and making sure that Dimitri stayed content with his life.

We both wondered if someday he would fall in love and request the woman's immortality. I knew I would want to do that for him, but Luke didn't like the idea. He feared that it would somehow leave me alone. I didn't want to think about what Luke really was or if the time I had with him was limited, so I insisted that we deal with it only if it came up.

"What about Denny?" Luke asked out of the blue. "His passing will be devastating to you. Have you thought about asking for him too?"

"He doesn't want to be an immortal, Luke. He told me so himself."

"You offered him that?"

"I didn't offer exactly. I misunderstood what he was saying when I asked him about becoming immortal. It doesn't matter, he said he'd be too bored," I replied.

"Are you okay with that?"

"I'm fine," I lied. Every day I had to block the thought of never seeing him again after he died.

"I'm sorry." Luke took my hand. "I know how much he means to you."

"Well, I'm his friend. He wants to be with his family more. That's how it should be."

That night, I had a frightfully realistic dream from which I had difficulty waking. It was many years in the future and all my friends had passed away. Luke, Dimitri and I shared a seaside cottage in Crovie, Aberdeenshire, Scotland. We had been living there for about ten years. Our life was peaceful and rewarding. We spent our days enjoying the beauty of the world while finding ways to help people in secret.

One evening, we sat on wooden porch chairs, looking out over the sea, as the sun began to set. Out of nowhere, a man dropped out of the sky and into the water right in front of our home. He was a beautiful being with jet black hair and had incredibly bright eyes like Luke's, except his were green. He told us his name was Sebastian. He had come to take his brother home to a place called Daska.

Luke was thrilled to learn that he had a family waiting for him. He hugged him without hesitation. The person he was and his life before his descent to earth came rushing back to him. When Luke eagerly asked us to go with them, his brother explained that we were not gods and would not be accepted in their realm. Luke explained that we were immortals too, but we were quickly dismissed. He told him that I was his wife. Sebastian then said that I alone would be allowed to join him. Somehow, I knew he lied, and it would close before I could get through.

Dimitri pressured me to leave with them. He assured us that he would be fine on his own, but Luke and I could feel the despair behind his words. Sebastian explained that the portal would only remain open for one hour. I could feel how devastated Luke was at the thought of never getting to see his family again but also didn't want to leave Dimitri behind.

When the portal opened, we said good-bye to our tear-filled friend and ascended. As it began pulling us up, I thought about how much I wished I could also see my family and friends again. The force from the portal pulled my hand away from Luke's, causing me to fall to the sand. Watching him disappear into the sky forever brought me more despair than I had ever known in my waking life. When I was finally able to escape from the nightmare, I was still sobbing.

Luke scooped me up and held on to me tightly. "It's okay. I'm here. It's just a bad dream."

I held on to him still shaking.

"Do you want to tell me about it?" he asked.

I shook my head. The dream embodied my deepest fears. I couldn't speak.

"Will you show me?"

I nodded.

I opened my mind and showed him everything while it was still clear in my head.

"Shit," he said, turning on the lamp next to the bed. "That was horrible."

"It felt so real."

"That's never going to happen," Luke said, trying to assure me. "It was just a really bad dream."

"I know this is probably a dumb question, but did anything in my dream seem familiar to you? The name of the place? The brother?"

"You need to find a way to stop thinking about that kind of stuff," Luke replied. "We can't worry all the time about what might happen to us. That's no way to live."

"If you found out that you have a family somewhere, you'd want to be with them. I couldn't be the reason you stay away," I said seriously. "You would eventually need to go home."

"Home is wherever we are." He put his arm around me. "And if I had a family somewhere that sent me here as some sort of punishment or wouldn't allow both you and Dimitri to come, I wouldn't go with them or want anything to do with them."

"You should never have to make that choice." I replied.

"Listen, none of us will ever have to choose. I put that vision in Isabelle's head. I'm not leaving you or Dimitri behind. We are together always."

I gave him a hug and said, "I hope you're right. I know it was just a dream, but we don't know if the book has power beyond this world."

"Well then, to be safe, we'll just never move to Scotland," he joked.

He masked his concerns and didn't want to discuss it any further. I decided to drop it and start getting ready for the day.

There was a lot of noise outside. We walked towards the window and peaked through the curtains. A group of adults dressed in Lord of the Rings costumes laughed as they walked towards the larger cottage nearby. We smiled at each other and then closed the curtains.

"They must have checked in last night," Luke said.

"They look like fun people," I said cheerfully. "We've definitely got to eat in the dining hall today."

"Absolutely."

After we showered and got dressed, we headed to breakfast a couple minutes before 9:00 am. The hall was crowded, and the aroma of sizzling sausage and bacon drifted through the air. It made my stomach rumble.

"There they are," Luke said, glancing at a large table near the center of the room.

"It would be cool if one of them spoke Elvish," I said. "Would it be too weird if we joined them?"

"We can make sure it's not." Luke winked. "Remember?"

After a few seconds, the group signaled for us to sit with them. I smiled at Luke, knowing what he had done, and we walked over and sat down at the table.

Shortly after, the waitress brought us our menus. The conversations revolved around the movies and the books. It was so much fun.

"Is she supposed to be Arwen?" a young woman with platinum blonde hair mumbled.

"God, I hope not," the rock star looking boyfriend snickered. "Arwen was hot, not dumpy."

The woman at our table overheard them and began to remove her long brunette wig. Her husband, who was dressed like Aragorn, complimented her on how pretty she looked and told her to ignore them. She adjusted it and kissed his cheek.

The couple continued making fun of everyone in costume. My face turned red. I channeled Luke, wondering what we should do. He winked at me and then worked his magic.

"Hey!" the whole table said cheerfully to the couple. "Come sit with us."

The young woman rolled her eyes. "As if."

The costumed guests continued to ask them nicely to join us.

"No thanks," the rock star boyfriend replied, looking annoyed.

"Please. It will be fun." The Arwen lady grinned.

Next, the waitress asked the couple if they would like her to push our tables together. They still declined.

"Come on Grima and Saruman," a man dressed like Frodo said cheerfully. "The more the merrier."

The young woman became angry. "What did you call us? And which one am I supposed to be?"

"We love your costumes," Luke said. "My wife and I feel like the odd ones out here, but we're joining in. Please, come sit with us."

The rock star boyfriend laughed, looked at his girlfriend and said, "Come on Saruman."

She smiled and said, "Sounds fun, Grima."

Through the rest of their stay, everyone called each other by their character names. Although Luke using people as puppets would have normally made me angry, I thought it was a great idea. It made the couple behave much better and everyone had a genuinely good time.

Chapter Eleven

The next few years were especially difficult for us. Denny fell in love with a religious man named Craig who forbade him from speaking to me, after learning about my powers and immortality. My grandmother had fallen ill and then died of a heart attack. Within the same month, both of Dimitri's parents perished in a small airplane accident. This devastated him. The day after their funeral, Dimitri texted us to let us know that he needed time away to heal on his own. He could not get past the fact that they still were not on speaking terms at the time of their death. He rarely came home, and when he did, it was for a couple of days. I missed him terribly and hated that he was slipping away from us.

With no more ties to New Orleans other than Luke's shop, I asked him if we could move somewhere else to have a fresh start where no one knew us. We sold both my grandmother's house and our home and decided to travel until we found somewhere that was a good fit. It took about three months before we bought a nice home on the beautiful Oregon coast.

We carefully chose a beach house that was placed between a few rental properties.

Years passed and neighbors would come and go around us without noticing we stayed the same. We remodeled the house several times, until there were no more ideas left. To make sure I was always giving back to the world—especially when we weren't traveling—I volunteered at the local children's hospital. I healed in secret but over time it was torn down to build a hotel. I longed to find a greater purpose.

One evening, while Luke had gone to a specialty market to purchase some wine and cheese, I decided to go for a swim. I kept going further out—watching dolphins at play—not realizing how far I had gone. I swam back as fast as I could when I saw Luke standing on the beach next to Dimitri. As I got closer to the shore, he walked away.

"Who was that?" I asked disappointedly.

"Some guy looking for his dog," Luke answered.

"I thought he was Dimitri," I said sadly.

Luke hugged me. "Why don't you ask your ancestors to send him to us?"

"I want him here, but I won't force him to come." I walked towards the house. "Besides, it's no use. The book of power doesn't always work, and I don't like using it. I asked for us to have an indestructible bond, but he isn't here."

"Maybe they interpreted the words differently," Luke said. "Can't hurt to ask again."

"If he wanted to be here, he would."

I went inside, took a shower and got dressed in my pajama shorts and tank top. I came out to find Luke finishing up a call with Dimitri. It was as if he didn't want to speak to me.

"How's he doing?" I asked. "Is he coming to visit soon?"

"No." Luke looked concerned. "He's in Nepal seeking assistance to end his immortality."

"He wants to die?" I gasped.

"No, no, not now. He just doesn't want to live forever. He's been travelling, looking for answers on how to undo what was done to him. He just wants to have the option."

"He told them about my book?" I asked.

"He didn't mention your name, only that he willfully agreed to it, but wants it undone."

"Is that even possible?"

"I don't know, but he's trying to find out."

I should have been happy knowing there was a small chance that someone could undo what I did to him, but I wasn't. He had been away from us for a long time, but I always thought that we had forever, so I could wait it out. I wondered if he hated me for what I had done.

I felt guilty. "I shouldn't have done it in the first place."

Despite the things that had gone wrong for so many years, Luke was the true constant in my life—my unending love. He treated me with immense kindness and incredible affection but was never smothering. He had told me once that Dimitri was my soulmate. I never believed in such a thing, but if I could imagine what that might look like, it would be my Luke.

Early one morning, I woke up to an empty bed. I thought Luke might have gone surfing. I brushed my teeth, took a shower and got dressed. When I came out, he still wasn't back. I looked through the windows towards the water, but no one was there. I was about to text him when I heard voices near the side of the house.

"A promise is a promise," a man told Luke. "I'm so happy for you. I gladly surrender it. The throne is yours brother. It will be so nice to have you home for good."

"Has that much time passed already?" Luke asked, sounding surprised.

"You've been on Earth for nearly two hundred years," he answered. "You know, you cut things pretty close. If you had married her more than a few weeks later, you'd becoming home as a prince, not the king."

My heart sank. I didn't want to believe what I heard.

"When am I to return for my coronation?"

"Today, tomorrow, as soon as you're ready," he answered happily. "You know Lucas, that was pretty clever of you to choose a witch powerful enough to keep herself young forever. I bet that made the whole husbandly duties thing a bit more enticing."

I waited for Luke to say something to take it all away, but he didn't. Although I was angry and heartbroken, I forced myself to block out every feeling I had to keep Luke out of my head. I grabbed a couple changes of clothing, my book, phone, jacket, wallet and passport and put them in my backpack. I snuck out the back patio door, through the backyard and climbed over the fence into another neighbor's yard.

"Hey there," a woman called out from her bedroom window. "Are you alright?"

I kept running until I passed through her gate and to the front of her house. I jogged down the road trying to figure out where to go. I didn't know whether Luke would even bother to say goodbye, but I didn't want to be there if he did. I was the butt of some stupid cosmic joke and just a player in a dumb bet. Rage filled my soul. The ground beneath me shook. I panicked at the thought of him ever being able to read my thoughts again. I quickly took out the book of power and wrote, '*Please keep Luke from getting in my head.*' I immediately sensed my ancestors' protection, and my thoughts were completely guarded.

I decided to call for a ride to the Portland airport. When I arrived, I studied the screens trying to figure out where to go. A woman in her late forties was standing behind me with her teen-aged daughter. They were headed to Dublin, Ireland. The woman had a terminal illness, and their trip was her last wish. I memorized the flight number on the boarding passes they were holding.

I walked up to the ticket counter and asked, "Are there any seats available on flight 4987?"

The woman checked on her computer. "Yes, business class. Would you like to purchase a ticket?"

I bought the ticket and sat down nearby to wait for the flight. About an hour later, they called my group and we boarded.

A while after take-off, the flight attendant asked, "Would you like anything to drink?"

"Water, please," I replied.

A couple hours into the flight, I got up to use the restroom while passing the woman and her daughter. Her pain was strong—though she managed to smile—trying to make the trip as pleasant as possible for her daughter. While I washed my hands, I focused on the woman and saw a similar type of goopy darkness I had seen in Anna. It would be difficult to remove but I begged my ancestors to ask God to help us take it out of her. When I was vacuuming it away, I became extremely nauseous and threw up a lot.

"Are you okay in there?" someone asked at the door.

"Yes, it's just motion sickness. Thanks." I flushed the toilet.

I opened the door. The person stood back a few feet.

"I'm sorry," I said politely. "I forgot to take medicine before we took off."

"Well, I hope you feel better," the man said.

I walked back to my seat, passing the woman and her daughter who were laughing at their inflight movie. It made me smile.

When we began the second half of the journey, my stomach was still upset. I declined the inflight meal and went to sleep.

When we landed in Dublin early the next morning, it was cold. I zipped up my jacket, walked out of the terminal and called for a ride. I asked the driver to take me to a hotel I had booked online. Once I checked in, I headed for my room. I had been holding in my emotions for many hours. I didn't want to see anyone or do anything, so I turned off my phone.

There was a knock at the door. I walked towards it but didn't open it.

"Yes?" I asked.

"Excuse me miss, but I forgot to give you our services guide," a man said with a beautiful Irish accent.

"Oh." I opened the door.

He handed me a paper with a list of fancy concierge and spa services. "If you need anything at all, ring downstairs and we'll be happy to help."

"Thank you," I said, trying to sound appreciative.

After I closed the door, I decided to take a hot bath. I climbed into the tub and slid back, leaning my head against the wall. I closed my eyes and tried to focus on anything positive in my life, but I couldn't. All I could picture was Luke's perfect face and his hypnotic eyes that had deceived me for many years. My soul ached for a love that wasn't real. As I had predicted years ago, I was completely alone.

The next morning, I checked out of the hotel and decided to face my future the best I could. It took up most of the day travelling—by a few different means of transportation—to Crovie, Scotland. Upon arrival, I was quite surprised by how similar it was to my dream. The town was charming and so were its people. Being an American citizen, I wasn't sure how long I would be allowed to stay.

I walked down a path parallel to the beach, studying the older buildings. I stopped and stared when I spotted one that was almost identical to the house in my dream. It appeared to have been recently renovated.

"Hello there," an older gentleman said, cheerfully walking from the porch with his cane. "Are you here to take a tour of the house?"

"Oh, no" I said. "But I do think it's lovely."

"Are you interested in renting or buying?" he asked.

"Honestly, I'm not really sure what I'm doing." I smiled awkwardly. "My life's gone a bit wonky. Does anyone even say that?"

"You seem a bit lost. Why don't you come inside for some tea and scones? I'll show you around."

I followed him inside and immediately loved it. It was a place that gave off a peaceful energy. Everything was done in shades of sky blue and pale yellow, and it had a large living room window that looked right out at the sea.

"Please sit down," he said, pouring me a cup of tea. "What do you think?"

"It's absolutely perfect. I wouldn't change a thing." I smiled. "Makes me wish I were Scottish."

"You're American, right?" he asked, sipping his tea.

"Yes."

"Are you here with your husband?" he asked while looking at my wedding ring.

"No." I did my best to not get emotional. "He's gone."

"Oh, I see. I'm sorry. Didn't mean to pry," he said kindly.

I sipped my tea and took a bite of the scone. "This is delicious. Thank you."

"My wife made those, been making them since she was a wee girl. She'll be along shortly."

"I've never tasted its equal."

"We're not needing this place anymore. The sea air is too cold for our old bones. We're looking to sell or lease it out, but we haven't had any luck so far."

"Really? I don't see how anyone could turn this place down."

"Then you'll take it?" he asked eagerly.

"I wish. I love this house but I'm American."

"So." He laughed. "Your money's good here."

"I thought you had to be Scottish to own property."

"Hello." A sweet older woman came through the front door. "Has Walter given you the grand tour?"

"He has. You have a beautiful home, and these scones are scrumptious," I said cheerfully.

She sat down at the table. "Have you discussed the price yet? We're willing to drop it a bit if it helps. We just want someone here who will take good care of it."

"No, Agnes. We haven't discussed that yet," Walter said.

"Well then, why don't you try this place out for a couple weeks and see what you think? If you decide to buy, we'll take what you've already paid off the price. If you decide not to, then you're welcome to lease it for as long as you'd like." She smiled at me. "How does that sound?"

She pushed a paper with the deposit, monthly rate and purchase price written down towards me.

"Really?" I asked, instantly tearing up with joy. "You'd let me do that?"

"We'd love to have you here," the man said kindly. "I think you'll be a good fit."

I didn't even know those people, but I sensed they had much compassion, I wanted to give them a Denny-sized hug. That might have seemed a bit much, so I thanked them by secretly healing their achy joints.

"Where did you buy your furniture? Is there a place in a nearby town that I could find something similar? It's absolutely perfect."

"We didn't plan on taking the furniture with us. It was a chore just getting each piece here," the man said. "We have a small place, a couple miles from here that's already furnished. We don't need any of this. You're welcome to it."

I thanked God for bringing them into my life, giving me some hope and a new place to call home for a while. I knew I would need to handle the issue of staying long term but channeling the person who handled citizenship would be easy.

"Thank you so much."

Walter reached for his cane but stood without issue. He took a few steps and then leaned it against the wall. I pretended not to notice.

I reached into my backpack and gave them two thousand pounds. I let them know that I would pay the full asking price for their home as soon as I could work it out with my bank. I was thankful Luke had insisted I always kept my own bank account, so I would not need his signature on anything. At the time, I thought he was doing it to make things easier for me, but it turned out it was because he wasn't planning on sticking around.

Walter and Agnes were kind enough to drive me to a nearby town to shop for groceries, clothes and supplies before dropping me back off at a road closest to the house. After they left, I got everything put away, washed my clothes and all the linens and wiped everything down.

Around 7:00 pm, a storm came in with high winds. The waves were enormous and didn't seem far from the shore. A normal person would probably have been concerned but I couldn't drown or be harmed. I enjoyed some soup, took a shower, turned my phone back on and went to bed for the night.

I guess the jet lag and time difference had caught up with me, because I didn't wake up the next day until almost 1:00 pm. I walked into the kitchen to get a drink of water and noticed my phone flashed. Dimitri had been trying to call me. I dreaded talking about Luke and immediately assumed it was to tell me that he somehow got his immortality issue resolved. I decided to wait until after I had a bowl of cereal to call him back.

"Alice?" Dimitri asked, concerned.

"Yes," I answered. "How are you?"

"I'm fine. Where are you? I've been worried about you."

"I'm at home."

"Uh, no you're not," he replied, sounding annoyed. "I'm at your house right now."

"I'm sorry." I wasn't sure how to begin to explain things. "I moved away. I'm at my new home."

"You moved? Why? To where?"

"Scotland."

"Scotland?! You're on the other side of the world! What the hell? Were you not going to bother telling me? What's going on? Why are you over there?"

"How was I supposed to know you were coming to visit? You've barely spoken to me in months. Why would it even matter to you where I am?" I asked, getting frustrated. "You could avoid talking to me from anywhere."

"Because I care about you." He was offended.

"You always call Luke but never me. I know I screwed up, but I didn't do it on purpose, and I didn't force you into anything. I'm terribly sorry for what I did but I'm not the one who shut the other out." I hung up the phone.

A couple minutes later, he called back. "I'm sorry. I didn't mean to go off on you. I know I should have stayed in touch better, but I've been worried about you. I thought something awful happened."

I didn't know what to say. I walked out to the front porch and sat down on one of the chairs, forgetting that it had rained. My pants were instantly soaked.

"Where are you exactly?" he asked.

"A small village in Scotland, but I don't want to see anyone right now. I need some time alone to heal. I'm sorry."

"When you're ready to talk, please call me," he said sadly. "Do you need anything?"

"No, I have everything I need. The couple that sold me this house have been kind to me." I paused for a moment then continued. "Dimitri, may I ask you something?"

"Of course."

"Do you think God will forgive me if I ask my ancestors to help me forget Luke?" I asked with my voice shaking. "I tried to heal myself, but my power doesn't work on me. I fear this pain will stay with me forever. I just want to stop hurting, Dimitri. My soul aches to its core. I need to forget him."

"I'm sorry, Alice. Can you hold on for just a minute?" he asked, before muting the phone.

After a couple minutes, he started talking again. "Honestly, I don't know what God forgives, but I don't think you should do that. You're not supposed to forget the person you're married to—even if you're apart—no matter how painful it is."

It wasn't the answer I hoped to hear.

"If you'd like, I can mail you a healing charm," he said sympathetically. "If you text me your address, I can get it out today. I can expedite the shipping, but it will still take a few days. Would you like me to do that for you?"

"Yes, please. Thank you, Dimitri. I'll send it to you as soon as we end the call."

Later that day, I got the money transferred to Walter and Agnes' account. By the end of the next month, the house would be officially mine and I would also have dual citizenship. Although my sadness seemed to be overwhelming, it was the little things that helped me move forward with my life.

Chapter Twelve

In eighth grade, a boy in my class frequently snuck up behind me. He pulled on the back of my bra strap, making it snap against my skin. Although it never hurt, it was extremely irritating. The last day before summer break, I asked why he kept doing that. He told me he was trying to teach me to never let my guard down. While lying in my bed that Saturday night, he randomly popped into my head. This made me wonder if it was a warning.

As the sun began to rise, I woke up with a sick feeling in the pit of my stomach. Remembering what that boy had said, I tossed my covers back, got up and double-checked to make sure everything was locked. When I reached the living room, the front door flew open. A tall, slender man stood on the porch. He had light brown hair and large green eyes that glowed. I knew he couldn't hurt me, yet I was frightened.

"What do you want?" my voice trembled.

He held up an object that somewhat resembled a small television remote controller. He pointed the mirrored side towards my face and clicked one of the buttons on the side. A couple seconds later, a green light came on. He reached through the doorway, grabbed my wrist and yanked me outside away from my house. I tried to pull my hand away but couldn't.

"Help!" I yelled, hoping someone might hear me.

Before I could make another sound, a strong force from above pulled us up. The pressure was so strong, I couldn't keep my eyes open. I knew my body was ascending but it was more like the feeling you get on a large rollercoaster when the steep drop happens.

Eventually, everything slowed down, and I could open my eyes again. It was as if we had a parachute tied to us and were about to reach the ground. Below us were white marble pillars supporting a tall white building adorned with colorful plants. The sky was both blue and purple, and many of the trees had fruit that were not normally seen in nature. It was oddly beautiful. I wondered if I had died somehow and faced judgment.

The man let go of my hand and asked me to follow him. I didn't know what else to do, so I did. We went inside the building and he directed me to an empty room with glass on all sides.

"Step inside, please," he said politely.

As soon as I walked into the room, a thick piece of glass came down from the ceiling and sealed the doorway. Realizing there was no way out, I paced back and forth. I wondered how much trouble I was in for any of the less-than-stellar things I had done in my life. When I thought about Dimitri's immortality curse, my heart began to race.

I'm not sure how much time had passed before a woman in white opened the doorway. "This way," she said, holding her head high.

I got up and followed her out. She led me down several long halls and into a room with white marble walls. A curved black and white marble bench sat beside a pool about ten feet wide. It was filled with some type of purple-colored liquid. A white and gold gown was laid out on a small black marble table beside it.

"Will you get in on your own?" she asked. "Or would you like some help?"

"Get in?" I asked cautiously. "What is this?"

"Your bath," she answered as if it were normal.

"My bath? Why is the water that color?"

"To wash away any ancestral magic you have left from Earth and bathe you in the star dust from Sajet."

"What is Sajet?"

"This realm," she answered. "Please get in."

"This is to wash away my magic? Why?" I asked. "I don't use it to hurt people. It's only for healing. Please, I just want to go home."

"You are home, and it is what he commanded," she said firmly. "You must."

"Who commanded?"

"The king." She took a step towards me. "Do you need help getting in?"

"No. I'm not getting in that. Please, explain to your king that I'm a healer. I won't hurt anyone." I pleaded.

"We know you can't possibly hurt anyone here with your Earthly magic."

"If I'm no threat, then why does he want me to do this? Will it hurt me? Could this kill me?"

She walked out of the room without answering. I didn't know what to do. I ran for the door but was stopped when she returned with two men. They closed the door behind them. My heart seemed as though it could pound right through my chest.

They walked towards me. I kept stepping away from them until my back bumped up against a wall. They effortlessly picked me up from under my arms and carried me back towards the deep pool. I started to scream and tried desperately to get away, but they were too strong. Electricity built inside me and then everything began to shake. The purple goop started to splash up from the edges.

Something moved above me. I turned my head. Luke stood with his arms crossed on another level watching what was happening below. He wore a golden crown and dressed in black, purple and gold.

"Luke!" I yelled. "Please help me!"

He glared at me and shook his head. "You shouldn't have left!" he yelled angrily.

"Left?!" I cried out. "What are you talking about?!"

"You thought you could run away and hide from me! You will never be able to do that again!"

They tossed me into the pool like they were throwing out the garbage. The gel-like substance was the same temperature as my body. As I sank to the bottom, the strange liquid seemed to invade my every pore. My ancestors fought to stay with me, but my thoughts faded away as my lungs ran out of air. The harder I fought it, the thicker the liquid felt. Everything started to flash between light and darkness as my lungs began to fill. There were voices in the distance, but I couldn't understand what was being said. I quit trying to struggle and began to float back up. Then, everything went black.

When I woke, I was laying on the ground next to the pool, completely dry and everyone was gone. I was extremely weak but managed to pull myself up and walk out the open door. The halls were empty, so I kept moving, not knowing where to go. Luke's actions of betrayal confused me. I left the building and followed a long path made of lime-colored stones that led me to the edge of the area where we landed. Several hundred feet below the railing was something that resembled an ocean.

"You can't jump from there," I heard the man say that took me. "And you'll never be allowed to leave without the king's consent."

"So, I'm stuck here until I die then?" I asked, feeling sick to my stomach.

"No, forever," he replied, taking a step closer. "You are immortal. You can't die."

"I thought that purple goop took that away from me."

"It took away your Earth magic but bathed you in ours, giving you a new everlasting life. It may take a little while for you to become strong again, but you'll be fine."

"I don't understand. What was the point? Why did he have that done to me?" I sat down on the ground.

"You should be thankful. He could have rightfully done much worse." He spoke to me as if I were some sort of criminal.

"Thankful? I heard what he said to his brother. He lied to me, tricked me and then left me!" I said angrily. "All I did was block him out of my head so he couldn't feel how much I was suffering and take pleasure from it. I loved him and he fooled me into thinking he loved me too. He used me to get the crown, yet I am the one being punished. For what exactly? What have I actually done to be sentenced to this place for eternity?"

"You committed a crime. You ran away from your husband and blocked him from your mind so that he couldn't find you," the man said. "His brother came and took him home for his coronation. He was only here for a couple hours before he came back for you. He thought you would still be asleep, but you were gone. He was furious and used your friend to find out where you were."

"Wow," I said sadly. "Dimitri betrayed me too. That's just great."

Denny and I had many talks about heaven and hell. Until he met Craig, he never believed in either. At that moment, I wished I could tell him we were both wrong. Hell did exist and it was my new home.

"Is there somewhere I can go to rest without bothering anyone?" I asked. "I'm so tired. Not that anyone here cares, but I'd like to be alone and have a good long cry."

"I'll show you to your room," he said, putting his hand out to help me up. "My name is Tharius."

"My room?"

"You are still the queen," he replied.

"Oh no," I said sadly.

He took me back into the palace and showed me to a room that was bigger than my entire house. Everything was decorated gold and green with fine silks. In the center of the room was a bed twice the size of a king bed. Sitting on one of the side tables was Luke's stupid vampire doll that he took with him everywhere.

"Is there somewhere else I can go? Anywhere? I don't want to be here."

"No, you are the queen," he said as he started to walk away. "This is where you stay."

"Great," I mumbled. "I'm the queen of hell."

He turned back around and said kindly, "The king has left to handle an issue in Adersta. You will have a little time alone before he returns."

Unfortunately, Luke was only away for two days. The morning that I learned that he was returning, I forced myself to sing songs in my head over and over to keep him from hearing my thoughts. I found a quiet place in a garden on the farthest edge of the land to hide. In between songs, I could hear into his mind without trying. He asked people if they had seen me. I sat on the grass, leaned against a tree and focused on the small house

I bought in Scotland. I daydreamed I was there having tea and scones with Walter and Agnes until I fell asleep.

When I woke up, it was already dark. I was famished but didn't want to go back to the palace to eat. I picked a few apple-like fruits from a nearby tree and ate them as I slowly headed back. I hoped that by the time I got there, he would be asleep or had gone somewhere else. I didn't want to see his face, smell his cologne or even hear his voice.

"May I fix you anything to eat?" the cook asked as I walked past the massive dining room, trying to find my way around.

"No thank you," I answered. "I've already eaten."

As I approached the bedroom, Luke stood in the hall speaking with Tharius. I made no eye contact with either of them, put my fingers in my ears and started humming. I washed myself up for the night and put on the ridiculously lavish nightgown that was laid out on the bed, because I didn't have my own normal people sleepwear. I climbed into the bed, scooted to the very edge opposite Luke's nightstand, covered myself up and put one of the many pillows over my head. I kept singing songs in my head until I fell asleep.

When I woke up early the next morning, I got dressed in the next extravagant thing that was laid out for me. I ignored the purple gem covered tiara and tiptoed out of the room. The last thing I wanted was to wake Luke.

I headed back to the garden for the day. This time, I brought a book I found on a shelf in the palace library. I read it quietly out loud to keep my thoughts focused on what I was reading. It was interesting to see how similar the story was to one I had to read in high school. The biggest difference was the author on Earth made the villain out to be the hero. It made me laugh.

As the afternoon approached, I became hungry for something more than fruit. I realized that I would have to go back to the palace to eat, but also wondered why I needed food or felt hunger if I was immortal. I took a different way back to view part of the realm I hadn't seen. Laughter and a delightful sound of stringed instruments I had never heard before drew my attention. When the people came into view, it took my breath away. Dozens of children of all ages ran around playing in the village square.

A woman noticed me, smiled and announced, "The queen has come to see us."

I quickly straightened my messy hair when I realized she was talking about me. I wasn't wearing a crown or the stupid tiara, so I wondered how she knew who I was. I suppose it was the dress.

"Hello," I said humbly.

A little girl ran up to me, took me by the hand and lead me towards the group. She bent down, picked some flowers, tied them together and handed them to me.

"May I put these on your head?" she asked in her sweet tiny voice.

I smiled. "I would love that."

She placed them on my head like a crown and began singing a beautiful song about stars and wishes. It warmed my heart to tears.

"Are you okay, your majesty?" a red-headed woman asked.

"Oh yes," I said happily. "These are the first children I've seen since I arrived. I didn't think there were any in this realm."

"There are many children here," the woman replied.

"Are they—immortal?" I whispered.

"Yes. Everyone here is. They're born, grow until adulthood and then stop aging somewhere between thirty and thirty-five years old."

"That's remarkable."

"Are you hungry? Would you like some lunch?" she asked cheerfully. "I'd love for you to try my vegetable stew."

"Oh, my goodness, yes please. I'm famished. Thank you."

I sat down at one of the large tables in the middle of the courtyard surrounded by many families, smiling, eating and sharing their day. It reminded me of the many Fourth of July picnics I went to with Denny's family.

"This is delicious." I was amazed by how yummy and satisfying a meatless dish could taste.

I enjoyed listening to their stories and shared some good memories of my childhood. After lunch, the older children pushed the younger ones on swings that hung from tall flowering trees.

"Your majesty," several villagers said at once looking past me.

I turned around. Luke stood behind me carrying two enormous baskets full of lavender-colored fruit. He walked past me without saying a word and sat them down on the table. The kids cheered and a few of them ran up to hug him by his long legs.

I didn't want to make a scene, so I thanked her for her hospitality and said that I hoped to see them again soon. I bowed to Luke without making any eye contact and went on my way. I realized at that moment, there really was no where I could hide from him.

When I got back to the palace, a beautiful dark-haired couple stood in the entry dressed in extravagant clothing. I wasn't sure who they were, but they seemed to be waiting for me.

"I'll let you two have a word." The man smiled and then walked away.

"Please, come sit with me," the woman said.

She walked towards a seating area inside the entry. I followed her in.

"I've waited a long time to meet you, Alice," she said smiling.

"Oh?" I replied, not knowing who she was or why she wanted to meet me.

"I'm Lucas' mother."

"His mother?" I was perplexed. "I thought his parents had died."

"We're immortal. Why would you think that?" she asked confused.

"Well, because Luke is king now. How is that possible?"

"No one here must die before someone else can become king or queen," she said almost laughing. "The throne is usually passed down to the eldest child when the king or queen no longer wants to rule."

"If Luke was meant to have the throne, then why did he and his brother have a wager for it?"

"Because Liam was born a few minutes before Luke," she replied. "You see. I love both of my sons dearly, but Luke has always been a bit self-serving. When Liam told us that he didn't want to rule Sajet, he asked that we make Luke the king if he could prove himself worthy. He'd need to find a kind-hearted wife who could love him for ten years. We agreed, but only on the condition that if Luke failed, Liam would have to take the throne. Quite honestly—as much as we love him—we never expected him to succeed."

I wasn't sure how to respond. He was her son, and I didn't want to say anything negative about him to her, but I could not fathom why they allowed someone so deceitful to take up the throne. I wondered how much worse Liam must have been for them to approve Luke.

"I understand that you're upset with him, but you should know that he wasn't allowed to say anything about his life here or mention the crown. No one visiting Earth can mention their home," she said, taking my hands. "I hope you can give him another chance."

I started to cry. "I don't know if I can. I'm so angry. He's lied to me so many times, my heart's broken. I don't see how I will ever trust him."

"You still love him. I can see it." She smiled. "You can work with that."

"I do, but I don't want to love him anymore. His version of love always brings me sadness." I tried to hold back the tears. "I saw how he looked at me when they threw me into the pool.

He looked down at me with disgust. I didn't see any love in him, only rage."

"Then you didn't look deep enough. He still needs to grow and that requires you by his side, as well as patience and time." She looked at me in the eyes. "Forgiveness is one of the greatest gifts we can give others but even more for ourselves."

Luke and his father approached.

"When my son returned to Earth and you were gone, he thought you ran away and blocked him out, because you didn't love him. I know that's not an excuse for his actions, but it's why he behaved so poorly," she said quietly. "You were not the only one whose heart felt broken."

His father smiled, "Did you beautiful ladies have a nice chat?"

His mother looked at me for my reaction.

"Yes, she's absolutely lovely," I replied, smiling at his father.

I still could not quite bring myself to look at Luke, but I tried to be as pleasant as possible.

"Wonderful," his father said. "Let's have some tea, shall we?"

His parents only stayed until nightfall, but it was nice to get to meet them. I looked forward to their next visit and getting to know them better.

Once they were gone, Luke and I were left alone at the table. As angry as I was, I thought about everything his mother had said. I hoped he would apologize or at least try to talk to me, but he didn't. After a few minutes of uncomfortable silence, I got up and went for a walk outside. Although there were no lemons on Sajet, the air seemed to be filled with the marvelous, fresh citrus scent.

"Aren't you cold?" Liam asked as he walked by.

"Hi Liam," I smiled. "It's a little chilly but it's so peaceful out here and the night sky is breathtaking."

"What did you think of my parents?" he asked, stopping to talk.

"Your mother is kind, insightful and classy and your father's so funny and charming. They're both ridiculously intelligent."

"Exactly. I could've never replaced them nor had any interest in being king and dealing with inter-realm issues. I have always wanted a simple life," he said. "Speaking of which, my wife really took a liking to you today."

"Your wife? Who was she?" I thought about all the people I had met. "Was she the beautiful, curly-haired brunette?"

"You're thinking of her sister, Laurien. She's still a maiden," he replied. "Greta, the gorgeous red-head that made the stew is my wife."

"Oh my gosh, I just love her. She's so sweet and funny," I smiled. "And your children are adorable. You have three, right?"

"A fourth on its way," he said proudly.

"Congratulations, that's wonderful."

"Thank you," he said, taking a step away. "I better head home. I don't want to miss reading their bedtime stories."

"Have a good night, Liam and please thank Greta again for her hospitality."

"Come see us any time you'd like. You're always welcome."

Once Liam was out of view, I decided to go inside. I reached our room; Luke was sound asleep on his side as close to the edge as possible. I was relieved. I got cleaned up and slipped into my side of the bed.

That night, I had a dream about Dimitri. He sat alone on the beach looking as if he hadn't bathed or trimmed his facial hair in weeks. He stared out at the sea and wept. I kept trying to go to him, but the faster I ran, the further away he would seem. I yelled for him, but he couldn't hear me. There was a loud rushing sound and with it, a giant hourglass appeared behind him. The sand moved extremely fast to the bottom, but just before it would run out, it would flip over and start again. I could feel his soul aching for it to stop turning but there was nothing I could do to help him.

I woke up shaking and in tears. Luke saw how upset I was, but he said nothing—did nothing. My heart sank. I threw on my clothing and ran outside into the darkness. Although it was a dream, his suffering seemed genuine, and it was clear that he had not gotten his mortality back. In that moment, I believed that I was being punished for what I did to Dimitri. I deserved every bit of pain in my heart because no one could undo what I did to him. I ran as fast as I could to find a place where no one could hear me scream.

I reached an opening in a meadow. I noticed two gigantic moons and a sky full of more stars than I had ever seen. God and Heaven never seemed so far away in that strange land. I fell to my knees, cried out from the depths of my soul and wept until my eyes burned.

Once I calmed down, I considered trying to find my way back, but I was too tired to walk, and the palace seemed too far away. I laid my tired body on the grass and closed my eyes.

A few minutes later, footsteps approached. I turned over. Luke walked towards me carrying a stack of warm blankets. He squatted down on the ground next to me and handed me one.

"Thanks," I said while wiping my sore eyes.

He grabbed a folded one and placed it under my head. He took another, laid it down next to me, rest his head on it and then covered himself up with the other. He never said a word but stayed beside me the whole night.

When I woke up, Luke sat nearby on a large rock pulling petals off a bright blue flower. As each fell to the ground and new one took its place. I folded all the blankets and walked towards him carrying them.

"You really thought I just left you behind?" he asked, sounding ashamed of his behavior.

"Yes," I said with my voice shaking.

"I thought you left me too," he said sadly.

I didn't know what to say. I was still angry and hurt.

"Do you hate me?" he asked.

"I should."

"Fair enough," he replied.

He took the blankets from my hands and carried them. As we headed back to the palace, we passed people who smiled, assuming we had a romantic night sleeping under the stars.

About half-way there, Luke stopped walking. "I can't undo what I did to you and I don't know how to make things right between us."

His words caught me off guard.

"I cursed Dimitri and you've made it so we're all apart. We can't fix this—so no—I don't see how anything will ever be right." I looked at him directly in the eyes.

227

Luke started walking again. "I'm sorry."

"What I did to Dimitri is far worse than anything you've done," I said, tearing up. "I'll never forgive myself until I can find a way to do right by him."

Chapter Thirteen

The next few weeks, Luke did everything he could to mend our marriage. I was no longer angry with him, but my sadness and self-loathing consumed me, no matter how hard he tried to fix things. Although I never turned him away, he didn't put pressure on me to resume intimacy, but always kissed my cheek before climbing into his side of the bed each night. He tried to make me feel beautiful and wanted but all I could think about was what I had done. I didn't deserve affection and happiness while Dimitri suffered alone on Earth.

The nightmares continued but Luke was there, inside my mind, helping to pull me out of them. He did what he could, but I fell back into them as soon as I went to sleep. They were almost always about Dimitri's agony, but sometimes they would be about Denny hating me for being a witch. I could not escape them and missed them both terribly.

Late on a Sunday night, I woke up to find Luke coming out of the bathroom. He was dressed like the day I first met him. I was half-asleep but it made me smile. "Where are you going Dracula?" I asked while yawning.

"I need to take care of something in another realm," he said, kissing my cheek. "Try to get some rest. We've got a party to attend for Liam's birthday tomorrow."

"You're twins. Why don't you celebrate yours too?" I asked.

"He was born first and gave me the throne." He smiled. "Besides, I'm the king. I'm celebrated every day. I don't need a party. I get enough attention already."

"Luke?"

"Yeah?"

"I am trying," I said.

"I know," he replied.

I stood up and kissed him softly on the mouth. "Thank you for being patient with me."

He was pleasantly surprised. "Get some rest."

When I woke up the next morning, I got dressed, ate some breakfast and headed over to help Greta prepare the food for Liam's party. I had fun learning how to make desserts with the unusual but delicious ingredients they farmed.

The whole courtyard was decorated with his favorite colors and birthday messages painted by his older children. I was so excited to see Liam's face when he saw all the love that was poured out for him on his special day.

"You've got perfalamen on your chin," Liam's daughter told me while laughing.

"Thank you for telling me, Arbie. I better wash that off." I went to the fountain to clean up.

"Surprise!" everyone yelled.

Liam pretended he had no idea he would be coming back home to a party. Music played and most everyone sang. I stood back and clapped along as people danced. Through the joyous sounds, Luke called my name. I turned around. He stood near the side of one of the houses.

I walked up to him and gave him a hug. "Why are you hiding over here?" I asked.

"I need to pull you away for a few minutes," he replied, sounding giddy. "I brought you some souvenirs."

"It's your birthday and you bring me something," I smiled. "That's not fair. You said you didn't want to celebrate your birthday."

"Come with me," he said cheerfully taking me by the hand.

"All right," I replied curiously.

As soon as we were away from where anyone could see or here us, he asked me to close my eyes and hold out my hands.

I did as he asked. He placed something flat and relatively light on them.

"Okay," he said in a cheerful voice. "You can open them."

I opened my eyes. He had brought back my book of power.

"It likely won't work here but I thought you should have it back, as it belonged to your father. It could be a journal or something." He waited for my reaction.

"Thank you," I said, realizing the huge gesture he tried to make. "I really appreciate you doing this, Luke."

I reached out to give him a well-deserved hug, but he took a step back.

"Wait. There's more," he said excitedly. "Close your eyes and hold out your hands."

I closed them and put my hands out again. I wondered what else I might have left at the house that he could have brought me, but nothing came to mind. Then, something rested on my hands, but I wasn't sure what it could be. I was intrigued.

"You can open them now," Luke said cheerfully.

I almost fell over. Dimitri stood in front of me with his hands on mine. "Dimitri!" I said loudly. "Is this real? Are you really here?"

He started laughing and gave me a big hug.

"What's going on?" I asked with joyful tears. "How long can you stay?"

"He can stay until he asks me to take him back," Luke said.

"What about your quest?" I asked Dimitri.

"I'm tired of searching so I'm taking a break. No one has any answers, so Luke suggested I come here and be around other immortals. Maybe we'll figure something out, maybe not but at least we can all be together until then. It sounded rather good to me," he answered cheerfully. "Besides, I've missed you terribly."

I couldn't believe what Luke had done. I was happier than I could remember. I gave him a hug and cried tears of joy. "Thank you so much."

Luke smiled and said, "I would do anything to see you happy again."

I pulled him close and kissed him passionately.

Dimitri chuckled. "I think she's forgiven you."

We both laughed.

The three of us spent the rest of the day and well into the night at Liam's birthday party. I don't think I ever stopped smiling. We danced, drank and ate far too much, then headed to the palace a few minutes after midnight. Dimitri was given the grand bedroom that Liam had before he got married and moved to the village. It was so nice to have him staying with us.

As I got ready for bed, I thought about Luke and everything he had done for my happiness. I don't believe I ever yearned for him more than I did that night. When I came into the bedroom, he sat on his side of the bed. His legs were over the edge, and he read a new book. The more time passed, the thirstier I got for his touch. I wished that he would stop focusing on the vampire story, get inside my head and feel what I felt.

Ten minutes passed, but it felt like hours before he finally put the book down and walked over to me. He gently kissed me on the cheek, as he had done for weeks and then headed back to his side. I wanted to pull him close and yell, '*Take me!*', but I couldn't expect him to instantly behave any differently.

Luke started to laugh.

"What's so funny?" I asked.

He rushed back to my side, climbed under the covers and rolled me to the center of our enormous bed. Every touch made me quiver with anticipation of the next. The thought of being able to be with him like that forever fueled my desire and my love for him renewed with each caress. There was overwhelming joy and elation—it was as if we might float away.

We spent the next few days giving Dimitri a tour of the realm. He became close friends with Liam, as they were much alike. Although he would always start and end the day with us, he spent most of his time with the villagers.

After a few weeks, he stopped mentioning wanting to give up his immortality. I wondered if he lost hope in ever finding a cure or was so happy in Sajet that living forever didn't seem like such a bad thing after all. Either way, the longer he was there, the more contented he appeared.

One afternoon while Luke was away visiting his parents, Dimitri and I decided to have a picnic next to Teal Lake. We hadn't spent time alone in many years and talked mostly about our lives on earth. He wondered if I missed it and if I thought about my old friends that were now entering middle-aged, likely with families of their own. I told him that they came to mind many times a year, but Denny was in my thoughts and prayers every day.

"You miss him?" he asked.

"Yes. I miss him terribly, but he isn't the same person anymore. I miss the guy that was my best friend."

"Don't you wonder if he misses you too? He was your best friend for many years."

"Maybe a small part of him misses who I was before, but I looked into his mind when I tried to visit him. He was afraid to speak to me, as if I were possessed by some sort of demonic monster. He believes that if he associates with me, he'll be damned. This, coming from someone who was an agnostic. I can't imagine that we'll ever be friends again," I said sadly. "You're actually my closest friend now, Dimitri."

After a moment of silence, Dimitri asked, "Have you tried to use your book since you got it back?"

"No. I appreciate that Luke brought it here, but I don't see anything to ask for and I feel funny asking for things anyway. Even if it works, I worry it will backfire like it did on you. I'd rather just keep it hidden. I don't want to hurt anyone else."

"Hello," Greta said as she approached with her sister. They carried a small clay tray.

"Would you like to join us?" Dimitri asked without hesitation.

"Thank you, no," Laurien replied smiling. "We created a new recipe and they turned out quite well. We wanted to share and brighten up your picnic."

"You're too kind. Thank you," I said as she handed me the treats that resembled oatmeal cookies. "Please sit with us for a while."

They both sat down. After about twenty minutes of chatting, Laurien mentioned that she needed to go home to fix her door that had come loose from the hinges.

"Would you like me to help?" Greta asked as she stood.

"Thank you, sister, but I'll get it figured out," Laurien replied.

Dimitri stood and offered to help, letting her know that he was quite handy. "Is that all right with you Alice? We end our picnic a little early?"

"Oh no, I don't want to pull you away. Please stay with your friend," she said sounding nervous. "I'm sorry, your majesty. I didn't mean to disrupt your picnic."

"Please, call me Alice and do let him help you. I've taken up a lot of his time already today and he loves doing kind things. My friend and I can have many more picnics while he's here."

As soon as I stood, everything started to spin. I tried to focus but couldn't and passed out. When I woke up, many people stood around with concerned eyes. I composed myself and slowly stood again.

"Let me walk you home," Dimitri said, hanging on to support me.

Although I was still a bit light-headed, I insisted he help Laurien before it got too late. He reluctantly agreed and Tharius made sure I made it back safely. When we reached the palace, I could smell some strong herb cooking in the kitchen. It made me feel extremely nauseous. I went to my room, closed the door and opened the windows. I wondered if it was my stomach disagreeing with so many new foods. I brushed my teeth and climbed into bed.

A couple hours later, someone knocked at my door.

"Alice, may I come in?" Dimitri asked.

I sat up and pulled the covers over the top part of my gown. "Come in," I said loudly.

"I just wanted to see if you're feeling better." He walked in.

I wanted to ask him to close the door so the smell would stay out, but I knew that wouldn't be proper and might be some sort of punishable crime. "I'm okay. I think my body's still adjusting to this place and the foods."

He put his hand on my forehead. "Good, you don't have a fever."

"Doesn't that smell bother you?" I began to feel nauseous again.

"What smell?"

"The herbs the cook is using."

He took in a deep breath through his nose. "It actually smells really good to me."

My stomach started to turn.

"Would you like me to close the door?" he asked, reaching for it.

"No, thank you. It has to remain open if anyone other than Luke is alone with me." I rolled my eyes.

"Alright, I'm going to go then. I'll close it behind me. Would you like me to ask the cook to make you something else to eat?"

"No thank you. I'm just going to rest. I don't think I could keep anything down."

"I'll check on you in the morning. I hope you feel better soon."

"Thanks, Dimitri. I'm glad you're here."

"Me too." He smiled and closed the door.

I slept for about two hours and then had trouble falling back asleep. I sat on my bed thinking about Dimitri. Although he seemed much happier, I still hadn't fixed what I had done to him. I took out my book of power and thought carefully about what to write. I knew I couldn't undo anything, and that magic may not work in that realm, but I had to try. After much consideration of all possible outcomes, I wrote *Please help me find a way to offer Dimitri his mortality back.'*

The next morning, my stomach had settled, and the dreadful smell was gone from the palace. I got dressed and met Dimitri in the dining hall for breakfast.

"Are you feeling better?" he asked.

"Yes, much," I replied cheerfully.

When we were done eating, I stood up and the dizziness returned. I sat back down. I wondered if I had something going on with my inner ear. I had a similar feeling as a teenager when I kept getting swimmer's ear. I told the palace staff what was going on and asked if there was anyone that could look at my ears. Before they could answer, Luke came walking into the room.

"What's going on?" he asked me. "Liam told me that you haven't been feeling well."

"I've been having an issue with my equilibrium when I get up too quickly. I think it's an inner ear issue. It's been making me dizzy and a bit nauseous," I replied. "I was just asking if there's someone here with medical knowledge that can take a look at my ear."

"No one gets sick here and neither should you," he answered, sounding concerned. "I don't know of anyone here who could help. Maybe someone on Geordia could look at you."

"Another realm? Hopefully, it will just get better on its own." I was a little concerned.

"Can't you just take her back to Earth to have her checked?" Dimitri asked, as if it were the obvious thing to do.

I looked at Luke hoping he would agree but I could tell he was apprehensive.

"It's fine," I said. "I probably just need some fresh air."

I walked out the door. A moment later, Luke caught up with me and took me by the hand. He typed something into his transport device and the next thing I knew, there was a freefalling sensation. I closed my eyes. Before long, we were landing a block away from a hospital where no one would notice us showing up. We checked into the emergency room and sat in the empty waiting room.

"Thank you, Luke," I said quietly. "I know you don't like coming back here."

"I had no choice. You need help." He held my hand.

After ten minutes of waiting, the nurse called me to be seen. We went into a small room connected to the emergency room and the nurse checked my vitals. Everything seemed normal. A couple minutes after she left, the doctor came in.

"You're having dizzy spells and a bit of nausea?" he asked while holding a clipboard.

"Yes," I replied.

"You have a history of ear infections as a child, but no tubes?"

"Yes."

"Alright, I'll take a look to see what's going on in there." The doctor scooted close to me using an otoscope to examine my left ear. "Okay. Please turn your head so I can see the other side."

I turned it while he finished up.

"Both ears look healthy," he said as he typed into the computer. "When was your last menstrual cycle?"

I had to think about it for a bit. "I'm not sure exactly. It's been a while."

"Has it been more than a few weeks?" he asked with raised eyebrows.

"Uh, yeah. I suppose it has. Is there something wrong?"

He stood up, grabbed a urine sample cup, a cleansing wipe from a cabinet and handed them to me. "I want you to go into the bathroom and get a clean catch, then place it on the metal tray next to the sliding door. Then wait to be called in the waiting room."

I had enough friends go through this to understand why the doctor ordered the test, but I knew I couldn't be pregnant. I began to worry. I had vacuumed illnesses out of people so many times, I wondered if I may have absorbed their illnesses into my own cells. Being an immortal, that shouldn't be possible. I took the test anyway and sat with Luke in the waiting room.

"If I'm immortal like you now, I can't have a disease, can I?" I asked Luke. "I thought no one in Sajet could ever get sick. Maybe that pool didn't work for me, maybe it just took away my immortality."

Luke knew that I shouldn't be able to get sick. "It'll be okay." He tried to reassure me.

Although we held hands tightly, they both managed to shake.

"Alice Varlett?" the nurse called after about an hour.

I followed her back to another room where the doctor sat waiting for me.

"Have a seat," he said. "I have the results of your test. It's as I suspected. You're with child."

"What?" I asked, not believing what I heard. "That's not possible."

"Your symptoms are related to the pregnancy," he replied. "Dizziness and aversion to certain foods is fairly common but should pass over the next few months. Try avoiding spicy or new foods until your body adjusts and get up slowly to help with the dizziness."

"There must be a mistake. Did my urine sample get mixed up with someone else?"

"There's no mistake." He handed me a prescription for prenatal vitamins. "Congratulations."

I walked out to the waiting room to find Luke reading a magazine. I took him by the hand. He dropped it on the seat, walked with me outside and immediately saw into my mind.

"You never wanted children. How is this possible?" I asked. "Everyone told me conception was impossible on Sajet unless both people wanted it."

"That's true," he smiled.

"What?" I couldn't believe what was happening. "This is what you want? Are you sure?"

He pulled me close to him. "More than anything."

I couldn't contain my excitement. My eyes filled with happy tears. I didn't want to stop hugging him. I never believed this would ever happen and I couldn't have been happier about it.

Chapter Fourteen

The night we returned, I had a vivid dream about my grandmother, Moana. I spoke with her as if she were alive sitting by my side. I told her about everything that had been going on since she passed and my lingering guilt about Dimitri. When I told her about the purple pool of Sajet star dust, she told me if it could take away my ancestral magic, it should do the same for the book of power. If I tossed it into the pool, it might give Dimitri back his mortality.

I woke up the next morning thinking about what I had dreamed and wondered if it would work. As soon as I saw Dimitri at breakfast, I thought about telling him but couldn't get the words out. I would like to say it was because I wanted to be sure before getting his hopes up, but it wasn't. Although I wanted to do the right thing and tell him, I didn't want to ever have to say good-bye to my friend. I justified my behavior by thinking he was so happy that I was doing him a favor by not mentioning it.

Time flew by and Luke and I focused on preparing our home for the baby's birth. Dimitri helped put together the nursery but shared much of the rest of his days with Liam's family. One afternoon, I headed off to see if my friend Greta would like me to teach her how to paint. As I passed an orchard, Dimitri stood alone facing the village.

"Dimitri." I approached him. "Are you okay?"

He turned to face me with sad eyes.

I walked up and hugged him. "What's going on?"

"I want to go home, back to New Orleans," he said sadly.

"Today?" I asked, hoping he would say no.

He nodded and walked away.

"Did something happen?" I tried to keep up with him.

"I don't belong here."

"Of course, you do," I said kindly. "You're family. We love you."

He took longer strides. I could no longer keep up.

By the time I reached the palace, he had already asked Luke to take him home. He tried—without success—to talk him out of leaving.

"You promised, Lucas," Dimitri reminded him.

"Okay, I will," he said sadly. "But can't you stay until after the baby's born? You're meant to be the godfather."

"I just want to go home. Please," Dimitri pleaded with teary eyes.

"Can he take you back tomorrow?" I asked. "Let us have one more night here together? I really need to tell you something before you leave."

Dimitri agreed.

Shortly after dinner, I went with him for a walk alone. As we overlooked the waves crashing below, I told him about the dream I had about the book of power. I could barely get the words out before he begged me to toss it in the purple pool.

"Are you sure?" I asked. "Once I do this—if it works—I'll never be able to use the book again. I won't be able to undo it."

"I know it's a lot to ask but please do it," he said. "I just can't do forever. Please, Alice."

"What will you do?" I asked teary eyed.

"Live the life I was meant to live."

"Without me?" I asked sadly.

"You and Luke can visit me after the baby's born. That device can bring you to me any time. We'll still see each other. That doesn't sound too bad, does it?"

I wanted to tell him that it sounded terrible and how much my heart ached at the thought of him going home, but I didn't. I wanted my friend to be happy, even if it would cost me some of my own happiness.

"Come with me," I said, taking him by the hand.

We went and got Luke and the book of power, then headed for the pool together to undo something the three of us had started many years ago. As we stood over the purple goop looking down into it, a deep sadness washed over me. I kissed Dimitri on the cheek and told him how lucky we were to have him in our lives. Then, I tossed the book in and watched it slowly sink below the surface.

"Thank you," Dimitri said.

We all hugged.

After a few minutes, the book slowly floated back up. As I pulled it out, it immediately dried. I carefully opened it. Everything I had ever written had washed away.

"What are you going to do with it now?" Dimitri asked.

"I think I'll write about our story," I said, smiling gently. "A tale of three unlikely friends."

We stayed up that night until nearly dawn talking. When it was time for Luke to take him home, I gave Dimitri a big hug.

"I don't want to let go," I said sadly.

"You're going to come visit soon. Remember?" Dimitri smiled. "I want to meet vampire wannabe junior as soon as it's safe for you to come."

We all laughed and then Luke took him home.

A short while after they left, Laurien came to the palace looking for Dimitri to see if he wanted to meet her brave, handsome, Cousin Everett. He had come in the day before and was visiting for a few days. When I told her that he had returned to earth as a mortal, she wept. Although he was well-liked by everyone in Sajet, I hadn't realized they had gotten that close.

"Is he coming back?" she asked with teary eyes.

"I don't think he means to. I'm sorry."

"Why?"

"I don't know. Out of nowhere, he asked Luke to take him home. He said he didn't belong here and wouldn't listen."

"How is he a mortal now? I thought that wasn't possible," she said, sounding upset.

"We found a way. He asked for me to undo the magic."

"He's gone there to die then?" She sounded like she was beginning to hyperventilate.

When I tried to console her, she ran away, crying.

During the weeks approaching the baby's birth, Laurien stayed in her home, barely eating or sleeping. No one could comfort her.

On a stormy night, our beautiful daughter Elsbeth was born. She much resembled Luke's mother but had sparkling eyes that were the same shade of brown as mine. Everyone was so happy to welcome the new princess, especially Liam and

Greta. They were glad that their youngest and our daughter were so close in age. They would have fun growing up together.

When Elsbeth—who we nicknamed Bethie—was three months old, Luke felt it was safe enough to take her to visit Dimitri.

The moment he saw her, his whole face lit up.

"She's perfect," he smiled. "And no fangs."

We laughed.

Dimitri didn't wait long to let us know that Denny's deceased mother had channeled him. Craig had fallen asleep while driving home from a long road trip, causing them to crash into an oak tree. The accident took his partner's life, but Denny wasn't aware, as he hadn't yet regained consciousness. He suffered broken bones, a punctured lung and some internal bleeding. The doctors had him on around the clock pain medication and antibiotics. Denny had once told his mother what I was able to do, and she wanted to see if I could heal her son.

I started to tear up. "I have no magic to heal. I can't help him."

"How do you know you can't heal? Have you tried? You never used the book to ask for healing power, you learned it from Lucas teaching you channeling. Shouldn't you at least try?" Dimitri asked.

"Denny thinks I'm evil. He wouldn't allow me to do it even if I could."

"If you can do it, he wouldn't have to know. You'd do it in secret just as you have many times before," Luke said, trying to help. "I know you still care about him."

"What if I try and it doesn't work?" I asked.

"Then I'll do what I can to make him as comfortable as possible," Luke said as he took our baby from my arms.

"Try it on me," Dimitri said.

"Are you hurt?" I asked. "What is there to heal?"

"I'll let you in my head," he answered.

"Really? You'd let me do that?" I was surprised. "Are you sure?"

"Yes, but only you Alice," Dimitri said as he closed his eyes. "You have to try to save him."

I closed my eyes and focused. Nothing happened right away, but eventually, my head started to feel tingly and warm. Slowly, the doors to his mind opened and I could see into his soul. There was so much light but there was also darkness and sorrow. I felt the pain of when he lost his parents and the moment, he learned that I married Luke. His love for me wasn't friendship alone. He was angry at Luke for taking me from him. Then, I saw a brief lighted moment when he met Laurien and could feel his hope of loving someone new. It faded when he saw her hugging another man. He felt angry, jealous and darkness washed over him.

I opened my eyes. Dimitri's eyes were still shut. I went back inside his mind and took away all the sorrow he felt. I showed him how broken Laurien had become since he left and gave up his mortality. I let him feel that my love for him was great and pure, and that Luke loved him as if he were his own brother. He was our family. I could feel his heart become light again and the darkness faded away.

When Dimitri opened his eyes, he waited to see if I would say anything to Luke about what he revealed, but I didn't.

"Did it work?" Luke asked. "Was she able to see into your soul?"

"Yes," he smiled.

Luke handed me Bethie and gave him a big hug. "Do you feel better though?"

"Yes."

"It doesn't prove I can heal physical wounds," I said, feeling unsure.

Dimitri left the room and came back with a carving knife.

"What are you going to do with that?" I asked with raised brows.

"I'm not going to stab myself," he replied. "I'm just going to give my finger a small cut."

He took the knife and slowly pressed the pointed tip into his left index finger until it started to bleed. I watched as tiny drops of blood rolled down the sides of his finger and onto his wooden floor.

"Any time now." He laughed nervously. "I just mopped."

I focused as hard as I could, but nothing happened. Dimitri went into the other room, grabbed a band aid and put it on his finger. "It was worth a shot," he said as he cleaned the floor.

"We can still help him to feel better," Luke said, trying to sound positive. "That's something."

Bethie fell asleep. I put her in the travel bed and sat down on the couch.

"Wait a minute," Luke said. "I want you to try again, Alice."

Luke and Dimitri sat down on the couches.

"Alice was only able to get in your head because you let her. Right?" Luke asked.

"Yes. She can't get in unless I let her. I put a protection spell on me years ago. Mostly to keep you out actually," he said, joking with Luke.

"Can't blame you for that," Luke laughed. "Try letting her in again and see if she can heal your finger."

"All right," Dimitri said. "It's worth a shot."

I was able to get in much faster this time and could feel the throbbing of his finger. I focused on it and told his body to heal. My ancestors were inside again helping. I laughed.

Dimitri opened his eyes and tore off the band aid. "You did it," he said cheerfully, showing us his healed finger.

"You'll be able to get in Denny's head much faster," Luke said. "We should go now."

I walked over to pick up the baby but because she was asleep, Dimitri offered to watch her until we got back.

When we reached the hospital, we learned that Denny was in the ICU and wasn't allowed visitors. We asked if it would be okay to sit in the empty waiting room nearby and pray for a while. With it being a Catholic hospital, we knew they wouldn't say no to that.

"I'll focus on his mood while you concentrate on healing," Luke whispered as he took my hands and we both closed our eyes.

I prayed that God would help heal his body and his heart. I couldn't imagine how I would feel if I lost Luke.

"Ready," Luke whispered.

"Yes," I replied.

I had trouble channeling Denny because it had been too long. He was now into his forties and I was not sure what he looked like. I could hear Luke telling me not to focus on his appearance but his soul as I remembered him. It would be the only way to get through. I did what he suggested and in a couple minutes, I was in. There was so much damage to his poor body. I wanted to cry knowing how much he suffered and how sad he would feel when he learns that Craig had died.

"Focus," Luke whispered.

I called on my ancestors and asked them to intercede to God to allow him to be healed. There was an enormous feeling of pressure against the inside of my body, and I could see swirls of black and red goop. I kept pulling at it trying to vacuum it away from him. It was exhausting. When I thought I had no strength left inside, Denny's parents' spirits lent their energy to help heal him.

When I opened my eyes, everything was red. I kept blinking and tried to wipe my eyes clear, but my hands were wet and smelled of blood. Luke tried to help but when I stood up, I slipped, pulling Luke down with me.

"Help!" Luke called.

"Oh my God!" Someone yelled.

"Luke?" I could barely see him.

He took my hand. "I'm here."

Two nurses tried to help me to my feet, but I asked them not to move me. Blood ran from my eyes and nose into my mouth faster than I could stop it.

"Please step back," I said. "I feel sick."

I tried to make sure they weren't too close to me and held it in as long as I could. Then, the vomiting started. The more I tasted the blood, the more violently I threw up. Eventually, it slowed down, but I blacked out anyway.

When I regained consciousness, my eyes were clear, and everything seemed like normal again, except I was lying in a hospital bed. Luke was on the phone with Dimitri telling him what happened.

"We'd like to run some tests on you," the doctor said.

"I'd rather not," I replied. "I'm fine now."

The doctor kept insisting that I stay but I knew it was a part of healing. It happened to be the worst episode I had ever experienced.

"She gets nose bleeds sometimes," Luke said as he went into the doctor's mind to manipulate him into releasing me. "She can go home."

The doctor left the room.

"I should have known," I heard someone say.

A man with neatly cut pepper-colored hair stood in the doorway. He wore a hospital gown and had multiple casts. He walked like Frankenstein into the room.

"Denny?" I asked, recognizing his big brown eyes.

"How did you find me?" he wondered.

"Your mom went to Dimitri asking for my help," I replied. "She wanted me to heal you."

"My mom?" Denny leaned down on the chair while trying unsuccessfully to take the cast off his right arm.

"Yes, your mom," I replied.

"Still, you shouldn't have come," he said, sounding annoyed. "If I was meant to die or be in pain, that was part of God's plan. I didn't give you permission to use your hoodoo on me."

"Knowing everything you do about me; how could you possibly think I would purposely do anything I thought went against God? You proclaim to be a Christian now, so why haven't you learned to let God alone judge people? You can hate me forever; It doesn't change how I feel about you. But I can almost guarantee that when you face God, you're going to feel shame for how you've treated me. God knows my heart and my intentions," I said firmly. "That's all that matters."

"I never hated you, Alice, but I will continue to pray for your soul," Denny said, looking at me with pity. "Can't you see that there's something gravely wrong? We're nearly the same age, but you still look the way you did when you were in your twenties. What happened to our dreams? We were supposed to live next door to each other, raise our families and go gray together. You chose to throw it all away for someone who

257

deceived you many times. You may go on forever or until God puts a stop to it, but you can never have the life you wanted."

"I may not have gotten the Little House on the Prairie life I wanted, but what I have isn't far from that dream. I live in a place surrounded by extraordinarily good people; I have a husband whom I'm thankful for every day and we have the most beautiful baby girl I could have imagined. The only thing missing in my life has been you and that was by your choice, not mine." I grabbed my blood-stained clothes out of the plastic bag they were tossed in and headed into the bathroom to get changed.

"You have a child?" Denny asked as I closed the door.

When I stepped back into the room, a nurse helped Denny into a wheelchair to take him back to his room.

"Do you have a pen and paper I could borrow for just a minute?" I asked the nurse.

She reached into her pocket, tore off a page from her note pad and handed it to me along with a pen.

"Thank you," I said, laying the paper on the sliding table.

I wrote a message, handed the paper to Denny and then gave the pen back to the nurse.

"What's this?" he asked.

"It's Dimitri's phone number. If you ever find *my* Denny someday, give him a call and he'll let me know," I said. "I would love to see him again."

"Why don't you just give me your phone number?" he asked.

"I don't have one," I replied.

As he left the room, I wondered if I would ever hear from him. Although I wished he would be his old self again, I didn't have much hope in that ever happening. At least, I tried one last time.

Luke whisked us back to Dimitri's house where he was holding little Bethie on the couch, smiling and cooing at her. It made us happy to find them together like that.

"Wow, you weren't kidding." Dimitri looked at my clothes and laughed. "Are you sure you two weren't out draining some necks?"

"Would you mind if I take a shower and get changed?" I asked laughing.

"I'd mind if you didn't." He grinned.

We spent the next two weeks with Dimitri soaking up all the time we had. When the morning came for us to return, I asked him again if he would like to come home with us. I explained how I knew everyone would be so happy to see him, but he declined. I wondered if Dimitri would have kept his immortality if he had known that Laurien had growing feelings for him.

Chapter Fifteen

Many months passed and Bethie's first birthday arrived. Luke and I were excited for her party but especially because Dimitri had finally agreed to come visit. He said he couldn't miss his goddaughter's big day and brought with him a large bag full of wrapped toys.

"They're here," Luke said cheerfully as his parents walked up—looking regal as always.

As soon as they were close enough, I sat Bethie down on the ground so she could walk to them. Luke's mother scooped her up and gave her a big hug.

"I've missed you, Bethie," she said, grinning from ear to ear.

Bethie kissed both of her cheeks.

"You do plan on having another one, right?" his father asked while looking at my flat stomach. "The palace will be far too lonely for her. You should think about getting on with that."

"Right now?" Luke leaned in and whispered in my ear. "Okay."

We started giggling like a couple of love-struck teenagers.

Laurien approached, holding hands with Greta and Everett. Dimitri took a few steps back. I walked over to him and took his sweaty hand.

"Dimitri," Laurien said as she let go of their hands.

Being the gentleman he was, Dimitri graciously asked to be introduced to her beau.

She laughed. "My beau?"

Dimitri was confused but attempted to smile.

"This is Everett. He's my cousin," she said cheerfully.

"Your cousin?" Dimitri asked. "I thought—"

"She has no beau," I whispered in his ear. "She's still a maiden."

Dimitri went from delightfully pleased to instantly unhappy in less than a minute. In that moment, I realized that I had once again hurt him. If I hadn't tossed the book in the pool, he would have stayed an immortal and they could have been together forever.

Dimitri shook Everett's hand. "It's nice to meet you."

"Dance with me?" she asked him.

"I'd be honored," he replied, and they walked away together.

Luke's mother handed Bethie to Luke and then walked towards me. "I know that look," she said. "What can I do to help?"

"Nothing, thank you though," I said with a heavy sigh. "It seems like no matter what I do, I always make things worse for my friend."

"He looks pretty happy right now," she said, gesturing to him out on the dance floor.

"For now, but it won't last forever."

I watched him and Laurien walk away, disappearing behind the trees.

"I think I might need to know a little bit more. Why are you being so hard on yourself? What have you done?" she asked kindly.

"I asked for his immortality and he got it. But when his parents died, he realized he didn't want to live forever. I was finally able to undo the spell, but now their time together will be short. Although he asked me to do it, I ultimately took away his forever with Laurien."

"Listen." She took me by the hands. "Time is precious whether it's one day, fifty years or an eternity. All that matters is how we spend the time we have together. God makes the final decision, not us."

I knew she tried to help, but it did not make me feel any better.

"See that couple adorned in flowers standing with Luke and Bethie?" she asked. "He's an immortal but she's a Geordian. She'll be lucky to live a thousand years, but I promise you, they'll make the most of every single one."

I couldn't help but think of how difficult the last years together would be for them.

"The best thing anyone can do is be kind, appreciate what you have every day and don't fear what comes next. Life is a gift." She smiled as we watched Bethie smother her father's cheeks with kisses. "That's why we're celebrating today."

We got up and started walking back over towards them. As we got closer, I noticed a woman with long brown hair dressed in ivory staring at me. It made me uncomfortable, so I looked away.

"May I hold the birthday girl?" Luke's mother asked, reaching out for her.

"Of course." Luke handed her over.

The woman's eyes were fixed on me, but I didn't make eye contact.

"Do I know you?" the woman asked.

"Aidra, this is Alice. The birthday girl's mother," Luke's father introduced us. "She's married to my son, Lucas."

She took a couple steps closer and looked into my eyes, studying them.

"Forgive me," she said, taking a step back.

"No need," I replied, feeling a little less uneasy.

"Curious though," she said.

"What is?" Luke asked.

"She reminds me of someone I knew on Earth," she said, squinting her eyes.

"She is from Earth. They say everyone there has a doppelganger," Luke's father joked.

"Who were you? Before?" she asked curiously. "What's your maiden-name?"

"Gordon," I replied.

"Oh." She sounded somewhat disappointed.

"Gordon?" Luke's mother was surprised. "I thought it was Cabot?"

I clarified, "That's my biological father's last name but I've always gone by Gordon."

"Antony Cabot?" Aidra asked inquisitively. "Mother's name was Moana?"

"Yes," I said excitedly. "Did you know them?"

Her faced turned red. She rushed away to an older woman standing about thirty feet away. They whispered and stared at me.

"I guess she knew them," Luke said.

After a couple minutes, the two walked towards us. As soon as they were close, the woman used her silver-tipped pinky nail to cut into the palm of Aidra's hand. Before anyone could stop her, she grabbed my hand and did the same thing.

"Why did you do that?" I asked angrily.

She didn't answer. Aidra put her palm up in front of mine and the woman grabbed my hand forcing it on top of Aidra's. The blood on her palm squashed against mine.

"Eww!" I yanked my hand away. "What's wrong with you?! Get them out of here!"

The guards restrained them immediately.

"Wait!" the woman shouted. "Look at their hands."

Our blood had turned a bright copper color.

"What did you do to me?" I asked, shaking.

Aidra's eyes filled with tears. "I'm so sorry. Please forgive me," she said as the cut on my hand healed. "I just had to know for sure."

"Know what?" Luke asked angrily.

"That she's my daughter," she replied.

"I am not your daughter."

"You are." She pulled away from the guards.

She walked towards me. I took a few steps back.

"Your father told me that you died during childbirth," she said, crying. "He lied to me, used his power to blind me from knowing that you survived."

"No. My mother's name was Lucy Gordon. It's on my birth certificate. She died about forty years ago," I insisted. "You've mistaken me for someone else. I'm not who you think I am."

"Your blood glowed when ours touched. That only happens to our people," she said. "The color proves that you're my child."

Everyone around me believed it to be true. My stomach turned.

"You're a healer too. Aren't you?" she asked. "It's a gift unique to our people."

"I need to sit down," I said, taking a seat at a long table.

"You are so much more than any of us here," she said excitedly. "You have both Geordian and ancestral Earth blood magic running through your veins. We can only heal, but you have the power to cause pain as easily as you can take it away. Once you learn to fully harness those powers, you'll be unstoppable. Let me take you to where you can grow into whom you were meant to become."

I was terribly frightened by her and channeled Luke asking him for help.

"She's been immersed in Sajet stardust," Luke said defensively. "Whatever she was before, she is one of us now."

"Oh, my. Even better! That's wonderful!" she cheered raising her hands in the air. "You can't simply wash away who she is nor her power. It's in her blood. She now has the power of three. With her added immortality, her sands of time shall never run out. One day she will rule all realms without end."

"No, that's not true. I'm not what you say," I insisted.

Aidra gave Luke a suspicious gaze. "Oh, but you already knew this, didn't you? Clever prince who spent a century on Earth learning to read and control minds. You knew exactly who she was. That's why you chose her for your queen."

"That's absurd," Liam interjected.

"But heed my warning: should you ever betray my daughter—without her given proper training—she won't be able to contain her fury. Immortal or not, she will destroy you without effort."

Luke's mother spoke up. "They love each other. Even with great power, Alice would never harm him."

"I don't care about power. I never have," I said firmly. "I only care about helping people."

"That's because you never understood how much of it you have. Gaining immense power always changes a person. It may take hundreds of years, but it will change you." Aidra stepped closer. "Your father was an incredible sorcerer, as was his father before him and that's in your blood. As soon as I realized what he was, I knew that it was our destiny to create you together. Your husband, Lucas only made you mightier by bringing you here. By baptizing you in Sajet stardust, he has made you a god. No wonder it took him so long to find a wife he felt worthy enough to make him a king."

"My father knew what you are?" I asked, ignoring everything else she was saying.

"Of course not." She grinned. "He fell in love with a sweet, innocent schoolteacher. He only learned who I was and the incredible plans I had for our little family just before you were born."

"You tricked him into having me?" I asked angrily. "It's always bothered me that my father kept me hidden away. I thought he didn't care about me at all, but now I know, he was protecting me from you."

"Embrace me as your mother!" she demanded. "You owe me that much. I gave you life. Without me, you wouldn't exist, and neither would your child."

"I owe you nothing," I replied angrily. "I want you to leave right now."

"Show them how formidable you truly are," she said sinisterly. "If you want me to go, use your powers to send me home. Make me, Alice!"

Most everyone was watching, even the children. I didn't want to try to do anything or risk hurting anyone. I wanted her to leave and never return.

"Please go," I begged.

She rushed over and grabbed Bethie before anyone could stop her. Immediately, Luke leaped forward attempting to grab her back.

"If you take another step towards me, you will never see her again," she warned him.

Luke stood still trying to figure out what to do next.

"You cannot be my mother. No mother of mine would even think of taking her from us," I said angrily.

"Antony robbed me from raising you into who you were meant to be. An eye for an eye, as they say on earth. Elsbeth has great potential too," she threatened. "If you want your daughter back, do something about it!"

Bethie cried and my whole body began to heat up. I wasn't sure what to do, but the more I thought about Aidra taking her away from us, the hotter I became. It was like high voltage electricity ran through my veins but didn't hurt. I scowled at that horrible woman holding my precious daughter. I went into

Luke's mind and told him to be ready to catch her. Immediately after, I focused all my energy and forced Bethie out of her arms and into her father's.

"Outstanding!" Aidra stomped her feet and cheered. "That's only the beginning. Wait until you see what you can do with practice!"

I went over to Luke and Bethie to make sure she was unharmed. Then I turned back towards Aidra and watched as she celebrated. The angrier I got, the happier she became.

With fury in my soul and clenched fists, I screamed, "Leave!"

A massive portal opened and pulled her in. She cackled, up until it closed.

I turned to face everyone, afraid they would turn on me or cower with fear, but instead, they cheered.

I walked away from the crowd towards an orchard trying not to show any emotion. My legs wobbled from my nerves.

"Will you please watch her for a few minutes?" Luke asked his mother.

"I'd love to," she replied and took Bethie into her arms.

Luke followed me. As soon as we were out of ear shot, I broke down and cried. I couldn't believe that terrible woman was my birth mother or that I had so much power in me. I was relieved that she was gone but terrified about who I was.

271

Luke cautiously hugged me. "Are *we* good?"

"Why wouldn't we be?" I replied, looking at him. "Unless there's some other secret you haven't told me."

"No other surprises," he said nervously. "But aren't you curious to know if I already knew?"

"Not especially. You know I'll stay with you regardless. I always do. What would be the point?" I asked. "I stopped believing everything you tell me long ago."

Luke looked dejected.

"I'm not angry, Luke nor am I trying to hurt you. You are who you are, and I love you for it and despite it."

"But you don't trust me."

"I trust your actions, just not your words." I took a step closer to him. "I believe that you would do anything to keep Bethie and me safe, but I also wouldn't be surprised to hear a completely different version of your time on Earth."

"I'm your husband, I need you to believe in me." Luke sounded sincere.

"Then try never lying to me again. Stop keeping secrets," I said. "Whatever all this is that's going on inside me, it's escalating quickly. I need you beside me, helping me learn to control this storm. What if Aidra's right and I'm going to snap one day? I don't want to accidentally hurt you because you tricked me one too many times. We need to stay on the same side *all* the time. I can't be worrying about another curve ball being thrown at me."

"Is there anything I can do to help?" Dimitri asked, overhearing the end of our conversation.

I wanted to beg him to stay with us for the rest of his life and use his magic to help us, but I knew that was selfish.

"Be our dearest friend for all your days and visit as much as you'd like," I replied.

"Until my last breath." He smiled and gave me a hug.

"I'm glad you're here with us, Dimitri," Luke said, joining the hug. "Being around you always brightens her spirit."

"Do you think cloning is one of my superpowers?" I joked. "Could I have a strand of your hair or a drop of your blood before you go home, just in case?"

We all laughed.

"I know you're going through a lot. I'm happy to come here as often as you wish," Dimitri said.

"Well then, you're next to get tossed into the pool," Luke laughed. "She will *always* want you here."

Dimitri smiled.

"Very funny, Luke. I would never force him back into immortality."

"If you're feeling better, we should head back now," Luke said. "It's time for her birthday cake and presents. You know she's going to be covered with frosting. It's going to be great."

We headed back to the party giving Bethie the best first birthday a one-year-old would never remember.

As night fell, everyone headed back to their homes. Luke's parents and the other visitors went back to their realms. When it was time to take Dimitri back, Luke spoke with him alone at the palace entrance. I took Bethie to her room, cleaned her up and put her to bed for the night.

"Dimitri's deeply concerned about you and Bethie. He's asked to come back in a few days," Luke said as he entered our bedroom.

"Of course, I want him to come back, but I don't want him to feel like he has to be here," I said, getting my things ready for my bath.

"I already promised I'd bring him back here on Thursday," Luke replied. "He has magical abilities that could help us."

"Why didn't he just stay then?"

"He needed to go home and take care of some things."

"Hmm. Okay. Well, I'll never complain about getting more time with him."

"You know, Alice," Luke said intensely. "I've said this before, but I believe it to be true more than ever. Dimitri would do anything for you. You have no idea."

"He's a good man. I'm extremely grateful for his friendship." I smiled. "I hope he knows that."

"He does and it just makes him even fonder of you," Luke said as he took off his shirt.

"Can I ask you something and have you answer honestly?"

"Uh, oh," he said nervously. "Sure."

"Would you be willing to go back with me to Earth for a while when Dimitri gets old? You know, to stay with him if he ever needs someone to take care of him or just to keep him company?" I asked. "Hopefully, he'll have a wife and children long before then, but I wouldn't be able to bear it if I knew he were alone."

"You've got to be the most caring person I've ever known." He leaned forward and kissed me. "We will always look out for him."

"Thank you," I said, hugging him.

"Care for some company in your bath?" he asked flirtatiously.

"Well, I was planning on just relaxing."

"All right, we can just relax."

"We *never* just relax when you join me." I smiled.

"True." He grinned. "So—may I?"

"You know I can't resist your charm," I said, taking him by the hand. "If I didn't know better, I would think you've gotten me under some spell."

"Perhaps it's the other way around." He smiled.

Chapter Sixteen

The following morning, Liam and Greta came by during breakfast. They asked us to allow Bethie to enjoy an all-day playdate with their family in the village. We thanked them and immediately Bethie climbed down from her seat, held their hands and they left.

"I had a dream about my mother, Lucy last night. She was at the house I grew up in, hiding something under a large stepping-stone next to our old outdoor drinking fountain," I said, remembering it quite well. "But I wasn't able to see what it was."

"Are you sure it was her?" Luke asked. "You were very young when she died."

"I never saw her face, but I know it was her. She was trying to show me something."

"And you want to see what's hidden there?" Luke asked. "It's going to drive you crazy if we don't check. Isn't it?"

I started to laugh because he was right. From the moment I woke up, that was all I could think about. As soon as I found out that Lucy wasn't my birth mother, I wondered how she ended up with me. I knew she had been living in New Orleans before showing up at my Grandma's house with a brand-new baby, but there was so much that I didn't know.

"How soon do you want to go?" Luke asked.

I smiled.

"Now," he laughed.

"Well, as soon as you're done eating."

"All right," he replied, taking his last bite. "I am curious to see if she actually did bury something in the yard too."

Luke whisked us away, but the city had gotten crowded over the years, which made it more difficult to find a remote place to show up unnoticed. We landed in a clearing near the American River and walked the few blocks to my old house.

"It looks so different. I barely recognize it," I said, feeling a bit disappointed. "When I lived here, it was painted an off-white color with a dark green trim. The rocks look nice, but I miss the lush green lawn and my Grandma's beautiful roses. It's a shame they took them out."

A woman in her thirties holding a toddler watched us from the kitchen window. I immediately went into her head to have her invite us in for a tour.

"Good morning," she greeted us. "Come on in."

Luke and I smiled at each other.

"Thank you," I said cheerfully.

We all walked inside, and she showed us around the house while carrying her child on her hip. The inside hadn't changed much. Even the chip in the sliding glass door remained from when I accidentally rolled Denny's skateboard against it when we were eleven.

"May we see the backyard too?" Luke asked.

"Of course." She smiled. "This way."

We followed her outside. Most of the grass had been ripped out and replaced with wood chips. In the middle of the yard was a fenced in playground with slide. Her child immediately asked to be put down to play.

"Didn't there used to be a drinking fountain out here?" I asked.

"Yes, it's on the other side of the big oak tree," she replied. "It gets so hot here in the summer. The shade really helps keep the spigot from getting too hot."

"Do you mind if I take a look?" I asked. "My family lived here long ago."

"Please do," she said cheerfully.

When I reached the first stone in the path, I was surprised they were the original ones—even my tiny handprint and name was still there. In my dream, my mother buried something under the stone closest to the fountain. I walked to it, tried to pull it up from the ground, but it wouldn't budge. I channeled Luke letting him know that I would need a shovel to get it up.

A few minutes later, Luke walked towards me carrying a garden spade. "She went inside to put her son down for a nap," he said as he handed it to me.

I laughed, feeling surprised that she was fine with me digging it up. "Thanks."

I dug around the edge on one side, but the ground was hard as stone. I couldn't get it to budge.

"Would you like me to try?" Luke asked.

"Please."

He tried for about five minutes without success.

"We can come back another time and bring some tools." Luke said, trying to help.

I didn't want to have to come back. I was terribly impatient and wanted to move the stupid thing out of the way and check. I began to get angry and wondered why I would dream such a thing and then not be able to see what she was hiding.

"Ugh!" I slammed both of my fists against the stepping-stone.

"Whoa!"

The ground began to shake, and the stone loosened itself.

Luke moved it out of the way, and I knew exactly where to dig. It took about five minutes before the spade hit something hard. The excitement made me dig faster.

"You found something," Luke said cheerfully, as I pried a metal box from the ground.

"I can't believe there was actually something there." I was eager to open it.

We put the dirt back in the ground, re-set the stone, and then Luke whisked us back to Sajet. Once we were in our bedroom with the door closed, I placed the box on my lap, undid the latch and opened it. Inside was a picture of my father and Aidra and a small, black diary. I picked up the book and turned to the first page. My mother's name, Lucy Gordon was written on the inside.

"She started writing in this just before I was born," I said, beginning to read.

Luke read along with me.

October 19ᵗʰ

> *Today I was asked to do the unthinkable. If what he's telling me is true about her and I accept, I pray God forgives me as I'm doing it for the greater good. I only have two days to let him know before he acts on his alternate plan. I told him I'd sleep on it, but knowing what the alternative is, I feel there is only one true choice.*

I turned to the next page and continued reading.

October 20th

    I made my decision and let him know. I could sense the relief in his eyes as I believe he was just trying to do what he thought would keep her safe. I forced myself to not think about his wife and how this would affect her.

October 21st

    I packed my bags and moved into the guest room of their home ready to assist with the birth. As I watched her go about her daily life, I began to question whether what we were doing was best. She seemed like a kind, loving person who wouldn't harm a soul. How could she possibly be dangerous?

October 22nd

    I woke in the night and can hear them arguing. She's going on a rant about how their unborn child is destined to be the most powerful sorceress. He keeps telling her that he doesn't want that life for their child, but she's trying to convince him of all the spoils they could have as she will grow to be a great ruler. She seems insanely obsessed with power, saying that their child will be even greater than he is once the book of power is in her hands. He's franticly telling her that he means to find a way to destroy the book, ensuring that their child can never use it.

After about an hour, he stopped responding to her and it went silent. I'm afraid that if his plan doesn't work, she's going to take that poor child away and corrupt it with her madness. I fear for this child.

October 23rd

Today was a long, terrible day. From the time he woke up, until he finally locked himself in the bathroom and fell asleep in the bathtub, she followed him around the house telling him that she plans to take the baby back with them to her realm as soon as she's born. Although, he finally agreed to go along with her plans, I knew the truth.

October 24th

Early this morning, I heard her calling out in pain from their room as her labor had begun. Unbeknown to her, Antony quickly put a protection spell on the house not allowing her to leave with their child.

As the contractions progressed throughout the day, she kept insisting on being taken to the hospital to deliver. He reassured her, explaining that I was there to help and when the contractions were closer together or her water broke, we would take her.

At a quarter to 8:00 pm, her water broke. To have a viable excuse for not leaving, he caused a storm to come through New Orleans. Although it appeared to be fierce, it was only a façade and caused no damage.

Their baby girl was born a few minutes before midnight, but Antony had spelled her to not see the baby move nor hear her cry. He needed her to believe that she had died. Immediately after, he lifted the protection spell from the house, calmed the storm and tearfully asked me to wrap up the baby until the coroner arrived. She screamed at him, blaming him for not taking her to the hospital. She walked slowly out the door telling him that she never loved him before disappearing into the night sky.

Once she was gone, Antony called a physician friend to come over. I took his wife's place on the bed, holding the baby as if she were my own just before he arrived. The doctor examined her and then signed the birth certificate naming me as the mother and omitting the father's name. I was fortunate that he never checked me before leaving or he would have known that I hadn't given birth.

As soon as it was done, Antony broke down and wept. He had loved his wife deeply before learning the truth and had dreams of a life with his new family. He held on to his daughter for nearly an hour. Watching his despair, I asked if he was sure about going through with the plan. He told me that we had no choice. Aidra was born without a soul and the only way his daughter could be safe was if she were kept hidden from all magic. He feared that their child too may have no soul and wanted her to have a strong Catholic upbringing, away from anything that could possibly trigger her powers.

October 25th

I arrived at mom's today with the baby in tow, explaining that I had gotten pregnant from a man in Louisiana who wanted little to do with our child. After giving me a good, long lecture about my promiscuity, she told me that all babies were a gift and that she was excited to finally be a grandmother.

October 26th

Today I will bury this diary and take this secret to my grave. I pray that I did the right thing and will be the best mother that sweet Alice could have. She will learn about God's love, kindness and become a caring person. Whether or not she has a soul, she will be a gift

to this world, and I am blessed to be her mother. I pray
that her father finds peace in his decision and that she
someday understands the incredible sacrifice he made and
the love he has for her.

I had tears in my eyes, as I finished reading her last entry. "It wasn't just about Aidra. He was trying to keep me away from all magic."

Luke hugged me.

"What if he's right?" I worried. "What if I don't have a soul? If I weren't an immortal, what would happen to me when I died? Where do people go without one?"

I became very frightened. I always considered myself to be close to God but wondered if it was because I was raised to feel that way. If I were soulless and wasn't supposed to be born, he may have never listened to my prayers.

"Your father was scared and didn't know what he was talking about," Luke said, trying to comfort me. "Everyone has a soul, whether they're a good or bad person. Aidra may not have a conscience but she has a soul. Maybe that's what he meant. A body can't exist without a soul. I'm sure your mother realized that as soon as she took you in."

"It's kind of strange reading her diary though. I've always worried about saving my soul but hearing I may not even have one, means I may not have needed to care," I replied, half-joking.

"I wouldn't give it another moment's thought." Luke hugged me. "You definitely have a good soul."

"I wonder what my father would think about you and me being together," I said curiously. "It was so important to him that I stay away from magic, but you found me anyway."

"I'm guessing he would have preferred that you married Denny instead, but I bet he sees how happy we are together and is probably okay with it all now."

I sat on the bed thinking about everything I had read and wondered what my life might have been like, had he chosen to keep me.

"I wonder how my grandmother never knew my father's wife was pregnant. I don't see how he could have kept that hidden from her," I said. "She never mentioned that he was ever married."

"Maybe he put some cloaking spell on her to keep the pregnancy hidden or made her forget," Luke replied.

"He was that powerful?" I asked.

"Your father was amazing. I don't think there was any spell he couldn't conjure, either on his own or by using the book of power."

"I wondered why he stopped using it and kept it locked away."

"Probably to keep you safe."

"I wish I could have known him when he was alive. I would have loved a letter. I don't understand why he couldn't do more than a card with a quick message," I said sadly. "He knew where I lived up until he died. He had almost twenty-nine years to get to know me."

"It was probably too painful for him. If I had to give Bethie away in order to give her a safe life, I can't imagine the mental state I would be in. I probably wouldn't be able to write more than I love you either. I think he did the best he could with what he knew."

"Bethie is so lucky to have you." I kissed him. "You're a wonderful father, Luke."

"And a decent husband?" he asked, kissing my neck.

"An amazing husband."

"They have her until around seven this evening, huh?" he asked flirtatiously.

"Yes, indeed." I smiled. "We have most of the day to ourselves."

"Wonderful," he said as he undressed.

Chapter Seventeen

A few days later, Luke brought Dimitri back. He arrived with two large chests and one small brief case full of his belongings. He unpacked and took back his old room in the palace. He had enough clothing to stay for more than a couple months. I tried not to act too excited or get my hopes up, but I was thankful to have him with us for as long as he wanted to stay.

The first night back, Luke and Dimitri stayed up late talking in the great hall. They discussed complex spells that were beyond my understanding. I was especially tired, so I headed to bed just after midnight. I woke up around 2:00 am. Luke still hadn't come to bed. I wandered the halls looking for him and Dimitri but couldn't find them. As I turned to go out into the courtyard, I noticed a light on in one of the rooms. Voices spoke softly. I followed the sounds into the room.

"What are you doing?!" I asked loudly.

Dimitri sat on the edge of the purple pool dressed in swim shorts.

Luke stood beside him. "This is what he wants," he said, trying to reassure me he wasn't doing something against his will.

"No, it's not. He asked me to take away his immortality. What could have possibly changed? I may not be able to take this back."

"I don't want you to undo this. It's my choice," Dimitri replied. "This is what I truly desire."

"What about your mom and dad?" I asked. "You're suddenly okay with spending an eternity without them and they without you?"

"I have faith I'll see them again someday. Besides, I can speak to the dead, remember? If they want to reach me, they can. I've never closed the door to them." Dimitri smiled. "I've weighed all my options, Alice. This is what I choose."

I realized his motivation and smiled. "This is about Laurien. You love her. This is so you can be with her forever."

"No. She's a dear friend, but nothing more. I don't love her, well not that way." Dimitri nodded at Luke. "Please."

Luke bent down, lifted him from under the arms and tossed him into the purple goo.

I watched as he went under the liquid with his eyes locked on mine. He didn't struggle—he let himself sink.

"This can't be what he really wanted. If he doesn't love her, why would you do that to him?" I asked sadly.

"You already know the answer." Luke raised his brows.

"I truly don't," I said as my eyes teared up. "But I do know what kind of life Dimitri wanted. He's told me many times. He is never going to have that now."

"You're right, but he knows that staying here with us is as close to that dream as he could possibly get. That's all he wants now," Luke said firmly.

Dimitri gradually came back to the surface. Luke reached down and helped him out of the pool. I couldn't comprehend why he would make such a choice. Earth was full of kind, beautiful women he could have loved. It would have been easy for him to find a wife and have the family he wanted. Sajet wasn't the type of place he would ever want to live forever. He had big dreams and loved magic. His decision made no sense.

As soon as Dimitri was able to catch his breath, he smiled at Luke and said, "Thank you."

I stood without saying a word. I didn't know what to say.

"Lots of godchildren," Dimitri said as Luke bent down to hug him. "I'll love them all, even if they turn out to be ridiculous vampire wannabes like you."

Luke laughed.

"What?" I asked.

"I'll explain later," Luke replied as he helped pull him to his feet.

"Good night," Dimitri said with little energy, then walked out of the room.

As soon as we were alone and behind closed doors, I asked Luke what all the god-children talk was about. He explained that part of his agreement of making Dimitri immortal was that he would be the godfather to every child we had.

"That's wonderful, but I still don't understand why you did this and why you didn't talk to me about it first. We just talked about not keeping secrets, Luke," I said as I climbed back into bed. "I don't like being kept in the dark, especially when it comes to big decisions like this."

"I'm sorry. He asked me not to tell you until after it was done," Luke said, getting undressed for his shower. "Besides, I agree with him. Having him here as an immortal is what's best for you."

"What about what's best for him?" I asked, thinking about how much Dimitri was giving up. "How can knowing he's missing the life he wanted be best for anyone? Do you both think I'm really that selfish?"

Luke walked over to me, kissed me on the forehead and said kindly, "Being apart wasn't good for anyone. Dimitri respects our marriage, but that man loves you, he told me he always will. So—being here with you in any capacity is what's best for him."

I wasn't sure how to respond. Although I was concerned that Dimitri had let go of his dreams to help protect our family, I was surprised Luke would make him an immortal and allow him to stay after confessing his feelings.

"Knowing what we both know now, let's try to keep our PDA to a minimum around him." Luke kissed me and then took his shower.

When Luke and I got up the next morning, Dimitri was already in the dining hall having breakfast with Bethie. The two laughed between bites.

"Good morning," he said cheerfully. "Look Bethie, mommy and daddy are awake."

I walked over, kissed her cheek and hugged him. "Thank you, Dimitri."

"So." Dimitri let out a heavy sigh as soon as we sat down. "Are you all up for a trip in the next couple days?"

"All?" Luke replied. "To where?"

"Denny's not doing well. His mother asked that we go see him."

"Oh no. What happened to him now?" I worried.

"He's becoming increasingly despondent. He's been taking medication since his partner died but it's not doing enough. His doctor already changed his meds a few times with no luck. His mom was hoping that you could try to heal him."

"Where is he?" I asked.

"He's at home. He lives in Simi Valley," Dimitri replied. "I wrote the address down."

"How am I supposed to help him when he doesn't want to see me? There's only so much I can do from a distance," I said.

"Luke will get the guard to let us in. His mom said he really misses you, so he's not going to throw us out."

"Okay," Luke said. "Liam and Greta are expecting us all for an early dinner, but we can go first thing in the morning."

"Do you think it's okay to wait until then?" I asked Dimitri. "How urgent did this seem?"

"Tomorrow should be fine," he replied. "She just thinks it would help to lift his spirit and getting to meet Bethie would be good for him."

When it was time to head to Liam's, Dimitri let us know that he would not be joining us. He planned on working on some protection charms and counter spells. I was glad to know he was still going to practice magic.

"Can we bring you back a plate?" I asked.

"Thank you, no," he replied politely. "I'm happy with some leftovers from last night."

At dinner, Laurien showed up around half-way through. She seemed disappointed that Dimitri didn't come and offered more than once to bring him some dinner. Luke explained that he was working on an important project and should not be disturbed.

"We can save him a plate and I'll bring it to him tomorrow," she insisted.

"He's going with us to take care of some personal stuff in the morning. I'm not sure when we'll be back," Luke said.

"Oh." She sounded disappointed. "I guess I'll just have to wait to see him when he returns."

"Dimitri." I was surprised to see him approaching. "Did you finish early?"

"No, but may I speak to you two alone for a couple minutes?" he asked and then picked up Bethie who was reaching for him.

"Excuse us," I said as we followed Dimitri to a place where we were out of ear shot.

"What's up?" I asked.

"I can't seem to make the spells work without a strand of your hair," he replied.

"Whose hair?" Luke asked.

"All of yours, including Bethie's."

"Oh, I don't want to pull hair from her head. Is there another way?" I asked.

"We can just cut a small strand off, if that's okay," he said, taking out a small pair of shears.

I took the scissors, carefully cut a strand of her dark hair and handed it to Dimitri.

"Ouch," I said, as Luke yanked a single strand from my head and then his.

Dimitri handed Bethie to Luke, put the hair in little pouches and then started walking away. "All right. I'll get back to it."

"Thanks Dimitri." I replied.

Luke, Bethie and I walked back to rejoin the group. Before we sat down, Laurien got up and went after Dimitri, calling his name. He stopped to speak with her.

"He keeps his thoughts well-guarded," Greta said, looking at Dimitri. "Not that I've been prying."

"That's my fault, I suppose," Luke said. "I had too much fun messing with his head for a long time. Well, until he figured out a way to only let me see what he wants. He's actually quite a brilliant wizard, more than I ever gave him credit."

"I can see how much he loves you three and Bethie always lights up when he's around," she replied. "I'm glad he chose to stay here with us."

"Me too." Luke smiled.

After about five minutes, Laurien walked back. "I'm really tired. I hope you don't mind if I call it a night," she said to Greta and Liam.

"Of course not. Is everything all right?" Greta asked.

"I'm fine," she replied. "Enjoy the rest of your evening."

"Good night, Laurien," I said.

"Your majesty." She bowed.

"Your majesty?" I asked, feeling uncomfortable. "Just Alice, please. You know I don't like being addressed so formally."

She didn't respond and continued walking home.

The next morning, we arrived at Denny's home shortly before 10:00 am. Luke manipulated the guard into letting us through the gate. He made his staff believe that he was expecting a visit from his old friends. We sat in his foyer waiting while we were announced. Denny came downstairs but then turned around to walk away.

"Wait, please!" I called to him. "I want you to meet my daughter."

He turned back around and saw Bethie smiling at him. "Wow," he said. "She's adorable."

Bethie kicked her feet to have Luke put her down on the floor. As soon as he did, she waddled towards Denny with her arms reaching up for him. He smiled, bent down and picked her up.

"This sweet little girl actually came from you two?" he joked.

We all smiled.

"God, she's perfect," he said, tearing up.

Bethie wrapped her tiny arms around his neck and kissed his cheek.

"Oh, my goodness. She's so cute," he said smiling. "How old is she?"

"She's one." I was so pleased to see him holding her.

Bethie and Denny smiled at each other like long-time friends.

Denny turned and looked at me with tears in his eyes. "I'm so sorry. Can you ever forgive me?"

"Of course, I've missed my Denny." I walked towards him. "I love you."

Luke followed behind me to take Bethie while I gave Denny a long hug. We both wept. I never thought I would ever get my friend back and I could tell that neither did he. It almost felt unreal.

"I love you more." Denny smiled.

We both laughed.

"How long can you stay?" he asked us.

I turned to Luke for an answer.

"A few days, maybe a week?" Luke replied.

"Okay, we will just have to make the most of the time we have," Denny replied.

"But—if you come home with us, you are welcome to stay as long as you'd like," Luke smiled. "We have plenty of room."

"Thank you. That would be nice. It's been really rough lately," he said with teary eyes.

I hugged him again. "I know it has."

"I could definitely use a change of scenery. Do you all still live in New Orleans?"

"Not quite," Dimitri chuckled.

Denny looked confused.

"I don't think you would believe me without seeing it," I said, remembering we weren't allowed to mention Sajet to anyone on Earth.

"Well, now I have to come visit," he replied.

I grinned. "It may come as a bit of a shock. It's nothing like anything you could ever imagine."

"I think I'll be fine," Denny said cheerfully. "I've been all over the world."

Dimitri laughed.

"How soon can you be ready to go?" Luke asked.

"Twenty minutes," he said eagerly.

Denny left the room, and I could feel his knees hurting as he climbed the stairs. I healed his joints and helped lift his depression. The four of us sat down waiting on his crushed-velvet couches.

"He's done really well for himself," Dimitri said. "This place is stunning."

"Denny's always been brilliant at tech stuff and it doesn't hurt that he's a people person. I knew he would be successful," I said, feeling proud of my old friend.

After about fifteen minutes, Denny came back into the foyer carrying two pieces of fine luggage and a toiletries bag.

"Let's do this," he said cheerfully.

We all walked together out the front door and on to the large circular driveway.

"Did you call for a ride?" he asked as he looked around for a car.

"No, but I'll get us there." Luke replied.

"Are you sure about this?" I asked Denny, being in shock this was happening. "Ready for an adventure?"

"Yes." He held onto his things.

"All right," Luke said, reaching into his pocket to grab his device.

We all hung onto each other and Luke clicked us up and away. Denny's mouth was wide open.

"Just breathe," I said while trying to calm him down.

He closed his eyes and gritted his teeth.

"It's okay." I reassured him. "We're almost there."

As soon as we arrived, Denny opened his eyes. He shook in disbelief, but as soon as he heard Bethie giggle, he calmed down.

"Where are we?" he asked nervously. "What is this place?"

"This is Sajet," Luke said cheerfully. "This is our home. It's where I come from."

"What?" Denny asked, almost falling over.

Right away, a bunch of people rushed over to see who we brought with us. The children were especially interested because they were fascinated by anyone with gray in their hair.

Denny faced the crowd and asked, "Where are all the people my age?"

"Our age." I corrected him. "There are many here, but Sajet people don't age past thirty to thirty-five. They're immortals."

"You mean your bodies stay young and you could just keep having babies forever?" he asked with his mouth wide open. "Well, you always wanted a big family, Alice. You could like give her like ten thousand siblings?"

I laughed.

"We can have as many children as we both want," Luke replied. "Some people chose to have dozens, some a few but many would rather not have any. Everyone's different, but technically, there's no limit to the number of children Alice and I could have over time."

"Wow. What about population control? Won't you run out of room here eventually if no one ever dies?"

"This realm grows as more space is needed but many choose to go on and explore other realms, even Earth," Luke replied. "My parents aren't here any longer either. They live in a magnificent land of great beauty where many kings and queens go to retire."

"So, does that make you a prince or duke or something?" Denny asked.

"Thankfully for us, he's the king," Liam said proudly, approaching with Greta, Laurien and their children.

"Denny, this is my brother, Liam and his family," Luke said cheerfully.

"Where are you from?" Liam asked.

"Earth?" Denny chuckled.

"Another earthling friend of the queen?" Laurien said, sounding a bit off.

"Wonderful. We're always happy to meet Alice's friends," Greta said, ignoring her sister's snide tone. "How long will you be staying?"

"Uh, I don't know," Denny said, sounding a bit overwhelmed and looking at Luke for an answer.

"As long as he'd like," Luke replied cheerfully.

"Are you married?" Liam's daughter, Arbie asked. "Do you have any kids?"

"I'm widowed," Denny replied sadly. "And no children, my partner never wanted any."

"Oh," Arbie said sadly, then gave him a hug.

"It's okay," he replied. "We had many good years together and we were able to do a lot of things that we both wanted. It was worth it."

Bethie kicked to be put down on the ground when she spotted Liam's youngest. She rushed over to hug her and kiss her cheek.

"We should probably let Denny get settled in," I said, reading Denny's nervousness.

"Yes," Luke said. "Good idea."

"Nice to meet you," Greta said.

"Nice to meet you too," Denny replied.

We picked up Bethie, walked back to the palace and showed him to one of the spare bedrooms where he would be staying. The whole way there, I couldn't stop smiling. I never thought that Denny and I would be friends again or even be under the same roof.

"None of this seems real. I can't believe you came from another world, Luke or that this place exists at all. I guess that kind of explains some of your secrecy and why you made up such outlandish stories," Denny said in disbelief. "Though I don't understand why you asked Alice to use her book to make you an immortal when you already were."

"I was forbidden to discuss Sajet which made it difficult to be honest. Sorry about that," Luke said as he patted him on the back. "After you get your things put away, let us know. We'll be waiting in the dining hall. We can all have lunch together and then show you around."

During lunch, we got Denny caught up on what had happened over the years, including my birth mother, Aidra. Although he surprisingly seemed to be taking everything in stride, I could sense that he still had concerns about Luke and his past trickery.

We spent the rest of the day helping him become acquainted with our world. In the evening, a group of villagers put on an impromptu show for us with singing, dancing and short skits. The highlight of the night was a group of five-year-old children who performed a juggling act while their teacher played a bamboo flute.

"I love it here," Denny said, welling up. "Thank you for coming for me. I can't tell you how much this means to me."

"Thank you for giving our friendship another chance," I said with tears in my eyes. "It's so good to have you here."

I gave Denny a big hug.

That night was the happiest I had felt in years. Everyone I loved most was all in one place and my heart finally felt whole again.

When I fell asleep, I had a dream about my father. I don't know if it was a creation of my mind or if he was reaching out to me. He told me that everything he did was to protect me but wished he had found a safe way to be a part of my life. Last of all, he warned me to never trust my birth mother and to work diligently on controlling my powers.

That morning, I thought about the dream a lot but didn't talk about it. I had never been one to take much credence in dreams, but I also thought it was odd that the image of my father would warn me in one.

After breakfast, we took Denny to the stardust pool, he was fascinated by it. Luke offered to baptize him in it so he could stay with us without ever growing any older, but he was apprehensive about anything involving magic.

"Do you have something that could just make me look and feel younger without signing up for an eternity?" Denny joked.

"No, but Alice can heal you as you grow older," Luke said.

"We can also use colstra leaves to dye your hair black," I said, sensing a little vanity.

"What happens if I just touch it? Would that smooth away a few fine lines?" He laughed hysterically. "Can I scoop some up and add some purple streaks to my hair?

"The pool?" Luke laughed.

Denny nodded, still laughing.

"I don't know," Luke said. "We rarely use this pool and when we have, the person or object has been completely submerged."

"Could it hurt him?" I asked, sensing how much Denny was feeling drawn to the pool.

"I don't see how it would. You and Dimitri both went in and retained your magical abilities while gaining a new immortality."

"I thought you said you put your book of power in there?" Denny asked me. "Didn't you say that the pages were empty when you took it out and Dimitri became mortal again?"

"Yes," I answered curiously. "Why do you ask?"

"It just seems odd that you were able to keep your power, but the book didn't," Denny said staring at the purple goo. "Have you tried to use it since?"

"No, I assumed it didn't work because everything was erased," I replied. "I was just going to use it to write a story or as a journal someday."

"What if it does work but whatever is written can be undone by the pool?" Dimitri asked.

"Would you mind if I tried writing something in it?" I asked Luke.

"As long as it's not blocking me out again," he half-joked.

"Really?" I was annoyed with his response. "You know why I did that, and I promised I'd never do it again."

Everyone looked uncomfortable.

"I'll be back in a few minutes." I handed Bethie to Luke.

I returned with the book and a pen. They all sat on the floor next to the water. Bethie hummed.

"What are you going to write?" Dimitri asked curiously.

"I'd rather not say," I replied. "Just wait and see what happens. If you notice anything, say something right away."

I wrote asking for Denny to turn back to how he looked and felt when he was in his early thirties. Once I was done, I closed the book. Everyone waited for something to happen, but nothing did.

"Guess it doesn't work," Dimitri said. "Sorry Alice."

I opened the book back up to check if the words were erased or if I had somehow written it in a way that wasn't clear.

"Ouch!" I said loudly. The corner of the page cut my index finger dripping blood onto the book. The words I had written only moments before were covered with my blood. Seconds later, the blood faded away and the writing reappeared.

"Denny," Dimitri said, pointing at him.

Bethie quickly climbed off Luke's lap, went up to Denny and touched his face, giggling hysterically. He had changed back to the way he looked when he was younger.

"Oh my gosh." I put my hands on my cheeks. "It actually worked."

"What's going on?" Denny asked. "I feel funny."

Luke took out the transport device thing from his pocket and used the mirrored side to show Denny his reflection.

"Oh my God, Alice. What did you do to me?" he asked in shock. "I was just joking."

I opened the book and showed Denny what I had written. I wanted him to know that I didn't ask for his immortality.

"Can you change me back?" he asked nervously. "I just don't know about this."

"Probably—if I toss the book back in the pool," I answered. "But I'd rather not cut my finger again if I ever want to use it."

"But—do you really want her to do that?" Dimitri grinned. "Seems like a good compromise. You didn't want immortality, but you can look and feel like you did when you were younger."

Bethie kissed Denny's cheek and gave him a hug.

"I do feel better than I have in years. Maybe, I'll try this for a while." Denny laughed. "I never thought I'd be okay with you doing magic crap on me. Lord have mercy."

Later that day, we went to the village to bring baskets of cookies we made using my Grandma's recipe. When we arrived, everyone was surprised by Denny's appearance.

"Is this Denny?" Laurien asked, marching towards him.

"Yes, it is," I said cheerfully.

She stood still—studying his face and hands—then looked at Dimitri and then back at me again.

"Did you do this?" she asked, scolding me. "Dark magic is forbidden in this realm."

"Dark magic?" I was confused.

"How dare you speak that way to your queen!" Luke said, raising his voice.

"It's okay," I said, trying to calm him down. "She just doesn't understand."

"It's not for her to understand nor question what you do," Luke said angrily. "Apologize to her now!"

This made me extremely uncomfortable but knew it was better to not say anything else. Laurien turned toward me and quietly apologized. I nodded my head to reassure her that I wasn't the least bit angry with her.

"On your knees," Luke said firmly.

I went into Luke's head and tried to ask him to not make her do it, but I could feel him become angrier. He insisted that it was disrespectful for Laurien to speak to me in that tone and that she needed to remember her place.

"Alice is your queen. You must apologize on your knees!" he shouted.

Bethie began to cry and grabbed Dimitri's hand. He picked her up and she hugged him. Everyone stood around watching as Laurien knelt. I was terribly embarrassed.

"Please forgive me your majesty," she said with her voice shaking. "I'm sorry."

"Now was that so difficult?" Luke said cheerfully, as if that made everything alright again. He offered her a hand to help her stand back up. Laurien reluctantly took it, pulled herself up and then walked away from everyone without saying another word.

Chapter Eighteen

After three weeks of visiting and much to my surprise, Denny told us he wanted to spend the rest of his life on Sajet with us. I could not have been happier hearing that. We took him back to his house to tend to any final business he had and to gather his keepsakes with the most sentimental value. Being the generous person he was, he donated two million dollars, as well as any profits that would come from the sale of his mansion to help house and feed homeless people in California.

Before heading home, we went to Scotland and stayed for a few days in the house that I had bought on the beach. It was nice to be able to stare out at the beautiful sea and enjoy delicious earth meals with the people. I had planned on selling the place while we were there, but Luke insisted we keep it as a vacation home when he saw how much Bethie, and I loved it.

We returned to Sajet after being gone for nearly two weeks to a fully decorated courtyard lined with colorful ribbons and flowers.

"Surprise!" the villagers yelled.

"What's going on?" I asked.

"It's your birthday, Alice," Laurien said cheerfully.

"It is?" I asked. I hadn't paid attention to what day it was in a long time, but I was sure it wasn't October yet.

"Laurien organized all of this," Greta said, smiling. "She's been travelling with Tharius to other realms to bring new foods, drinks and gifts."

I was so touched by what she had done. I gave her a big hug. "Thank you so much for doing this."

"I'm happy to, Alice. I love you and want your special day to be perfect," Laurien said cheerfully.

"We need to unpack and then we'll be right out." Luke smiled at her. "Well done, Laurien."

We went inside, put our things away and got cleaned up. We came back out to the courtyard. Everyone sat in rows of long tables dressed in lavender linen and pink flowers. Place cards denoted where everyone should sit. It reminded me of a wedding setting and seemed a bit too extravagant for my fake birthday, but I was touched by the sentiment.

We found our seats and joined the feast. There were so many new types of foods and drinks to try, I wasn't sure where to begin. I waited a few minutes before eating, watching everyone enjoy their meals.

"I'm glad they sat us next to each other," Denny said quietly. "I want to try everything, but if I have an allergic reaction to any of this Martian food, please help me."

"I will." I giggled. "Try anything you'd like. I've got you covered."

About half-way through the meal, Denny randomly whispered in my ear. "It's not your birthday."

I cupped my hands over his ear and tried not to laugh. "I know. You never remember yours, but you always knew when mine was."

"What are you two whispering about?" Luke asked, leaning over my shoulder.

"I was just telling her that it's not her birthday," Denny said, laughing. "Her birthday is in October, a week before Halloween."

"That's right." Luke chuckled. "Let's tell Laurien."

"I don't want to embarrass her. She went through all this effort," I replied. "Please don't."

"Why do you think she thought it was today? It's not for almost two months," Denny asked.

"I don't know. I haven't celebrated my birthday in many years and never once here," I said. "Well, it was nice of her anyway. Maybe I'll let her know in a few days."

Right before we planned to get up from the table, Laurien and Greta passed out plates with a mini-layered dessert and tiny glasses of a lavender liquor served in edible cups. We thanked them, and then they sat back down at the table.

"I can't possibly eat another bite. I'm so full," Denny said. "Do any of you want mine?"

"No thanks. If I'd known they were serving more food, I wouldn't have eaten so much," I replied.

"Luke? Dimitri?" Denny asked, lifting his plate.

"I couldn't," Luke replied.

"Sure. She put a lot of effort into it," Dimitri responded. "I don't want her to feel bad."

Denny passed Dimitri his plate.

"You're not even going to try it?" Greta asked him.

"It looks divine but I'm too full," Denny replied.

Laurien came over, took the plate of food away from Dimitri and started to walk away. "I'll just put this away for Denny. He can have it later or tomorrow."

"Sounds good," Dimitri said, looking slightly uncomfortable but thankful not to have to eat his too.

"Okay, I'll try it," Denny said, seeing what a big deal was being made about it. "I might have a little room for it."

Greta took the plate and cup from Laurien and handed them back to Denny. The sisters sat back down in their seats smiling.

Denny whispered in my ear, "Was that weird or what?"

"Very," I replied.

"This better be *really* good," he whispered.

As soon as Denny took a sip of his drink, I had a strange feeling inside and channeled my concerns to Luke. We both looked at Denny. His face and hair began to change back to his older-looking self and then he kept growing even older. Everyone around watched in disbelief. Luke and I immediately thought the word *'Mirror'* at the same time. This stopped his aging and turned him back to looking young again.

Because Laurien had accused me of using dark magic on Denny, I immediately turned to see if she had somehow done it, but she was surprised as everyone else. Electricity rushed through me as my rage built over anyone trying to harm Denny. The table shook. With no real effort, it took me seconds to get into the minds of everyone there. Not one person knew anything about it.

"Who did this?!" Luke shouted, scanning the people to see if anyone had suddenly aged.

"No one here is to blame," I said loudly as the shaking stopped. "I can see into their minds. They didn't know."

"How were you able to do that so quickly?" Luke asked, while everyone watched nervously. "You could see everyone at once?"

"I don't know how I could, but yes," I responded.

Dimitri reached over to Denny and pulled a strand of hair from his head.

"Ouch," Denny said. "Why did you do that?"

"To make you a protection spell," Dimitri answered. "Do I have your permission?"

Before he could say yes, everyone began pulling a strand from their heads and their children's.

"Guess, I'm going to be busy for a while," Dimitri replied.

"Thank you, Dimitri," I said.

"If they're all immortals, why do they need a protection spell?" Denny asked curiously.

"We can't die, but there are many other ways to harm us," Liam replied while holding his youngest.

"Have you done this before?" Denny asked.

"Many times," he replied. "They've yet to fail."

With Luke's assistance, Dimitri completed the protection spells for everyone who requested them within three weeks.

"We can't thank you enough," Liam said, giving the men a big hug.

"Let's all go for a swim," Greta said cheerfully. "We can have a picnic by Teal Lake. We'll make sandwiches and you all can bring drinks."

"Sounds fun. I'll bring cookies," Laurien said smiling.

We all met back at the lake at noon and laid out blankets near the shore. We placed the food and drinks on nearby tables, then went into the water. Denny taught everyone how to play Marco Polo.

"Alice!" a man called.

He had long brown hair, dressed in an all-beige suit and walked alongside a blond-haired woman wearing a long, pale pink dress.

"Do you recognize them?" I asked Liam as they reached the shore.

"He seems familiar," he replied.

We walked out onto the shore and dried off. Everyone followed behind.

"May I help you?" Luke asked.

The man ignored the question and asked if my name was Alice.

"Yes," I replied.

He reached out with his right hand and said, "My name's Kedron. This is my wife, Relya. We come from Geordia seeking your assistance."

"With what?" I asked curiously while shaking his hand.

"We need you to reverse a spell," he replied, crossing his arms.

"What kind of spell?" Luke asked. "The queen isn't skilled at reversals."

"Are you able to reverse spells?" I asked Dimitri. "Could you help them?"

"I can only reverse the ones I cast," he replied.

"I'm terribly sorry, but we are unable to help," I said.

"You cast it, Alice. So, you must reverse it," the man said firmly.

"I don't know what you're talking about. I haven't cast any spells."

"You mirrored a spell back and it's caused one of our people to age close to her end days," the woman said.

"Oh—you're asking me to help the person who tried to kill my friend." I said angrily. "You shouldn't be surprised to hear that my answer is no."

"But you must!" the man yelled.

"No, I must not," I snapped back at him. "The spell was sent back just the way it was given. I did no more than what was trying to be done to him."

At that point, everyone in our group stood near me, hanging on every word.

The man stepped forward and said angrily, "You can either come with me and try to fix this or I will kill your people."

"You can't kill us." Luke laughed at him. "We're immortal, you idiot."

"What if I told you our people have secured a weapon that can take down any living being—including immortals—cell by cell?" the man asked sinisterly. "True, you will never die, but we can make it so that your atoms are scattered across many universes. It would take more than a million years to piece you back together. That's as close to death as you can get or perhaps worse. Don't you think?"

Denny took a step back. I went into his mind to assure him that Dimitri's protection spells work, and they wouldn't be able to harm any of us.

"Are you threatening us?" Luke took a step towards him.

"We're not leaving unless Alice comes with us," he insisted. "Come peacefully. I don't want to have to hurt anyone."

"Neither do I," I said, feeling the electricity building inside. "You need to leave now."

"No!" he shouted. "Help us!"

"I won't be able to hold this back much longer. You need to go," I said looking at him dead in the eye.

"Then you leave me no choice," he said angrily. "I will take your people down one by one until you agree to come with us!"

"Trust our words," Dimitri said as he watched the man's nose begin to bleed. "You cannot harm any of us, but you are not immortal. The queen is giving you a chance to live."

The man wiped the blood from his nose as the ground began to shake.

"Leave before it's too late!" I was afraid of what I might do to him.

"Do it," the man said, turning to his wife.

She opened her hands and showed us a small, black octagon-shaped box. She undid the latch and lifted the lid. Inside were what appeared to be a thousand micro-bots moving around.

"Are you sure we should do this?" she asked him fearfully. "Isn't there another way?"

"No, there isn't. She won't come otherwise!" the man screamed at her. "Just do it!"

"Adgressus," she said nervously as she slowly tipped the container towards the ground.

The tiny silver-legged things began crawling towards Luke's bare feet. Without any hesitation or worry, Luke and I both channeled 'Mirror'. The bot-looking things stopped as they reached the tip of Luke's toes and then turned back around.

Luke cocked his head sideways, squinted his eyes at them and watched curiously as the tiny things headed back their way.

The woman immediately took a few steps backwards and tripped over her own feet. Before she could get up, the bots were crawling all over her.

"Cover the children's eyes!" I shouted to our family and friends. "Don't let them see this."

Within a few seconds, small sections of her disappeared. It was if she were slowly being erased. She did not seem to be in pain but screamed in terror, begging for help. Her husband stood frozen in shock, unable to move.

"What have you done?!" he screamed as the last of her seemed to turn into vapor and float away.

"This is on you alone," I said calmly. "I warned you, but you wouldn't listen. No one here wanted this to happen. We are a peaceful people."

He picked up the octagon box with his hands shaking, said the word 'regressus' and the bots all crawled back inside.

"I just wanted to help our mother, Alice," he said tearfully as he closed the lid. "Why couldn't you just help us?"

"*Our* mother?"

"Aidra is my mother too," he said as he created a portal.

"Wait!" I called to him as he ascended.

I screamed into the sky, "Ah!"

Luke came over and hugged me. Before I knew it, we were all in a big circle, kids and all, hugging. I had so many thoughts running through my head. I wondered why Kedron didn't call the bots back until after his wife was gone or attempted to use his healing powers to save her. Perhaps they would not have stopped until they were finished or maybe it was sheer shock. What concerned me most of all, was realizing that *I* did nothing to try to stop them.

That night, when Luke and I were alone in our room, I told him I was concerned because I felt absolutely no remorse when I watched my brother's wife disintegrate. It wasn't normal for me to have no empathy, even for villains.

"Do you think I should try to help Aidra?" I asked.

"Honestly, no," he replied. "But I also know you well enough to understand why you would consider it."

"But shouldn't I do something? She did give birth to me. I don't know what the right thing is to do."

"How will you feel if you don't try to help her?" he asked kindly. "Could you live with that?"

"It sounds like you think I should try."

"If it were up to me, she would already be dead. I would have had her killed for threatening to take Bethie from us," Luke said coldly. "She has gotten far less than she deserves."

"That's not helpful at all," I replied. "You know I don't want anyone killed."

"You asked me to be honest. That's me being candid." He sat beside me on our bed. "I would rather you never saw her again and we just let God deal with her. We will never be able to trust her. God only knows what else she has planned."

Someone knocked at the door.

"Yes?" Luke asked.

"I saw your light's still on," Denny said anxiously. "May I speak with you both, please?"

Luke and I looked at each other and agreed.

"Sure, come in," Luke replied.

Denny took a seat in one of the chairs near the bed. "I know it's late, so I'll try not to take up much of your time."

"What's up?" I hoped he hadn't changed his mind and wasn't about to ask us to take him back to Earth.

"I figured you two were trying to figure out what to do about Alice's new sibling and birth mother. Right?" he asked.

"We've been discussing it," Luke responded. "But we haven't reached a decision."

"May I put in my two cents here?" he asked.

We both nodded.

"Okay—Alice, I know that you probably feel torn right now and are leaning towards helping her and getting to know your brother," he said with tears in his eyes. "I have always loved how big your heart is. You are the most forgiving person I have ever known, but you've always been a terrible judge of character. This is one of those times where you absolutely must walk away and never look back."

"You think I shouldn't try to at least give her the years back?" I asked. "Even if I never see her again."

"No, I most certainly do not," he said. "They're poison and will only use you for your power. They could destroy everything that's good in you and replace it with something horrible."

I didn't know what to say.

"How many times in your life did I tell you that I had a bad feeling about someone, but you didn't listen to me? I've had so many years to look back at everything that I did wrong, but I also remember a lot that I tried to do right," he said, scooting his chair closer to me. "You've always had trouble seeing clearly when your heart is involved. I need you to trust what I am telling you and try to see through my eyes."

"You've been right many more times than wrong. I know that," I said, looking into his mind. "But they're my blood. Am I not obligated to do something? How can I possibly do nothing? I didn't even think about trying to help save my brother's wife. I just stood there and watched it happen, fascinated and thankful it wasn't any of us. I fear my soul is at stake. You know better than anyone how much I've always worried about that. Wouldn't God want me to do something? How can I not try?"

"Because the decisions you make now don't just involve you. They affect your daughter, your husband, your friends and an entire realm. You're a queen and have great responsibilities. I see no way for you to help them without risking endangering everyone else," he said intensely. "Craig had me convinced that you shouldn't be in my life because you were a witch, but deep down, I always knew better. I know your soul and it is beautiful. I thought I understood what evil truly was, but I didn't until I heard about your birth mother and saw what your brother tried to do. *That* is evil, and you need to stay as far away from it as possible."

"What if not helping them makes everything worse? What if they retaliate? They have a weapon that is beyond any capabilities I have ever heard of. Where could they have gotten something so advanced and deadly?" I asked. "He was willing to kill all of us because I wouldn't go back with him to help. It isn't over because his wife died, and he left. I just made him angrier."

"That's exactly my point," Denny said kindly. "They were ready to kill everyone you care about, destroy a whole realm. Think about that for a minute."

I started to cry. "I'm just so scared."

"Hey, mind if I come in?" Dimitri asked, standing in the doorway. "I couldn't help but overhear."

"Come in," Luke said.

Dimitri walked in, knelt in front of me and held my hands. "There is nothing the four of us can't handle together. No harm will come to anyone here, no matter what you decide."

"I know this is a sensitive moment," Denny said, starting to snicker. "But the four of us, all here together, totally reminds me of the Wizard of Oz."

Dimitri laughed. "I call the scarecrow."

"Well, I'm definitely the cowardly lion," Denny said, grinning.

"And I suppose I'm the tin man?" Luke asked, amused by the thought.

Everyone laughed.

Chapter Nineteen

After much consideration, I decided to write in the book to ask my ancestors to give Aidra back half of what was mirrored at her. Other than that decision, I chose to cut off all ties with my birth mother, brother and anyone else that might be somehow related. To ensure this, I also requested they forget our realm and all our people.

The concern about the tiny war item they carried caused me many sleepless nights. Although our people were protected, it would be wrong to do nothing to stop them from using it against other realms. Much to my disappointment, my ancestors did not accept my request to destroy the tiny bot-like annihilators. My words were erased immediately after they were written. I understood that the book of power would not allow wishes requesting harm to anyone, but I was sure that the rule did not apply to the bots. This made figuring out a plan to prevent total genocide extremely difficult and required a deep dive into the history of the worlds around.

To aid with my studies, Luke's parents came to Sajet for two weeks. His mother spent most of her time enjoying Bethie's company while visiting with Luke, Liam and his family. Luke's father agreed to be my teacher on the condition that Luke and I would give Bethie a sibling once we resolved the inter-realm issue. We were more than happy to agree to it, as our concerns for other people's safety were the reason for our hesitation.

The first lessons were all about the connection between Sajet and Earth. He explained that a portal between the two was discovered approximately 40,000 years ago during an unusually volatile electric storm. Many of the Sajet people were excited to explore this new world, while others were apprehensive and waited to hear back from their people when they returned. After being there for a few days, most wanted to leave after witnessing human brutality and mortality first-hand. Some stayed behind for a while out of curiosity and to study the inhabitants. When they returned to where the portal dropped them, it opened, sucked them out and brought them home. It took another few thousand years before the Sajet people created a device enabling them to travel freely and to precise locations in any realm.

After Earth, it was only a matter of time before they discovered their neighboring inhabitable realms: Geordia, Adersta and Torleva. Geordians were Sajet's first inter-celestial friends. Both had much longer lifespans than humans with Geordians being millenniums and Sajet's having no record of death or illness, denoting the term immortal. While the people of Sajet never knew sickness or physical pain, Geordians were best known for their healing of any living thing.

A little further out was the Adersta realm. Although their people had no enemies and had never known battle, it was known as the Land of the Warriors. Each person, regardless of gender, was taught self-defense and combat skills as soon as they could walk. These people lived to be a couple hundred years old. Because they had a shorter lifespan than most other realms, they believed they were more vulnerable and needed to always be ready to protect themselves.

The most magnificent—yet smallest in size—of the neighboring realms was called Torleva, also known as "World of the Kings." The land was full of towering mountains with majestic waterfalls that seemed to fall from the heavens. It was completely uninhabited by people or animals but contained beautiful fruit trees and vegetable gardens that went on for miles. It was discovered after the portal device malfunctioned when the buttons labeled Earth and Sajet were accidentally pressed at the same time. Upon arrival, the king of Sajet, named Arsgrat, who had been ruling for 10,000 years, decided to leave the throne to his eldest daughter, Kamathria. He and his wife, Katharina returned a year later with their most precious keepsakes. Ever since, kings and queens from all realms, including Luke's parents, have been welcomed to call it their home.

Last of all, he told me about a realm called Danteba. It was discovered by the Sajet people only ten thousand years ago and has been kept a secret to protect the neighboring mortals from attempting to colonize there. The high concentration of sulfur and low oxygen levels made it so that no living thing could survive. It was known as the Land of the Damned.

After I completed my lessons, but before Luke's parents returned to their home in Torleva, they offered their counsel on the 'scatter bots', as Luke's father called them. He advised us to visit Geordia to investigate their origin. As they had no memory of any of us or the Sajet people, but Luke and I had the power to enter people's minds, we could get answers without drawing any attention to ourselves. We agreed but I wasn't looking forward to seeing Aidra or Kedron again. I would need to make it a point to show no reaction if we ran into them.

The following Monday, Luke and I set out on our journey. We planned to make the trip as swiftly as possible. Dimitri and Denny offered to take care of Bethie in the palace until we returned. As an extra precaution, Luke assigned eight guards to the perimeter.

We arrived at Geordia at ten in the morning. To blend in with their style of dress, we wore tan and gray clothing with no accessories. I was surprised to see that most of their realm consisted of green fields that seemed to go on for miles. It was beautiful and reminded me of Scotland.

The market was busy as people buzzed about their daily lives. No one seemed to notice us, so we kept walking and listening to their thoughts.

"There's got to be a faster way of doing this," I said.

A girl who appeared to be about eleven years old passed by. Luke immediately went into her head and told her to write in the dirt how to get to Kedron's home.

She asked an older man who passed by, "Do you know where Kedron's home is?"

"It's over the bridge at the end of the road. It has a white roof, green paint and a large sundial on the front," he answered. "You can't miss it."

The girl found a stick, bent down and began to write. Luke and I headed towards the bridge.

"How are we going to get him to tell us anything?" I asked. "Are we going to go up to the door?"

"No, we're just going to get close enough to get into his head."

As we approached the house, Kedron came out the front door and walked straight towards us.

"What do we do?" I asked nervously. "I don't want him to see my face."

"He's forgotten you exist. What is there to worry about?" Luke asked as if I were being silly. "Just relax."

"My head," I said loudly, covering my face with my hands. "It hurts."

"What?" Luke asked confused. "What are you doing?"

"Can I help you?" Kedron asked rushing towards us. "Is she okay?"

This is a realm of healers. You can't have a headache here. What are you doing?' Luke asked me while channeling.

'I'm sorry. I wasn't thinking. He makes me nervous.'

"She just has a slight headache," Luke said, trying to cover for my mistake. "She'll be fine after she has some water."

While Luke talked to him, I went into his mind and learned that he had burned the scatter bots late the night he went home. He had stolen them from a weapon designer named Trobert from Adersta, who had yet to present them to their king. As soon as he went back inside to get me a drink, Luke whisked us home.

"That was fast," Dimitri said while helping Bethie pick up her toys.

"What did you find out?" Denny asked, carrying a glass of water.

"He burned them, but there are more on Adersta," I said.

"We can't just show up there unexpected. We'll need a plausible reason," Luke said.

"They aren't our adversaries," I said. "Why can't we approach them directly?"

"How can we do that without exposing what we know?" Luke asked, picking up Bethie and kissing her on the cheek. "They'll ask how we knew about them."

"Only the inventor knows about them now," I said. "He's the only one we would need to deal with."

"Hmm," Luke said.

"We could go there and get into his mind to make him destroy them," I said.

"Can you imagine the destruction those could cause if they were let loose? They could wipe out entire species," Dimitri said seriously. "The sooner you two can handle this, the better."

"You're right," Luke replied. "But I think it's best that I go alone. It will draw less attention since their people already know who I am."

"Isn't it safer for us to go together, in case something goes wrong?" I asked. "Magic can be unpredictable."

"I'm immortal, can control minds and am guarded by a powerful protection spell. What have I to fear?" Luke asked, then handed Bethie to me.

"I don't know, but I also don't want to find out," I replied. "I really feel like we should both go."

He came over and whispered in my ear, "Have some faith in me."

Although I still had my concerns, I didn't say another word about coming along. I knew how important it was to believe in him.

"When will you be leaving? Dimitri asked.

"Tomorrow morning," he replied excitedly.

"Is there anything else I can do to help ensure your safety?" Dimitri offered his help.

"Perhaps there is." Luke was deep in thought. "Could you conjure up something that will keep *anyone* from reading my thoughts, even a powerful sorcerer? It's highly unlikely that any of them could get into my head but it would be best if they don't know the reason behind my visit."

"Good idea," Dimitri said cheerfully. "I can do that."

"And you're sure that it will work?" I asked.

"Of course, it will," he said. "Luke, try getting into my head."

Luke concentrated as hard as he could. "I can't." He laughed. "I can only sense your feelings, nothing more."

"I'll work on it this afternoon," Dimitri said. "But it will work best if you're also blocking it on your own."

"That's good to know," Luke said. "Thank you."

"Is it a spell or something?" I asked curiously.

"Or something," he laughed.

"I don't want to know," Denny said, smiling nervously.

Right before we all headed to bed for the night, Dimitri handed Luke a green gem with a crescent shaped hole in the center. He reached into his pocket and gave him a black string to use to wear it as a necklace. Luke immediately put it on.

"Want to try it out?" Dimitri asked.

"I suppose I should." He pulled the string through and tied it around his neck. "Alice, try to read my thoughts."

I tried but nothing happened.

"Focus as hard as you can," Luke said. "Don't hold back."

I concentrated on everything I knew about him, but nothing worked at first. Tiny sparks inside me tried to break through as I remembered his code words: Bridge, Blue, Ekul. I could start to make out an image. "I'm seeing something, but it's very fuzzy."

"Keep focusing," Luke insisted. "Describe what you see."

"I see a shape of a person holding something in their arms. It's so staticky I can't make it out." The connection dropped. "And now I see nothing. It's gone."

"Wow! Good job Dimitri," Luke said, hugging him. "She could read the minds of an entire village at once but couldn't see clearly into my mind."

"What were you thinking about?" Dimitri asked curiously.

"I was remembering Alice holding Bethie right after she was born," he said, smiling. "It's one of my favorite memories."

"But isn't her magic the strongest when she's angry?" Denny asked. "What if you come across someone who fuels their power that way?"

"Are you saying he should try to provoke her?" Dimitri asked, concerned. "That might not be safe. We don't know how strong her powers are. She could hurt him."

"I don't want him to get hurt. I'm only saying you can't fully test that thing if she's calm," Denny said. "It's not that I want to see him make you angry or anything. I just don't think it's been fully assessed."

"You're right," Luke agreed. "I'm going to put Bethie to bed and then we'll try again."

After about ten minutes, he came back into the common area where we sat together waiting for him.

"Have any ideas?" Luke asked before sitting down next to me.

"What does he do that gets on your nerves the most?" Dimitri asked.

"Nothing that I haven't already discussed with him," I replied. "It's not going to be enough to make me angry."

"Luke, can you think of anything that might make her *really* angry, but not the want to kill you type of angry?" Denny asked. "Something you've done, perhaps some secret you've kept?"

"What are you trying to do, Denny? I don't want to be angry with him before he leaves," I said firmly. "What if something somehow goes wrong? It would be the last conversation we had."

"If you can't find a way to test it completely, then maybe she should go with you," Dimitri interjected. "You are much stronger together anyway."

There was a long moment of silence.

"I used a love potion on you on our wedding night," Luke blurted out. "I put it in the glass of wine I gave you right before we consummated our marriage."

"Oh shit." Denny stepped back.

"What?" I asked in disbelief. "No, you didn't. I don't believe you. You would never do that to me. You made that up. You're just trying to make me angry."

"I'm so sorry, Alice," he said, taking me by the hands. "I know I shouldn't have but I knew how much you were dreading being intimate with me."

"Oh my God, Luke!" Dimitri shouted angrily.

Denny and Dimitri stood there watching me with pity in their eyes. There was nothing more I hated than having anyone feel sorry for me.

"How could you do that to me?!" I felt my insides starting to fire up and I pushed his hands away. "I trusted you!"

Bethie started to cry from her room.

"I'll go check on her," Denny said, relieved to have an excuse to leave the room.

"All this time, I thought we had something extraordinary between us, something that made me forgive you and believe in you, no matter what lies you told and all the crap you pulled on me and everyone else. But it was all just another one of your tricks?!" The fury inside intensified. "None of this immense love or this unbelievable attraction I've felt for you is real?! I've just been under some damn spell this whole time?! How dare you!"

Everything in the room shook as if there were an earthquake.

"Ahh!!" I screamed as an electrical storm built inside me.

"You should go outside. Take a walk," Dimitri warned Luke angrily. "Give her some space."

"I'm not going outside," Luke replied, taking my hands.

"Why Luke?!" I cried in anger. "Answer me!"

It took all my energy to not crush his hands, but his nose began to bleed any way.

"Luke, run!" Dimitri shouted. He knew Luke should not be able to be harmed.

"Look into my mind," he said calmly as the blood ran over his lips.

"Dimitri, take him outside, please," I begged. "I'm hurting him, and I can't stop."

"Focus, Alice," Luke said, not letting go of my hands. "See into my soul."

My fury grew. I worried my eyes could burn a hole right through the center of his brain. I tore down every barrier blocking my mind from reading him. The necklace came undone, and the charm fell, landing on the marble floor.

"Focus," Luke repeated as the blood dripped onto his shirt.

I immediately saw Luke dressed for our wedding in his black pants, light blue dress shirt and slim black tie. He looked so handsome as he stared into the mirror with his big, sparkling blue eyes trying to fix his shiny dark hair. Next, he stepped out of the bathroom, unzipped his suitcase and held a small amber bottle full of a clear liquid. He took out a bottle of wine and uncorked it. With shaking hands, he opened the small bottle and poured it into the wine, gently shook it and then re-corked it.

After pacing back and forth and pulling at his hair, he grabbed the wine bottle and took the cork back out. He rushed back into the bathroom and flushed it all down the toilet. He looked back in the mirror, fixed his hair again and went back into the room. Before he walked out the door to head to our wedding, he took out another bottle of wine and sat it along with two glasses on the small table. I immediately calmed down.

After I finished channeling him, I said with happy tears in my eyes, "You didn't do it."

"I couldn't do it." He smiled. "I was afraid, but I needed our marriage to be real for both of us."

I hugged him tightly.

"I take it you didn't really give her a love potion?" Dimitri asked, sighing with relief.

"No. I didn't." Luke grabbed a tissue and cleaned the blood off his face. "I was going to, but I never did."

"Oh, thank God," Denny said as he walked back into the room. "By the way, you are terrifying when you're angry, Alice."

"I'm sorry that I scared you guys and for the nosebleed, Luke. I was fighting the energy inside, but some slipped through anyway," I said feeling both embarrassed and worried. "I really need to work on controlling it. I'm going to need a lot of help with that."

"I guess Aidra was right in warning me to never cross you," Luke said.

"I'm so sorry, Luke."

He kissed me on the cheek.

"I drove you to it. I'm sorry for putting you through that," Luke said lovingly.

"But that means the charm didn't completely work," Dimitri said. "Someone may still be able to read your thoughts."

"I'll take my chances," Luke said. "The odds of there being someone as powerful as her are slim to none."

"Still, be careful. Try not to provoke anyone while you're there," Dimitri said. "No magic is foolproof."

Chapter Twenty

A week passed since Luke had left for his trip to Adersta. Because of the charm Dimitri had made for him, I was unable to channel him to find out how things were going or make sure he was safe. I decided to give him one more day before trying to use my power to open a portal to go find him.

In the short time he was away, Bethie began putting full sentences together. I was excited for him to see how extensive her vocabulary had become and how well she was able to understand multistep instructions. I was amazed by how advanced she was at such a young age.

Early the next morning, just before 2:00 am, Luke stumbled into our bedroom carrying a strange smell on him that I couldn't put my finger on. It resembled a combination of garlic, asparagus, onion and fish all at once.

"What is that smell?" I asked, plugging my nose.

He walked towards me getting undressed. "I missed you."

"No, no, no," I said. "You need to take a shower first. No offense but you stink. What have you been doing?"

He bent his head down, sniffing himself. "I don't smell anything." He shrugged his shoulders.

"How can you possibly not smell that?" I asked. "Please go take a shower."

"Fine." He let the rest of his stinky clothes drop on the floor.

"Please don't leave those there." I tried not to gag.

He bent down, picked them up and left to get cleaned up.

Ten minutes later, he came back into the bedroom smelling fresh.

"How did it go?" I asked. "Were you able to take care of it?"

"Yes and no one will remember they even existed or know how to create new ones," Luke said, sitting on the edge of my side of the bed.

"You were gone a while. I was beginning to get worried about you."

"Do you want me to tell you everything?" he asked. "Or should I just show you?"

"Not really, unless you want to," I replied. "I'd rather we never talk or even think about those dreadful things again."

"Good." He smiled and then climbed under the covers next to me.

"You're not tired after your long trip?"

"Nope." He put his arms around me—kissing my neck.

"Are we really doing this?" I asked. "I mean, trying to have another baby?"

"Yep." He kissed me deeply while running his fingers through my hair. "I love you more than you will ever know."

"You are my forever, Luke. I will always love you."

After a few minutes, he randomly asked, "Are you hoping for another girl or a boy?"

"Either would be wonderful."

"But if you could choose?" he asked, nibbling on my ear. "Which then?"

"A boy this time, but a little sister would be nice for Bethie too. What about you?"

"I want whatever you want." He smiled as he undressed me.

Several weeks later, we had a community picnic in the village to announce the pregnancy and invited Luke's parents to attend. It was a beautiful day surrounded by cheerful faces. As a gentle breeze came through, the lime-colored leaves and the enormous midnight blue flowers in the towering trees swayed in the sunlight. I realized in that moment they stayed the same all year. Even the fruit trees were always full of fresh fruit. Other than occasional storms, there were no significant weather changes nor seasons on Sajet.

"What's wrong?" Denny asked, gently elbowing me.

"It's October 20th."

"Oh, you never told Laurien when your real birthday is," he whispered. "It's in a few days. Do you want to do something this year?"

"No. I was just thinking about how spectacular the trees would be on earth right now," I said quietly. "I used to paint pictures of the trees every fall. I loved all the colors. The red, orange, yellow and even the brown leaves. It was my favorite season."

"You miss it," Denny said. "It's really pretty here too though. Everything always looks new and clean. It's like a world Walt Disney would have created."

"It's absolutely lovely here, but I miss watching the seasons change. Normally, right now I would have my whole place decorated for Halloween. The pumpkins would be ready to carve, and I'd drink and eat everything pumpkin spice that I could find. God, pumpkin anything sounds so good right now."

Luke and Dimitri walked back from the palace laughing about something. I forced a smile as they came and sat down with us.

"Are you alright?" Luke asked, putting his hand on my shoulder.

"Yeah, I'm fine. I just need to use the ladies' room," I said as I stood up. "I'll be back in a few minutes."

When I returned, Luke, Denny and Dimitri were huddled together at the table.

"What's up?" I asked curiously.

"Trying to decide on baby names," Dimitri said attempting not to laugh. "What do you think of Vladimir if it's a boy and Vladirie if it's a girl?"

I started busting up laughing. "We are not giving this child a vampire name."

Bethie got up from her seat, sat on my lap and placed her tiny hands on my stomach.

"Are you excited to have a little brother or sister?" Dimitri asked her cheerfully.

"My baby brother's name is Marcus," she said confidently.

"Marcus?" I asked. "Where did you hear a name like that?"

"I dreamed it. His name is Marcus," she said kissing my cheek.

"What if the baby is a girl?" Denny asked.

"It's not. The baby is a boy," she replied.

"Bethie, it's too soon to know what we're having," I said kindly.

"What else have you dreamed about?" Dimitri asked inquisitively. "Anything else that came true?"

"Uh, uh," she said, shaking her head. "My baby brother will be Marcus and my new baby cousin will be Arlan. Grandpa Antony told me in my dream. He can see stuff."

"What?" I asked surprised. We had never mentioned him to her.

"I want to play with Arbie and Arden," Bethie said as she climbed down from my lap.

"Well, that was weird," I said.

Denny nodded. "She sure has some imagination."

"Liam!" Luke called.

He came over and hugged Luke. "Congratulations, brother," he said.

"Is there anything *you* wanted to tell us?" Luke asked. "Any news?"

"Yes, but not today. Today is your day," he said quietly. "I will gladly tell you tomorrow. Okay?"

"You and Greta are expecting another child." Luke smiled.

Liam's face lit up. "Yes, but we didn't want to take away from your special announcement. How did you know? Did you go into our minds? She isn't even showing yet."

Luke, Denny, Dimitri and I all laughed.

"Congratulations to you too brother," Luke said cheerfully.

"We even have the name picked out already," Liam said excitedly. "Arla if it's a girl and—"

"Arlan if it's a boy?" Luke asked.

"Wow, Great guess," Liam said laughing. "Or should I say, nice mind reading?"

"Did you talk about that at all around Bethie?" I asked curiously.

"No, we haven't told a soul, not even our older children," he replied.

"Bethie! Come here for just a moment please," Luke called for her.

She rushed over. "What is it Daddy?"

"Tell Uncle Liam what you just told us about the babies," Luke said holding her hand.

"Okay," she said smiling. "My baby brother's name is Marcus and my new cousin's name is Arlan."

"Thanks, Bethie. You can go back and play now." Luke kissed her cheek.

"Whoa," Liam said. "That'll be weird if we both have boys. Were you planning on naming yours Marcus if it's a boy?"

"We hadn't discussed names yet," Luke answered. "But I do like it, actually."

"Me too," Denny and Dimitri said at the same time.

"What do you think Alice?" Luke asked.

"It's Denny's middle name," I replied. "What's not to like?"

"Mine too," Dimitri smiled.

"Well then we must name him Marcus," Luke said cheerfully.

"Now watch, we'll both have girls." Liam laughed.

After dinner of the following week, Luke, Bethie, Denny and Dimitri waited for me in the common area dressed in cool weather clothing.

"What's going on?" I asked. "It's like seventy-five degrees outside."

"Put on some pants, grab a light jacket and meet us out front," Luke said cheerfully.

"Okay." I went back to our room to change. Part of me wanted to read their minds but I could tell they wanted it to be a surprise.

When I came outside, Bethie jumped up and down hanging onto Denny and Dimitri's hands.

"Take my hand," Luke said eagerly.

I took his hand and we all hung onto each other. Before I knew it, we were being sucked up into the sky. Bethie giggled hysterically as we landed.

"We're here," Luke said.

"Burr, it's chilly." I zipped up Bethie's jacket and then mine.

We were in an empty alley, facing the back of some older-looking brick buildings.

"Where are we?" I asked.

Everyone smiled.

"This way." Luke took Bethie's and my hands.

We walked to the end of the alley and my eyes widened. Colorful autumn trees and Halloween decorations adorned the streets with petrichor in the air. There were people dressed in costumes and holiday treats being passed out by a group of women dressed as witches. I don't know if Bethie or I was more excited to be there.

She immediately pulled us towards the goodies. As soon as we got close to the ladies, one of them handed her a candy corn light-up necklace and another gave her a black witch hat to wear.

"Thank you," she squealed with delight. "I'm a witch!"

"Of course, you are," the gray-haired woman said. "This is Salem."

"Salem?" I asked, looking at Luke. "As in Salem, Massachusetts?"

"What better place to come celebrate Halloween?" He smiled.

I gave him the biggest hug. "Thank you! I've always wanted to come here."

Bethie reached towards a red candied apple.

"Those are too hard for your teeth," I said. "How about a cookie instead?"

"Can I get a cat?" she asked, looking at a tray of cookies.

One of the ladies handed her a cookie and quietly said, "Want to do a trick?"

"Yes," she said cheerfully.

Luke and I wondered what she might do.

The lady picked up a small jack-o'-lantern and held it in her hands. "Now say, ignis," she told Bethie.

"Ignis!" Bethie shouted.

The flame on the candle inside lit. She clapped.

"That was awesome!" Denny cheered.

Bethie laughed.

"That's a pretty good trick," Dimitri said. "You have a good night."

"You too," the woman said happily.

"Want to see something even better?" Dimitri asked Bethie as soon as we were far enough away, where the woman couldn't hear.

"Yes."

"Look back at the flame in the jack-o'-lantern," he replied.

We all turned back—the flame change to purple. The woman was stunned and nearly dropped it. She looked back at Dimitri and bowed to him. He smiled and bowed back to her.

"I didn't know you could do stuff like that," I told him. "I thought you mostly did hexes, charms and potions."

"True, but in places like Salem, West Africa and London, magic is much greater and I'm able to draw more power," he replied. "They're like extreme wi-fi hotspots for supernatural beings. You should be able to do even more if you concentrate. Cabots have incredibly strong blood magic."

"I wouldn't even begin to know how to," I replied.

"Just focus and think of something," Dimitri said.

"Like what?" I asked.

"If you could dress up as anything right now, what would it be?" he asked.

"Well, that's easy," Denny said. "She always goes as a pirate, ever since she was a kid. Even when we were supposed to go to a friend's party as Peter Pan and Wendy, she showed up as Captain Hook."

Luke laughed. "Got some sort of pirate fetish, huh?"

I gently elbowed him. "Maybe."

"All right then." Dimitri stepped close to me. "Close your eyes and picture what you want to wear. Once you've got a clear image in your head, feel the energy around you and tell it what to do."

I tried but nothing happened.

"Too bad," I said. "That would have been cool if it actually worked."

"Let's try this. Everyone, hold hands," Dimitri said.

We all held each other's hands.

"What now?" I asked curiously.

"On three, everyone shut your eyes and try to feel the energy around you," Dimitri said. "Draw from it, command it."

"Won't me doing this with you all interfere?" Denny said. "I'm not a supernatural being or magical like the rest of you."

"Luke's magic was entirely learned but he is quite powerful. If you focus too, it will help draw more energy," he replied.

Denny closed his eyes and nervously said, "Okay."

The rest of us closed our eyes too.

"One, two, three," Dimitri said.

I focused as hard as I could. It felt like there were tiny little gusts of cool air flowing all around my body. After a couple minutes, a bunch of people clapped loudly and cheered. It broke our concentration, and we opened our eyes.

"Where'd my witch hat go?" Bethie said as she pulled a red and white striped bandana from her head.

"Oh my gosh." I was astonished. "It really worked."

Our outfits had all changed into pirate costumes. The crowd grew and everyone was impressed by such a remarkable magic trick.

"How did they do that?" a little boy dressed like a werewolf asked his parents.

"I don't know, but that was amazing," his father said with his mouth wide open.

"Can you do another trick?" a teenage girl asked with her cell phone out.

"Sure," Dimitri said cheerfully. "Let me think a minute."

"Are you sure we should be doing this?" I asked him. "Is it safe to show our powers?"

"It's not the 1600s, Alice," Dimitri replied. "No one's going to hang us for it. They'll just think we're really good magicians."

"What are you going to do?" Luke asked curiously. "This type of magic is beyond my abilities."

"But you and Alice can get into everyone's heads and make them follow us," Dimitri said quietly. "Come with me!"

Everyone followed him as he walked down the street towards an enormous jack-o'-lantern display. There must have been a few thousand of the spooky faces glowing in the night.

As soon as he had the large crowd's attention, he took a deep breath and stared at the display. The flames all went out at once along with all the streetlights. The only light came from the bright moon above and the cell phones people were using to record.

"Boo!" someone shouted.

Dimitri laughed and then raised his hands. A bunch of the jack-o'-lanterns lit back up spelling Happy Halloween. The crowd clapped and stood at attention.

"Did you really just do that?" Denny asked in amazement.

"Just watch," Dimitri said proudly.

Next, they all went dark again, but this time, no one booed at him. One by one they all lit back up and the streetlights came back on.

The crowd clapped and cheered, but through it, I could hear the thoughts of some who expected more when he lit them all up again. They were almost mocking him saying that was an easy trick anyone could do. It made me angry to hear them and I could feel the electricity building inside me. Luke took my hand as soon as he felt my energy changing. I let him see what they were saying about Dimitri. I turned back, looked at the jack-o'-lanterns and put out all the flames.

The crowd immediately looked over at Dimitri.

"Are you doing this, Alice?" he whispered.

I could hear the voices again saying that he was going to do another lame trick, and the electricity inside grew. Then Luke was in my head telling me to control it before it got out of hand. I winked at Luke and then looked back at the display and made all the flames turn back on in black, orange, green and purple.

Dimitri laughed and then asked me, "What's your favorite Halloween song?"

"Monster Mash," I giggled.

Dimitri grabbed my other hand. The beginning of the song started playing loudly. As the beat picked up, the flames danced along with the music. The people cheered.

"This is amazing," Denny said while holding Bethie up so she could see better.

I noticed her witch hat was back on her head.

"Did you do that?" I asked Dimitri.

"No." He laughed.

"Bethie, what happened to your pirate bandana?" Luke asked.

"I changed it back." She smiled.

Luke and I laughed.

After the song ended, we turned the flames back to the way they were and then left to go on the hayride. When we got to the back of the line, everyone insisted that we cut in front of them.

"Luke, we could have just waited our turn," I said.

He smiled. "I didn't do anything."

During the hayride, a young woman with her two children sat across from us. I felt her worries about having enough money to get them costumes for Halloween. She was barely scraping by and was only able to bring them to the festival because the city sponsored it. It made my heart heavy.

"I like your costumes," the little boy said. "I want to be a pirate too, but I'll probably be a zombie again."

"And what do you want to be?" Denny asked the little girl.

"I'm going to be a princess," she said. "I'm going to make my crown out of aluminum foil and draw on gems with markers."

"That sounds perfect," Denny said cheerfully.

"That was quite a show you put on back there," their mother said. "Almost had me believing in magic too."

"Magic is real," Bethie said, sounding very matter of fact.

"She's adorable," the mother said. "How old is she? Two, three?"

"She's almost a year and a half," I replied.

"Wow," she said. "She's so bright. I never would have guessed."

"It's cause I'm an alien witch," she said.

"I thought you were a pirate witch," the woman said, looking at her costume.

I wanted to tell Bethie to not say any more about who she was, but then I realized that they wouldn't believe the ramblings of a toddler.

"It's just a costume," Bethie said. "But maybe we have ghost pirates in our family too."

The woman laughed. "I love her imagination."

"Why aren't you wearing a pirate hat?" the boy asked.

"Because I'm an alien witch," she said smiling.

"Then why aren't you wearing a witch or alien costume?" the boy asked curiously.

"Because my mum wanted us to all be pirates," Bethie said.

"Uh, okay—" The boy was confused.

I realized at that moment that I had selfishly wanted everyone to be a pirate. As soon as the other people had their backs turned, I changed Luke's outfit into an elaborate, Hollywood style vampire costume.

"Hey!" the boy noticed. "How'd you do that?"

Luke looked down at his clothes and laughed.

"That's more like it." Dimitri smiled at Luke.

By the time we reached the end of the hayride, a well-dressed man approached the tractor. We all stepped down and he handed a gift card to the mother.

"What's this?" she asked.

"Your family won our drawing, Ms. Chrissy," he said.

"I don't remember entering," she replied.

"Your name's Sarah Chrissy, right?" he asked.

"Yes," she replied curiously.

"Well, someone entered you and the grand prize is yours," he said. "I would take the prize. It's a $500 prepaid Visa gift card."

The woman's face lit right up, and her kids did too. We all smiled.

"Congratulations," I said.

"Thank you," she replied excitedly. "Have a great night."

We watched them as they walked away. After they were clear from the crowd, the boy's clothing turned into a high-quality swashbuckler costume and the girl's turned into a beautiful sparkly pink dress with a silver tiara with pink gems.

"Did you do that?" Dimitri and I asked each other at the same time.

We both shook our heads and then looked at Bethie who was nodding off to sleep in Denny's arms.

"Guess it's time to go home," Luke said, laughing.

"We should make coming here our Halloween time tradition," I said. "And stay for the whole week next time."

"That has nothing to do with the ridiculous level of magic here, does it?" Dimitri asked smiling.

"Maybe," I said. "This was so much fun.

Chapter Twenty-One

After we returned to Sajet, the strength of our magic went back to normal. Dimitri suggested there may be other hotspots on earth but hadn't heard of more than the three he mentioned. I thought it was odd that we could only do those things while we were there. It seemed like there must be another way to draw from the elements without being so close. I wondered if there was a hot spot on Sajet or any of the other neighboring realms.

Many months passed and it was the night of our second child's birth. There was a terrible storm, unlike any we had ever seen. Denny and Dimitri stayed up with Bethie playing games and listening to the thunder, while Luke helped me through the delivery. Around midnight the weather calmed and our son, Marcus was born. Two hours later came Liam and Greta's son Arlan—as Bethie and my father had predicted.

"He looks like a mini you." Dimitri smiled at Luke. "No fangs. That's two for two."

Luke laughed as he held him in his arms.

"He's perfect." I smiled.

"Would you like to hold him?" Luke asked.

I scooted up in the bed and reached for him. "Yes."

I was delighted and extremely thankful to be blessed with two beautiful children. I always wanted a big family but at that moment, it seemed like the perfect size. I wondered if we would want to have more in a couple years or maybe long after they grew up.

After Marcus' birth, time flew by. Before I knew it, many years had passed, and Denny began to tire more quickly. His age and family history of health conditions caught up with him. I spent more time healing, but no matter how much I tried, his heart grew weaker. I hoped that because he had become accustomed to magic by then, he might consider becoming an immortal, but his mind was unchangeable. He would spend the rest of his days with us but looked forward to seeing his family and Craig again.

We all sensed his time with us was coming to an end, so we offered to help him do as many bucket list items as time would allow. It turned out the thing he wanted the most, was to take the trip to Fiji we had planned when we were young. He said he never went with Craig because it was supposed to be our trip. Luke told us it was fine if Denny and I went by ourselves, but Denny wanted our whole family there together. This touched Luke's heart as he had grown to love him over the years.

The two weeks leading up to our trip, we spent teaching Bethie and Marcus how to become stronger swimmers. Although they were immortals with strong protection spells placed on them, we thought it would make the trip more fun if they improved their skills.

I spent every free moment I had with Denny trying to keep him as comfortable as possible. We soaked up each new memory. I did my best to not think about the inevitable.

"I almost want to stay here," he told me the day before the trip. "You know, you really make it hard to let go. If I didn't miss Craig and my family so much, I would probably stay with you forever."

I teared up. "I understand how much you love them, but I also can't imagine my world without you in it."

"Even though you won't be able to see me, I will always be watching over you, in any way I can," he said with teary eyes. "Well, maybe not *all* the time."

We laughed.

"Thank you for never giving up on me, Alice," he said as he held my hand.

"Never," I replied. "I have always loved you, Denny."

"I love you more." He smiled.

The next morning, the six of us got up early and Luke whisked us off for our trip. He surprised us with three overwater bungalow suites. Dimitri and Denny each had their own, while Luke, the kids and I shared a two-bedroom family suite between theirs. We felt how happy Denny was being there. As soon as he put his things away, he sat in a chair on his front deck staring out at the beautiful turquoise water. It was nice to see him smiling so brightly.

"This is paradise," Denny said loudly. "Thank you, guys."

The concierge walked up to see if we needed anything.

"Are we allowed to move one of their chairs to our deck, that way we can all sit together? Is that okay?" I asked.

"No need to move them," he said cheerfully. "I'll send down a couple chairs."

"Thank you so much," I said.

"If there's anything at all you need, please dial *999," he said, squinting his eyes.

"Are you okay?" I asked.

"I'm fine. Thank you," he replied. "I left my sunglasses at home and I've gotten a bit of a headache."

"Oh, I'm sorry," I said. "Can you wait here for just a minute while I run inside?"

"No problem," he said, rubbing his temples.

I took my unisex designer sunglasses from my suitcase and handed them to him.

"Thank you, but no," he said. "We're not allowed to accept gifts from our guests."

"What if you bought them?" I asked.

"I can't afford them, but thank you," he replied, stepping away.

I looked in his mind trying to find another option.

"I'll trade them for a seashell," I said cheerfully.

"You're not giving up, are you?" he asked, smiling.

"You're doing me a favor, giving me an excuse to buy a new pair on vacation," I continued, smiling. "I adore seashells. Can you bring me a shell?"

He laughed as he reached into his pocket and took one out.

"That's perfect." I handed him the sunglasses. "Thank you."

While he was putting them on, I took away his headache.

"Thank you so much," he said cheerfully. "I feel better already."

"I'm glad to hear it."

He walked away smiling, then I took the shell inside and put it in my bag.

Less than twenty minutes later, another man returned carrying two chairs.

"Thank you." Luke handed him a few dollars.

He smiled and then headed back down the long dock.

Luke arranged the six chairs in a slight u-shape facing the crystal-clear water. As soon as Denny noticed, he came over and sat down with us. We ordered tropical drinks for the adults and pineapple coconut smoothies for the kids, along with an array of snacks.

Once Bethie and Marcus were done with their drinks, they went inside and got changed into their swimsuits.

"Aren't they supposed to wait an hour or something before they swim?" Denny asked before remembering they don't get cramps. "Never mind."

When we had planned the trip with Samantha and Darren many years before, there were so many things we wanted to do like surfing, snorkeling and jet skiing. With Denny's heart the way it was, we couldn't risk it. However, he told us that he felt strong enough to go for a light swim. The water was about 68 degrees and just cool enough to feel refreshing.

"Let's try to talk underwater and see if we can understand each other," Denny said. "I'll go first."

Everyone agreed and we all went under. He said something I couldn't make out, but I easily read his thoughts underwater without trying.

As soon as we all came to the surface, Luke blurted out exactly what he said, "She sells seashells down by the seashore."

"Is that right?" Dimitri laughed. "It looked like you said something about cheeses or Jesus."

"Luke's right." Denny smiled.

"Wait a minute," Dimitri said as he turned to Luke. "Did you read his thoughts?"

Luke started laughing.

"That's cheating," Dimitri said.

"I didn't try to cheat, I just heard it before he even started talking," Luke chuckled.

"Me too," I said. "Being underwater made it effortless. I didn't even try."

"You two have an unfair advantage," Dimitri said. "I'll go next since I have a decent block. But if you can somehow read my thoughts, come back up right away. Promise?"

We agreed and then we all went back under.

After a few seconds, I went back to the surface. The rest followed shortly after.

"You could read my thoughts?" Dimitri sounded disappointed.

"Yeah," I replied. "The moment we went under. There's a lot of energy in the water."

"I couldn't," Luke seemed surprised.

"What was he thinking?" Denny asked me.

"He was deciding between saying Jaws or Orca," I said while rolling my eyes.

We all started laughing.

"Turtle!" Marcus said loudly.

A large green turtle swam past. Marcus dove under the water and swam alongside it for about ten minutes before swimming back towards us.

"Whew." Denny slowly dog paddled back towards the deck next to our bungalows.

The rest of us took the cue and followed him.

"You guys go on," he said. "I just need to sit and rest for a bit."

Bethie climbed onto the deck and dried off with her sparkly purple beach towel. "I'm hungry."

"Go ahead and grab the menu from the desk inside," Luke said. "We'll have them bring it out here to us."

"If you all want to eat at the restaurant, that's okay," Denny said. "Please don't let me hold you back."

"This is a family trip, Denny," Luke told him. "We are all eating together. Besides, they'll bring anything on the menu out to us."

The rest of the week, I stayed by Denny's side all day but swam with everyone else when he was taking a nap. We would watch them play while reminiscing. Sitting there by his side made me think of how I pictured us growing old together. Our dream of living next door to each other, hanging out on our front porches, sort of came true, but the view was much better. In that spectacular moment of gratitude, I thanked God for putting him in my life. I looked over at my sweet Denny and saw that he had fallen asleep again.

A few minutes later, Dimitri swam over towards us. He climbed up onto the dock and dried himself off. His eyes were full of tears.

I stood up. "What's wrong?"

Luke and our kids swam back too.

"He's gone," Dimitri said sadly.

"What?" I asked. "Who?"

"Denny's gone, Alice," he said, putting his hand on my shoulder.

I rushed over to Denny and started shaking him—trying to wake him. Luke quickly pulled himself out of the water and dried off.

"No." I shook my head in disbelief.

His chest didn't move. I tried to find a pulse but there was nothing. It felt as though all the goodness in the world had been sucked away. I dropped onto my knees and wept. Every breath was labored, and I felt like my chest was being crushed.

"Help her." Dimitri told Luke.

Luke wrapped his arms around me, and he tried to get into my head, but I could not let him. In that excruciating suffering, I had the most terrible thought: I wished the scatter bots would come take me apart, so I would never have to feel the pain.

"I can't get through to her," Luke told him in a panic. "She's much stronger than I am."

I worked so hard to focus on my family to pull me out of the darkness, but all I could see was Denny's face and imagine hearing his voice. I desperately tried to memorize it—wanting to never forget any detail of my precious friend. I thought about how it could be millions of years before I ever got to go to heaven—if I somehow didn't have a soul—I might never see him again. I wanted to die.

Luke and Dimitri kept talking and my kids were crying but it became like muffled sounds coming from far away. Everything went out of focus and all I could hear was my heart pounding violently in my chest.

I was soaking wet. I opened my eyes. Dimitri held me underwater. I could feel the darkness clearing and saw everything in his mind, as if through his eyes. Under the water, right in front of us was Denny. He looked young and healthy again and was standing with Craig, his brother, his parents and grandparents. They were all happy to be with him again. Denny smiled and told me that many years from now, we would all be together again. Until then, to love deeply, treasure every moment and to keep doing good whenever possible.

I heard a loud splash. Luke, Bethie and Marcus were under the water. They could all see what Dimitri saw too. The kids swam up to see Denny. They were grief stricken but immediately told him that they loved him. Luke quickly went into their minds and took away their suffering.

"I love you forever, Denny," I said with a broken heart.

"I will always love you more," he said as they all faded away.

When we came back to the surface, I looked over at where Denny's body was and asked Luke to take us all home. We quickly and quietly gathered our things, then Luke whisked us away.

The news of Denny's death brought a great deal of sorrow to our people. To honor his last wishes, we chose to take away their sadness but leave everyone with the good memories of a kind, generous and witty gentleman.

That night, when Luke and I went to bed, I asked him to take all my pain away. Losing him was a burden too heavy for me to bear and was something Denny and I had spoken about during his final days. He knew it would sit with me, festering over time, keeping me from being the wife, mother and ruler I needed to be.

"Are you sure you want all of it gone?" Luke asked.

"Please," I begged him in tears. "Leave me only with good feelings about him. I will always miss him, but I can't live like this. I feel as though I'm constantly falling."

"All right," he said. "Lay down and close your eyes."

I did as he asked and as soon as my head hit the pillow, the pain erupted again. I cried uncontrollably. Luke stroked my head as he slowly began to channel me. He could feel every ounce of my suffering, as well as his own loss of a dear friend. While he was focusing on me, I did my best to take his pain away from him. When we were finished, there were still remnants of sorrow that lingered, but it became much more bearable.

Luke had showed me how to enter the ocean that surrounded Sajet by jumping off from the most southern part of the realm. The color of the water appeared to be blue but upon entering, I could see it had lavender undertones. During the months that followed his death, I spent a lot of time underwater trying to feel and understand the energy it provided. We went there nearly every night after the kids went to sleep for a couple hours. It was as if my soul was getting a much-needed recharge. Even on Earth, I knew the ocean gave off so much more than oxygen to people with or without magical blood. There was an indescribable healing energy that could be felt simply by breathing in the sea air.

After Laurien felt that enough time had passed for everyone to mourn, she announced her secret engagement to Luke's highest ranked guard, Tharius. Although it was completely unexpected, this news brought much needed joy to everyone in the realm.

"We would love to be married as soon as possible," she said eagerly.

"How soon?" Luke asked cheerfully.

"Tomorrow?"

"That doesn't allow much time to plan," I said. "If you wait a week, we can give you a much nicer wedding."

"Thank you, Alice, but we want it to be simple," she replied, taking Tharius' hand. "Nothing grand."

"Tomorrow it is," Luke replied. "What time and where shall we meet?"

Laurien and Tharius whispered to each other giggling.

"Noon, and right here in the courtyard," Tharius replied.

I nervously awaited Dimitri's reaction, but he seemed nothing less than pleased for them.

The next day, Luke officiated the simple ceremony and afterwards everyone shared homecooked meals and desserts in the grand dining hall. As I watched Dimitri tossing a dinner roll to Marcus as if it were a baseball, I couldn't help but wonder if he wished for anything more in his deep, well-guarded thoughts. Being an immortal, time makes nothing feel too terribly pressing. Yet, I thought about his future happiness as I watched Laurien dance with her husband.

Chapter Twenty-Two

The day that would have been Denny's birthday came. To honor him, I asked Luke to take us to Sacramento so that we could let our children practice healing and altering emotions. We headed to a crowded park where there were at least a dozen different birthday parties and barbecues going on at once. There must have been a couple hundred people there that day.

"What's that smell?" Bethie asked curiously.

"It's meat cooking," Luke said. "Different types of animals. Like chicken, pigs and cows."

"Animals? Why do they eat that?" she asked. "It smells strange."

"People eat different types of food wherever you go," he responded. "You like to eat a lot of different plants they've never tried. If they came to visit us, they might think what we eat smells weird too."

"Don't be so judgmental," Marcus said to Bethie. "They aren't like us."

"We have ancestors from here too," she replied. "Maybe I'd like it."

"Well, maybe someday, but we're not here for that today, are we?" I asked.

"No, mum," Bethie replied.

Luke took out a large blanket and containers carrying our lunch from his bag and placed it on the grass. "Have a seat," he said, smiling. "Let's get started."

The children were quick learners and helped dozens of people throughout the day, from kids with small scrapes to a man who somehow burned his foot while barbecuing. I was so proud of them, not because of how skilled they were but by how much they genuinely enjoyed helping people. I knew that us spending his birthday that way would have made Denny smile.

"When I grow up, I want to live on Earth for a while," Bethie said. "There are so many people here to help. They're so fragile."

"Is she allowed to do that?" Marcus asked us.

"She can go wherever and be whatever she likes," Luke said hugging her. "As long as she always comes home to see us."

"Then can I go with her?" Marcus asked.

"That would be wonderful," Luke said proudly. "You can look out for each other."

Luke could feel that I did not like to think about the day when they would leave home. He scooted over, put his arm around me and kissed my cheek.

"Don't be sad, mum," Bethie said. "We wouldn't stay away too long."

"And you could come see us anytime," Marcus said kindly. "You can help heal people with us."

"I would love that," I said teary eyed.

We all hugged and then packed up to go home.

We arrived back at Sajet around five o'clock to find Luke's parents sitting in the palace common area. As soon as they saw us, they stood up, gave the kids a hug and asked Dimitri to take them outside.

"What's going on?" Luke asked nervously.

"Something's wrong. We went to Geordia to visit some old friends, but they were gone," Luke's mother said, sounding worried.

"Did they tell anyone where they were going?" Luke asked.

"No, they didn't. There are many others that have disappeared over the last two days. Entire households are missing."

"They have devices like ours to travel between realms," Luke said. "Maybe they all went together."

"There were only three given to that kingdom. Two of them were in the hands of the king and queen and the other was on the floor of Aidra's son's home," his father said seriously.

"Could someone from another realm have used theirs?" I asked, trying to figure out what happened.

"Possibly, but highly unlikely," his father replied. "We ask that you look into this right away. Something doesn't feel right."

"We shall, father," Luke said. "We'll leave this evening."

"We'd be happy to take Bethie and Marcus with us for a visit until you handle this," Luke's mother offered. "I would love some extra time with them anyway."

"Yes, sure," Luke said. "That would be great. I know they'd love that too."

After dinner, Luke's parents took our children to Torleva. When we told Dimitri what had happened, he insisted on coming along to help. Luke and I agreed, as there would be the same level of risk for him, and we could use an extra set of eyes.

When we arrived at Geordia, we first met with the king and queen who confirmed everything Luke's parents had said. We had them command everyone to stay in their homes while we investigated. They provided us with a list and map of all the residents, marking the houses where people went missing. In total, there were fourteen.

As soon as everyone was safely inside, we had a chance to study the diagram. The households who were unaccounted for were clustered near the bridge. This included Kedron's house, which we went to first. This time, I didn't worry about him recognizing me. We walked right up to the door and knocked, but there was no answer.

Dimitri reached for the doorknob. "It's unlocked."

We all went inside and looked around.

"He isn't here," I said.

Dimitri walked out of one of the bedrooms holding a black octagon-shaped box. "Isn't this the thing he was carrying those bots in?"

I rushed to him and studied it. "Looks like it, but he burned them all."

Dimitri put it in his pocket, and we continued to the next house. We noticed that each home was basically the same. There was no food left out and the beds were unmade.

As we reached the last house in the row, the sun set. We realized that if we followed the pattern, the next one down could be empty. We skipped ahead to the small, light blue house and knocked on the door.

I could feel that someone was sleeping. "Should we knock again?" I asked.

"Yes." Luke pounded on the door.

"It's Aidra's house. She's awake," I said nervously.

Luke immediately opened the door. There wasn't much light, but we saw what looked like tiny insects crawling all over the floor. He turned on the light as Aidra stepped into her living room.

"Don't move!" Dimitri shouted.

"What are you doing in my house?" she asked nervously.

Dimitri took a huge leap over them towards Aidra, picked her up and stood on the couch holding onto her. She screamed.

"What did he say to make those things go back in the box?" Dimitri asked loudly. "What was that word?"

I was confused for a second or two before I realized there were scatter bots crawling all over her floor. "Shit!" I panicked. "I don't remember. Dimitri, please carry her out of here!"

Aidra started to pull away from him—kicking, hitting and scratching him. "Let me go! Help, help!" she screamed.

"He's *trying* to help you," I said firmly. "Stop fighting him!"

She wouldn't listen. Before we knew it, she had broken free and was cowering in the corner. I quickly channeled her, calming her down and letting her know we came to help.

"What was the word?!" I shouted as they crawled towards her feet. "Please!"

"I can't remember," Dimitri said. "I'm sorry!"

The electricity built inside me, and I focused the energy on the bots. The ground shook and they slowed down a lot but didn't stop.

"No!" I screamed as they reached the tip of her toes.

"Regressus!" Luke shouted as he remembered the word.

Immediately they stopped. Dimitri tossed Luke the octagon box and he lowered it to the floor. One by one they all marched back inside and then he closed the lid.

"Thank you," Aidra said, realizing what had happened.

"I thought he burned them," I said with my voice shaking. "That's what I saw."

"So did I," Luke said.

Aidra came out of the corner and sat down on her couch, trembling. "Those things got my son. Didn't they?" she asked sadly.

"I think they did," Luke replied.

"He was the only family I had." She began to weep.

I didn't know what to say. Part of me felt pity and wanted to tell her she had a daughter and grandchildren, but my instincts told me she was still the same wicked person inside. I didn't want her to die but I could not allow her to be in our lives.

"I'm so sorry for your loss, ma'am." I channeled her, easing her suffering and leaving her with only happy memories of her son and the neighbors she had lost.

After we left her home, we went to visit their king and queen. We explained what had happened and let him know we would take the bots away from their realm. They were saddened for their loss but extremely grateful for our help. The king told us we were always welcome in their world.

Luke whisked us back home so we could have a chance to figure out what to do next before bringing our kids home.

"His thoughts were clear when we read them," I said. "He burned them. How are they still here?"

"When you burned the ones from Adersta what happened?" Dimitri asked. "Did they melt away or vaporize? Is it possible for them to reform?"

Luke took a moment before answering.

"You did destroy them, right?" I asked, feeling his hesitation to answer.

"No—I didn't," he replied, putting his hand over his mouth.

"What did you do with them?" I asked nervously. "Where are they? They aren't here, are they?"

"No, I hid them away," Luke replied.

"Why? You know the destruction they can cause. Why didn't you destroy them?" Dimitri asked.

"While I was visiting Adersta, I learned a lot about their people," Luke said, sounding anxious. "They're warriors and are trained to defend and kill. They have an armory large enough to weaponize an entire country."

"But your father told me they've never been in battle and have no enemies," I said. "They are a threat to no one."

"I heard them say their natural resources may only last a few thousand years or so. At that point, they would have no choice but to take what they need from other realms, including Earth," Luke said seriously. "We may be immortal, but we still need to eat and enjoy life. What they're talking about could cause inter-realm starvation. I couldn't just destroy a weapon that could save trillions of lives."

"What do you plan on doing with it?" I asked with worry. "We can't ever use those things."

"I will do what I must to protect our kingdom," he snapped back.

"By killing?" I asked.

"If they were to come here armed, then yes," Luke said, beginning to raise his voice. "I wouldn't think twice about it. It is my job to protect our people."

"There must be another way," I said.

"The bots are only a last resort. I hope to never need to use them, but I feel better knowing we have them and they don't," Luke said.

"Having that kind of power is far too dangerous," Dimitri said. "I understand you want to be the mightiest ruler, but at what cost?"

"Mightiest ruler? My parents thought that my thirst for power was the only reason I wanted to be king, but the truth is I'm willing to do what my brother won't to protect our people. That's why I live in the palace and deal with inter-realm issues while he lives in the village farming with his family."

"At what cost?" I asked, worried for our souls. "I admire your desire to keep us all safe and I love that about you, but we should find a way that doesn't involve killing."

"Can't you just get into their minds to get them to stop creating weapons?" Dimitri asked. "It would help them maintain their natural resources longer."

"We could get their rulers to believe that they've done enough with the weaponry and turn their focus on planting new trees and gardens. We could even bring them seeds from ours and the other realms that grow the easiest," I said, piggybacking on Dimitri's idea.

"What if it doesn't work and they still get close to using up all their resources? What then?" Luke asked.

"Then we reassess." I put my hand on his shoulder. "We can check in on them regularly to make sure they're improving their conditions. We have incredible power of mind control, Luke. We can do this."

"But if nothing else works, and they plan to attack any of the realms, you will consider the other option?" Luke asked.

"Yes, if there is no other way to protect everyone."

"Okay," Luke said, sounding relieved.

"But, because you didn't destroy them, we need to make sure no one can ever get them. Where are the rest of them now?" I asked.

"They are on Danteba," he replied. "No one is going to go there. Our people are the only ones that know of that place and how to get there."

"You hid them in the Land of the Damned?" I laughed. "The sulfur planet?"

"Yes. What's so funny about that?" Luke sounded annoyed.

"The night you came back, you smelled terrible." I smiled. "That explains a lot."

"Oh," Luke laughed.

"Not to put a hole in your theory but if you were willing to go there, someone else might someday," Dimitri said. "If anyone else were to discover Danteba, it sure sounds like a great place to hide something. How can you be sure it's safe?"

"You're right, but we can't keep them here," Luke replied.

"I could ask my ancestors that no one but us can find them or use them," I said, feeling brilliant. "They denied my request to destroy them, but it can't hurt to ask that they stay hidden."

We all agreed, and they followed me into our bedroom, watching as I wrote the request. Much to our surprise, as soon as the words were written, everything except for the words '*but us*' were erased.

"Write it again," Luke said, sounding upset.

I tried writing it three different times, but each time it removed the same part. We wouldn't be able to find them or use them.

"Where did that box go?" Dimitri asked, looking at the table that it was put on moments before.

We all looked around the room, but the octagon box and the bots were gone. We soon realized the request to hide them applied to all of them, not only the ones on Danteba.

"Throw the book back into the pool!" Luke demanded. "They've tricked us. Take back your wish."

"Maybe it's better this way." I thought about how no one would be able to ever use them. "We can stop them on our own. We have a good plan."

"No, we need to be able to protect ourselves," he said, grabbing the book and walking out of the room. "We need to be able to find them if we need them."

"Luke, don't!" I yelled. "If you do that, it will undo everything I wrote."

"Denny's gone now," he said coldly. "It won't matter."

I raced after him as he headed towards the pool. Dimitri followed closely behind.

"Please," I begged him. "If you toss that in, Aidra will remember who I am. She means to use me as a weapon. We can't have her in our lives."

"You can just write it in again." He stomped ahead of us.

"It may not work next time. My ancestors don't always give me what I ask. They could trick me again. You know this."

Luke got to the pool ahead of us and stared into the purple goo below deep in thought. "I have to protect our family and our people," he said while holding the book above the water. "It's my sworn duty."

"We will, together," I said. "But it will be much more difficult if we have to worry about what Aidra might do. She was married to my father and has some magical knowledge. You saw what she tried to do to Denny, and she threatened to take Bethie. What if she took our children, Luke? We can't have her in our lives again."

"Please just wait, Luke. Aidra will be dead long before they run out of resources," Dimitri said urgently. "If things seem too unsafe at that time, then Alice can toss it in and never use it to ask for anything. She will write her story about us."

I could feel how torn Luke was and how he was desperately trying to do the right thing for everyone. He stepped away from the pool and handed me the book.

"Thank you," I said.

Luke did not respond nor even look at me. He walked out of the room and went outside. We followed him, but when I tried to talk to him, he clicked the portal device and whooshed away into the starry sky.

"Where do you think he went?" I asked Dimitri.

"Maybe to get the kids."

"It's late and I think they were planning on staying longer. They would be disappointed if he came for them now."

"Or back to Danteba to look for the scatter bots," he said as he looked up.

"I hope not."

Dimitri and I waited outside the palace for him sitting on a stone bench. As the night got colder, he went back inside and grabbed us some blankets to keep us warm.

As dawn approached, I asked Dimitri about his happiness. I wondered if there was anything that he missed or could improve his life.

"Do you mean a woman?" he asked boldly.

I didn't know how to respond. I would have never mentioned that to him. I was thinking about his life, business on Earth and any dreams he may have still carried.

"No." He smiled. "There is nothing I am missing. My life is full."

"Are you sure? I want you to be happy, Dimitri."

"I know what Luke told you about my feelings for you and what you saw in my soul," he said as we watched a pair of shooting stars trail across the sky. "And it's true. I've loved you for a long time and probably always will. But I'm glad that you have Luke because I know that he genuinely loves you. Seeing you two together doesn't hurt anymore, because I know how incredibly happy he makes you. Sure, there was a time when I hoped that we would have what you two do, but that has left my mind long ago."

"How do you feel now?" I asked pulling a blanket over the top of my head, trying to stay warm. "Don't you want to try to meet someone you may love?"

"Would it be fair to court a woman when my heart desires someone else? How cruel would that be?" he asked. "Perhaps someday. Who knows? We are immortal after all. Today is only a blink in time."

I started to tear up.

"I'm not telling you this to have pity on me," Dimitri said, holding my hand. "I'm saying this because this amazing closeness that we have is enough for me. I'm not secretly wishing for anything more than what we already have. Being here with you, Luke and my beautiful, kind-hearted godchildren bring me more joy than I ever could have imagined. I regret absolutely nothing and am thankful every day to be in your life exactly the way I am."

"You're really quite remarkable," I said, looking at his eyes filled with joyful tears. "I love you, Dimitri. You are the kindest, most selfless person I have ever known. Thank you for choosing to be here with us and for being an amazing godfather. You make even the darkest days seem brighter."

He kissed my forehead and stood up. "We should probably go back inside and try to get some sleep."

"Okay, you're right. Thanks for waiting up with me."

We picked up the blankets and went back to our rooms.

The next morning, I woke around 10:00 am to find Luke asleep next to me. I never even heard him come in. I quietly got up, being careful not to wake him.

"Hey," he said, reaching for my hand.

"Did I wake you?"

"You seem tired," he said. "Did you wait up for me?"

"Yes. Dimitri and I both did." I yawned.

"I'm sorry. I should have asked you not to." He sat up. "I didn't realize it would take so long."

"What did?" I asked curiously.

"Convincing the king and queen to tell their people to stop making weapons and focus on restoring their natural resources," he said, sounding tired. "I also put in their heads that they should make those poor kids some better toys."

"That's where you went, to get the ball rolling on that?" I smiled. "I thought you took off because you were angry with me."

"I wasn't angry with you. I was upset and needed to do something."

"Why?"

"I'm supposed to protect you. I needed to take some type of action."

"Luke, we look out for each other. Everything doesn't fall on your shoulders alone." I sat down next to him. "There will be many challenges ahead but together we are stronger than anything we'll ever have to face."

Luke smiled and put his arms around me.

"I fear nothing as long as you are by my side," I said, looking at him in the eyes.

He was quiet for a moment.

"There was a time when I channeled you for a full day, he said nostalgically. "That's when I knew that I loved you."

"You channeled me for an entire day?" I asked curiously. "When was this?"

"I wasn't being a creeper. I didn't mean to," he said, almost laughing at himself. "I had planned to just check in on you as I had been, but I couldn't leave."

"What was different about that day?" I asked. "What made you stay?"

"It was the day that your Marine boyfriend, Charlie told you he was still in love with his ex, and that he was going to ask her to marry him," Luke went on. "You had been dating him for almost six months and were devastated by the news."

"You were in my mind when that happened?" I cringed.

"Yes, it was just the timing," he replied. "You had so many thoughts running through your head. I could feel how angry and hurt you were. I waited on pins and needles to hear what you'd say to him. I was sure you were going to tell him off."

"I don't even remember what I said any more."

"You held back all your emotions, told him that you forgave him and wished him a happy life."

"That's right." I remembered. "It wasn't what I wanted to say though. I wanted to slap him across the face and tell him to go to hell."

"But you didn't."

"What else happened? I honestly don't recall. It was so long ago."

"You drove back to your apartment and cried for hours. It was awful and seemed like you would never stop. But then Denny called you up in tears and told you that he was going to have to put his dog to sleep."

"Mr. Scruffers." I remembered. "He had that adorable cocker spaniel for ten years. Took him everywhere. His heart was broken that day."

"Then you remember what happened next," Luke said. "You told him that you'd go with him while it was being done. You washed your face, put on some makeup and stayed with him the rest of the day up until he fell asleep."

"That was a really bad day. I don't think I had ever seen him cry as much. My heart ached for him."

"The whole time you were beside him in his grief, you never once mentioned yours. You put all your energy into helping him get through his and didn't even tell him about your break-up until weeks later. That's love," Luke said warmly. "From that day on, the dream of having you love me someday became a far greater obsession than any desire I ever had for power."

"I wish I was half the person you give me credit to be," I said with teary eyes. "I've always tried to be a good person, Luke but I've made so many mistakes along the way."

"You know I've told you many times that I've always done what was best for me," Luke said. "Choosing you was one of those things. All I've wanted ever since was to become what was best for you."

"You have grown into the most amazing person and I absolutely adore you," I said with loving eyes. "We are what's best for each other."